D0310417

stichting
de nieuwe school
j. vermeerstraat 73hs
1071 dn amsterdam

MINE OWN EXECUTIONER

by
NIGEL BALCHIN

Collins
14 ST. JAMES'S PLACE LONDON
1945

There are too many Examples of men, that have been their own executioners, and that have made hard shrift to bee so ; some have alwayes had poyson about them, in a hollow ring upon their fingers, and some in their Pen that they used to write with ; some have beat out their braines at the wal of their prison, and some have eate the fire out of their chimneys ; But I do nothing upon my selfe, and yet am mine owne Executioner.

DONNE, *Devotions.*

PRINTED IN GREAT BRITAIN
COLLINS CLEAR-TYPE PRESS : LONDON AND GLASGOW
1945

PROLOGUE

THE University Lecturer in Abnormal Psychology lived in Old Court. The porter directed Milne to the staircase in the far corner and he read the list of names at the bottom of B. Staircase.

W. M. Tew.
A. J. P. Richmond.
Lord Islip.
J. W. Graham.
Dr. W. R. Field.

Milne paused for a moment just to make absolutely sure that his decision was made, and that it was the right decision. He had no real doubt about it. But he was just twenty-one, and it was an autumn evening, and Old Court was very impressive. He thought again of the words in which he had decided to put it to Dr. Field. " It seems to me, sir, that this stuff is so important that if one really believes in it, there isn't much choice but to devote one's life to it——" Simple, noble words, as became the response to a Call—the realisation of a vocation. And Dr. Field would stretch out a hand, in slightly emotional silence, to welcome this new recruit to the cause. . . .

Dr. Field's rooms were on the ground floor. The oak was unsported and the inner door half open. He knocked and went in.

Dr. Field was sitting at his writing desk. He did not look up.

Milne said, " Are you frightfully busy, sir ? "

There was a pause. Then Field looked up suddenly and said, " Ah ! Good-evening." He seemed rather startled.

" I'm sorry if I'm interrupting you," said Milne.

Field said, " Of course. Let's see, you're——"

" Milne."

" Again ? " said Field, picking up a pencil.

" Milne."

"Ah," said Field, writing something down. He gave a violent wriggle as though he were embedding himself more firmly in his chair, and stared at Milne through his bi-focal glasses rather uneasily. "Won't you sit down?" he said unsmilingly.

"Are you sure I'm not being a nuisance?" said Milne awkwardly.

Field said, "Ah yes. By all means," and motioned towards a chair. Milne hesitated and then sat down, with a vague hope that it would all come straight in a moment. Field leaned back in his chair and gazed at him inquiringly.

"Well now?" he said.

"Well," said Milne, "I've been attending your lectures . . ."

"Just a moment," said Field, leaning forward. "Could you bring your chair a little closer? You've got rather a quiet voice and my ears aren't too good." He smiled for the first time, fleetingly and rather pathetically.

"I'm sorry," said Milne loudly, pulling his chair forward. "I do mumble."

"No, no," said Field. "It's just that I have some difficulty in catching things nowadays." He said it with relief. It was the first bit of the conversation that he had heard.

Milne glanced from the intense, rather owlish face to the half-open door. There were some things which one could hardly send echoing round Old Court in a ringing shout.

"Do you mind if I shut the door?" he said helplessly.

"By all means," said Field. "I keep it open because otherwise I may miss the knocks."

Milne closed the door thankfully, and returning to his chair began the process of self-dedication in a steady and throat-skinning roar.

"Well, sir, I've been attending your Abnormal Psychology lectures, and doing a good deal of reading on my own, and I find the whole subject completely fascinating. It seems to me . . ."

"Just a minute," said Field, picking up his pencil. "I'd like to make sure that I've got all your particulars. Now your name . . . ?"

"*Milne!*"

"Milne. Initials?"

"F. J."

"College?"

"Jesus."

"And you're reading . . .?"

"I'm a third year medical."

"Are you taking Part I Natural Science?"

"I've taken it."

"Subjects?"

"Physiology, Anatomy, Chemistry."

"Class?"

"I got a First."

"In two years? Very good. Are you a scholar?"

"No. An exhibitioner."

There was a moment's pause.

"What I've been feeling . . ." Milne ventured.

"Just a moment. Your tutor will be . . .?"

"Dr. Gaskell," said Milne.

Field dug himself in a little further with his buttocks. "Right," he said, taking off his glasses and looking at Milne mistily. "Now—you wanted to ask me something?"

Milne took a deep breath. "I feel about this stuff," he roared, "rather as I do about religion. If it is of any importance at all, it must be far more important than anything else. If people really believe what they say they believe about God, I don't see how they can waste their time on anything else. In the same way, if one really believes that the methods of abnormal psychology can solve people's psychological problems, I don't see that there is any alternative but to devote one's life to solving them."

He paused and took a deep breath. Field still stared at him mistily and expressionlessly. Then he put on his glasses and gave a violent wriggle.

"Well," he said without noticeable emotion, "that's a point of view."

"What I wanted to ask you," said Milne rather irritably, "was what you think I should do if I decide to become an analyst."

"Ah," said Field, looking slightly surprised. "That's what you have in mind?"

"Yes," said Milne patiently.

There was a long pause.

"Well," said Field with a violent wriggle. "Of course you've got to qualify first."

"As a medical?"

"Of course."

Milne said, "That was one of the things I wanted to ask you. You think it's absolutely necessary for an analyst to have a medical degree?"

"Oh yes. Oh *yes*! Of course."

"Can you tell me about that? I've never quite seen *why* it was necessary. After all, it means spending three more years learning a lot of stuff which I should never use. I can see that an analyst needs a medical background—say up to second M.B. But I don't see that hospital work would help much."

"Well, of course," said Field. "If you don't qualify first you'll be a quack."

"Yes. But surely a quack is simply somebody who practises without a medical degree? It's a purely conventional difference, isn't it?"

"Possibly," said Field coldly. "But I think you'd find it made a good deal of difference to your prospects all the same."

"I wasn't thinking so much about my prospects," said Milne curtly. "I was thinking about being able to do my job."

"I can't hear you," said Field rather testily.

"I said I think we're at cross purposes. I wasn't thinking about my professional prospects, but about the best training in becoming a good analyst."

Field said, "Well, there's no doubt you'd have to qualify first. No doubt at all. It gives you"—he waved a hand—"all the background."

"Better than spending the three years in a psychiatric clinic?"

"You could do that afterwards."

Milne said, "I doubt if I can afford another six years' training."

"Well, of course, once you've qualified the rest of your

training is up to you. I don't know that you'd get a lot out of years in a clinic."

"You mean once I've qualified there's no reason why I shouldn't practise?"

"Well," said Field, "further training would be useful, of course. . . ." He took off his glasses again and said, "You feel that you are particularly suited for this work?"

"I don't know," said Milne. "That would be rather a large claim, wouldn't it?"

"It's difficult work," said Field. "Very few good practitioners. It attracts the wrong types of course. It needs great balance."

Milne said, "Do you practise at all yourself?"

"I have. My interest in the subject is mainly academic. But I used to have a few patients. Nowadays, of course, my hearing . . ." He smiled again momentarily.

"I should go on and qualify and then think it over," he said rather wearily. "You've got plenty of time."

"That's rather the difficulty. I think I can probably afford to qualify, but if I do that I shan't have time for any specialised training."

"But you're young. There's plenty of time."

"It's not time I'm short of. It's money."

"Scholarships," said Field vaguely.

"For post-graduate work in analysis?"

Field hesitated. "I should think so. I'm not absolutely sure about the details."

There was a pause. Milne said, "So if the choice is between qualifying and having special training in analysis, you'd advise me to spend the money on qualifying."

"Undoubtedly. A qualified man can always get a job. The other way . . ." he shrugged his shoulders. "In any case," he added brightly, "you may always change your mind in the next three years. And even if you don't, it's essential to have the background, absolutely essential. You can't divorce the mind from the body."

Milne opened his mouth to speak and then shut it again. Dr. Field gave a violent wriggle.

Milne said, "I know it's a silly question, but you see nothing against my going for analysis?"

"Oh no," said Field. "Why should there be? If you qualify and feel that it's your vocation, I see nothing against it." His eyes flickered to his wrist-watch.

"You see," said Milne as a last effort, "I like dealing with people. They seem to find it easy to talk to me. I wouldn't claim to be particularly well-balanced, Lord knows. But I think I know a fair amount about myself. I'm probably wrong about that, but . . ."

"Well, that's the important thing, of course," said Field.

There was a long pause. Milne rose and said, "Well, thank you very much, sir."

"Not at all," said Field. "I should get on and qualify. That's the main thing. Come and talk to me again if—if there's anything."

"Thank you," said Milne mechanically. "Good-night."

It was darker in the court now, and cold. He shivered slightly. As he came through the archway he saw the painted names gleaming in the dim lamplight. Milne reflected that whilst he was clearly not concerned with Dr. W. R. Field, there might still be some possibilities in W. M. Tew, A. J. P. Richmond, Lord Islip and J. W. Graham. This comforted him. But he still felt cold.

I

Lady Maresfield lay on the sofa. Her eyes were closed and her plump face was puckered up as though she was about to cry. Her restless movements had pulled her skirt up well above her knees, in a way which might have been attractive if she had been twenty years younger and four stones lighter.

"When he came back he was horrid to me," she said in a low, agonised voice. "I said nothing about it. Not a word of reproach. I always believe that a man should be handled tactfully. But from the way he behaved you would have thought I'd done *him* an injury. . . ."

Milne sat silently in his armchair, gazing at the Kashan

rug on the floor. The shortcomings and brutalities of Sir Pintner Maresfield flowed over and around him in a steady but ineffectual stream. As usual, the rug was the wrong way round. He must have pointed out to Pat at least a dozen times that the pile must lie away from the course of light to show its full lustre. Strictly speaking, that particular rug ought to be one way round in daylight and the other by artificial light.

He suddenly realised that Lady Maresfield had stopped.

"Yes?" he said gently and attentively.

She gave a groan and said, "I can't go on. It—it *hurts* me to think of it." She groaned again and turning her head restlessly, buried her face in the sofa cushions and began to sob.

"It's all right," said Milne quietly. "We'll stop for now. Don't worry yourself."

"I don't see how you can be so *damn* patient with me!" she said, suddenly sitting up and staring at him tearfully.

"It's quite easy," said Milne with a smile. "You might try it yourself some time."

"You mean I'm too impatient with myself?"

Milne smiled his practised smile of infinite wisdom and made no reply. He hadn't meant that. He hadn't meant anything in particular. It was just one of his standard replies. But it never failed.

Lady Maresfield said, "How incredibly wise you are! You're quite right. I *am* too impatient with myself. I set myself too high a standard. I always have." She sighed and pulled her skirt down four necessary inches.

"Well, as far as I'm concerned," said Milne, "the trouble at the moment is that you're trying too hard. You're thinking all the time, and trying to think of things which will help me. That's exactly what I don't want you to do. The whole idea of this free association business is that you should just relax completely and let your mind wander. Just say whatever comes into your head. It may sound silly or irrelevant but it won't be really."

"Yes," she said. "Of course my mind does rather tend to dwell on—on my relations with Pintner, because I have had such a *terrible* time in these last five years. . . ." She swung her legs off the sofa and passed a hand vaguely over her hair.

"Oh quite," said Milne, gazing at the rug. He was wondering whether this was the moment to say what clearly needed to be said.

"Sometimes I can be quite cheerful about it," she said. "I even think it's funny. You know sometimes I've told you things and laughed at them. And then suddenly they overwhelm me." She closed her eyes and shook her head reflectively.

"Quite," said Milne again. He paused for a moment and then added, "I think perhaps it's only fair to tell you what I've hinted at once or twice before. *Some* of your difficulties are things that nobody can do much about." He met her sudden frightened glance. "If a man suddenly shouts 'Fire!' and rushes out into the street when there is no fire, then he's acting abnormally in normal circumstances, and a psychiatrist may be able to help him. But if he shouts 'Fire!' and rushes out when the building *is* on fire, then he's acting quite normally. It is the circumstances which are abnormal. He doesn't want a psychiatrist. He wants a fire brigade."

"I don't *quite* see——" she said doubtfully.

"What I mean," said Milne patiently, "is that a lot of what you have told me about your married life can't be altered by curing *you* of something. There isn't anything to cure. You may be very unhappy. But in those circumstances it's quite normal to be unhappy. In fact, you'd be abnormal if you weren't."

Lady Maresfield's middle-aged baby face puckered threateningly.

"But what am I to *do* then? I—I——" She suddenly stopped and gazed at Milne in horror.

"You wouldn't stop seeing me?" she said breathlessly. "I couldn't stand that. I couldn't *stand* it! Not after all you've done for me. I've felt so much better and more cheerful since I've been coming. It's the one thing I have to look forward to——"

Milne hesitated. He had been trying for nearly fifteen

years now to think of the proper end to this conversation and he still hadn't found it.

"I know I don't do it well," she said pathetically. "Not what you want me to do. But I will try. I'll do anything so long as you won't give me up."

"Of course I shouldn't think of doing so as long as I felt that I could do any good," said Milne gravely. "But . . ."

"But you *are* doing me good!" said Lady Maresfield. "Of course you are. You've no idea how different I feel. I was telling a friend of mine only yesterday. I feel like a new woman. Don't *you* think I'm better than when I first came?"

"Oh yes," said Milne, rather helplessly. "I think you're a good deal better. It's been good for you to tell somebody all about it. But what's worrying me is how far further I can help you."

She said, "But surely, people go on for years, don't they? I've only been coming to you for about six months."

"Oh yes. People go on for years all right," said Milne. "But you don't want to keep coming to me for years if I don't get you any further, do you?"

"Yes," said Lady Maresfield simply.

Milne smiled. "That's very nicely and flatteringly put. But . . ."

She said, "You don't understand what it means to me," and began to cry.

Milne sighed. "Well, well," he said cheerfully. "Don't let's worry about it for the moment. Let's see how we get on in the next few weeks, eh?"

He smiled the infallible smile. Lady Maresfield wiped her eyes and smiled back rather wanly.

"I can go on coming?" she said.

"Yes, of course. I only felt that I must say that in case you felt you weren't getting on very fast."

Lady Maresfield heaved a deep sigh. "I don't mind *what* happens as long as I can still come," she said.

"All right," said Milne briskly. "Let's get on. Dreams?"

"I've had two really vivid ones," she said. "In the first one I was in a train. . . ."

Lady Maresfield and her sorrows went away in a large Daimler at five o'clock. Usually Milne stayed for a while in the consulting room after a patient had left him, making notes on the interview. But he was tired and hungry, and there was nothing new to say about Lady Maresfield. He put out the lights and went in search of tea.

Patricia was reading. She looked up and said, " Hallo. Long session ? "

" Yes," said Milne. " Any tea ? "

" I'll make you some fresh. This is stewed."

" No, this'll do," said Milne.

" But it'll be horrid, darling."

" No, it won't." He picked up the teapot and poured out some tea.

" Are you sure ? " said Pat. " I can make some more in a second."

Milne said irritably, " For Pete's sake don't *fuss*." He sat down, lit a cigarette and shut his eyes.

There was definitely something slightly odd about the atmosphere, and Patricia's face. For a moment he wondered what it was. Then he remembered the previous night. He shied quickly away from that and said, " Lady M. must go."

Patricia said, " Why ? "

" Because she bloody well wastes my time."

" Then tell her."

" I have told her. But she won't go." Milne opened his eyes.

Patricia was sitting on the floor in that queer adolescent way of hers, looking at the fire. " Won't go ? " she said, looking round.

" I suppose she would if I made her. But it's a darned difficult thing to do. She goes pathetic. It's my own fault. I ought never to have taken her on."

" Why ? "

" She's unhappy because there's something the matter with her marriage. And the only thing that's wrong with her marriage is that it ought never to have happened. But as it's been happening for about twenty years, there isn't much to be done."

It suddenly struck him as a queer thing for them to be discussing in the circumstances. He watched to see if Patricia thought so. But she just said, " You can't have her wasting your time. There are too many people you *can* help. By the way, a Mrs. Lucian rang up for an appointment. I said Thursday afternoon. Is that all right ? "

" I think so. Any idea who she is, or what, or who sent her ? "

" No. She just wanted to see you."

Milne said, " Mrs. Lucian. I'll tell you about Mrs. Lucian. In fact I'll bet you ten bob I know what Mrs. Lucian's like, and we can check it up afterwards." He leaned back and closed his eyes again. " Mrs. Lucian," he said, " is about forty-five. She was once pretty—fairly pretty anyhow. She has been married for twenty years to Mr. Lucian, who is definitely well-off. They have no children. Mrs. Lucian has never done a stroke of work since she married, or probably before that. She was brought up in the belief that one day she would marry someone like Mr. Lucian, and for the last twenty years she has done nothing much but *be* married to him. She did a little part-time voluntary work at the beginning of the war, but her health prevented her from doing *much*, of course. She now finds that Mr. Lucian does not love her as he once did. Perhaps he even runs after other women. Anyhow he neglects her or is cold to her or drinks or what have you. This worries her. She does not sleep well, and suffers from her nerves. Will I please do something about it ? "

Pat said, " But that's all pure Lady M."

" They're *all* pure Lady M," said Milne. " That's exactly the point. Or nearly all of them. I have at present twelve patients, outside the clinic, which is too many anyhow to let me do a decent job. Seven of them are just different editions of the Lady M story, and two more are the male version of her. I can hardly remember which is which, and it doesn't really matter much whether I do or not." He threw his cigarette away violently and said, " It's bloody well got to stop."

Pat said, " Well, then, stop it. Chuck them out. It's no good letting them come if you can't do anything for them."

"I dare say," said Milne. "But it's not as simple as all that. I *can* do something for them. I can give them somebody to talk to about it. It all comes pouring out and they feel much better, and as long as they can go on doing that once or twice a week they go on feeling much better."

Pat said, "But you can't just be a damp shoulder—not if you don't want to and it doesn't get them anywhere. Your time's too valuable."

"Yes, but the snag is that until I've been a damp shoulder for a bit, I can't be *sure* there's nothing to be done. I can make a damn good guess, of course. Taking it all round, people of that age are a pretty bad bet even if they have got something definitely funny. If you start digging around in their minds and generally clearing things up, you're liable to find that when you've finished there's no person at all left and nothing to make one out of. But I can't be sure. And by the time I *am* sure the good old transference situation is well under way, and they've decided that I, or what they've made me out to be, am the only thing in the world they want."

"Well, then, they just can't have it."

"No. But you see I can't kick them out at that stage. Once I've let them go so far, it would be an unpardonable thing to do technically." Milne passed his hand wearily over his eyes. "As far as I can see, most of the people practising in this country spend nine-tenths of their time and get nine-tenths of their income from rich, unhappy people, chiefly women, who're incurably normal and want something done about it. They don't matter a damn to society anyhow."

There was a pause. Patricia was looking into the fire again. She said, "Well, obviously you can't go on like this."

"No," said Milne. "But exactly what happens if I don't?"

"Well, you work at the Clinic and so on. You think that's worth while, don't you?"

"And what do we live on?"

Patricia's head came round quickly and he knew it was

coming. She looked at him for a moment and then turned away to the fire with a crooked little smile.

"Does that arise?" she said quietly.

"How d'you mean?" said Milne clumsily.

"Well, last night you were going to leave me anyway. So I don't see that I come into it."

Milne hesitated. "Putting aside the fact that that was last night and this is to-day, if we did break up we should still need money. More than we do now."

"Oh, no, we shouldn't," said Patricia decidedly. "If we break up you'll need exactly as much money as you want to live on. I haven't reached the pensionable stage yet, darling."

Milne said, "A proud and independent Rhinoceros." Her face lit up at the nickname, just as he had known it would. He went on quickly before she could speak, "Seriously though, I don't see how we get on without the Lady M's. They pay."

"Oh, damn that. You're not a grocer."

Milne said, "I'm not a grocer but I have to buy groceries."

"Well, I just don't think that ought to come into it at all." She hesitated. "I don't know whether you're talking about us together or us separated. But if—if we do carry on we could manage. Of course we could."

"It's all very well to talk like that," said Milne irritably. "But you know quite well that when it comes down to brass tacks you never have economised and never will. You're one of the people who needs a lot of money. I don't mean that you spend it on yourself, but you lose it and get rid of it somehow. What's the use of not facing it?"

Pat said, "I know I'm awful about money. But *honestly* I'd be better if it were a thing like this—where it meant that you could do what you wanted to." She put a tentative hand on his knee. "Honestly, Felix."

"I know," said Milne cynically. "Fire the charwoman and take on another maid in her place. I've had some of your economy before. I can't afford it."

"All right," said Patricia, offended and withdrawing the hand. "Then you're going to go on wasting your time on these rich old women because you can't take the chance of being poorer?"

"What I'm going to do is to think," said Milne rather feebly.

"But you won't take on any more of them? This new woman——"

"Not if she's like that."

There was a long silence. Then Patricia turned and looked at him steadily. He stared back as expressionlessly as he could. She said, "Look, just let me get this straight. *Am* I still under notice?" She said it lightly, but he saw her lips tremble slightly.

He said, "I told you. That was last night and this is to-day."

"I dare say," she said rather bitterly. "I dare say. But you said you thought you'd leave me. And—and——"

Milne said quickly, "Don't cry, Rhino." It was very important at the moment that she should not cry. It was very important that what had been said should be dropped. Not forgotten, perhaps. But not pursued now.

"I'm not going to cry," said Patricia rather huskily. "Only I must *know*, Felix. You can see I must."

"Of course," said Milne. "After all, there's packing to arrange and a ticket to buy and so on."

He leaned down and pulled her back against his knees. For a moment she tensed, and he thought he was going to be pinned down—challenged—forced to go into it. Then she said wearily, "That's right. And a room to book somewhere," and leaned back against him with a sigh. Milne bent and kissed her forehead. She turned her head and rested it on his knee.

"Oh God," she said, "I don't know where we are, honey. I just don't know where we are."

"Never mind," said Milne. "Don't let's bother about the map for a bit. It's very comfortable here."

Patricia said, "Yes. For the moment, anyhow."

Half an hour later Milne said, "Is it to-night Barbara and Peter are coming?"

"Yes. Sorry, but I couldn't very well get out of it."

Milne said, " Oh, that's all right. Why should you? You must see Barbara occasionally."

" Sure," said Patricia cynically. " I shall sit and admire her legs all the evening and have a lovely time."

" There's no need to be *bitter*, darling," said Milne with a grin.

" I'm not. I don't mind Bab a bit. After all, I've had to put up with having her around all my male acquaintances for years. But Peter *is* a bit hard."

" I don't know. He's not so bad really."

Patricia said, " I don't see how he could be much worse. Why she had to go and marry an ass like that I cannot see."

" No," said Milne absently.

* * * * *

" What seems so alarming," said Peter Edge, taking a large helping of roast potatoes, " is the utter lack of self-restraint we see all around us." He took a mouthful of food. " Greed," he added indistinctly. " Greed and selfishness. As much money as possible for doing as little as they can. That's what these people want."

" That's what we all want, darling," said Barbara cheerfully.

" But at least we have some sense of responsibility," said Peter. " The modern working man hasn't. He expects somebody else to plan for him—to provide for him—to carry all his burdens. And then if everything isn't exactly as he wants it, he turns round and abuses those of us in responsible positions."

Milne glanced at Patricia. She was looking at Peter with one eyebrow slightly raised. To raise one eyebrow at people was Patricia's rudest gesture, only to be used in extreme circumstances. To her it meant a notable loss of self-control. Milne had never been able to convince her that nobody else ever noticed, or knew it was an insult.

Barbara said, " Are you busy, Felix? "

" Yes. In a useless sort of way."

" You ought to be busy," said Peter morosely, " considering the number of people who're nearly off their heads with worry. I think I shall have to come and have a few guineas' worth myself, Felix. Might cheer me up."

"Felix doesn't exactly cheer people up, darling," said Barbara. "He deals with their complexes, don't you, Felix?" He caught her eyes and smiled a quick, secret smile; but the smile he got in return was completely public and uninteresting.

"D'you really think it's good for people?" said Peter. "All this digging about in their minds? I should have thought it'd make 'em morbid. You know—thinking too much about themselves."

Milne said, "I think it's good for some people to think about themselves. If they do it in the right way." He was looking at Barbara's fingers twined round the stem of her glass.

"Carlo was run over by a bicycle this morning," said Patricia. "He gets sillier about traffic every day."

"Hurt?" said Barbara.

"Oh no. It just biffed him. Carlo yelped and the man on the bike swore. But he didn't even come off."

"I saw a case the other day where a dog ran into the road in front of a car," said Peter. "Three dead and the driver crippled for life." He gazed sombrely at his plate.

Milne nodded absently. After dinner, he was reflecting, Pat would take Barbara away for a bit. Then they would listen to the news, and Peter would talk. About ten, Peter and Barbara would go. There was no way, between now and ten, by which he could get even a single word in private with Barbara.

"You know, you're getting more of an old misery every day, darling," said Barbara. She sat back and looked at Peter with her queer, mocking, patronising smile.

"Onset of a depressive phase," said Milne. "You can come to me for that if you like. Not that I'd take it on."

"Do people come to you because they're depressed?" said Barbara.

"Well, yes. They'd hardly come if they were happy, would they?"

"Most of them come because they find Felix is a nice damp shoulder to weep on," said Patricia.

Barbara said, " I should think he would be." She stared at Felix with the bold Siamese cat eyes. " I can imagine that he'd make a very nice person to tell your sins to."

" Oh yes, I'm good at that," said Felix quickly. " Unshockable, you see. That's the point. People don't mind telling you their sins if they find you aren't shocked. They always think they've done something quite uniquely wicked that nobody's ever done before."

" And haven't they ? "

Felix shook his head. " No. They've just done the same old things. The range of human sin is very limited, you know."

" I don't know that I should altogether *like* my husband to be father confessor to a lot of other females," said Barbara, turning to Pat.

Pat said, " I don't like it myself. Particularly the pretty ones."

" I never *get* any pretty ones," said Milne dejectedly. " Some of them were pretty once, but it was a long time ago."

" What d'you ask 'em ? " said Peter.

Milne said, " Oh, all sorts of things. The patient does the work, you know. I only have to talk if they won't."

" I should have thought it'd be an embarrassing business," said Peter. " Very embarrassing."

" But you're so easily embarrassed, darling," said Barbara. " I don't think I should be, really. Not if nobody laughed at what I told them."

" But you always were a shameless minx," said Patricia calmly. " I can remember thinking so the first time I ever saw you. We were both eighteen and it was at Roy Pearson's twenty-first birthday party. You were playing around with somebody and I know I was shocked to the core and green with envy."

" It's all rather like the Oxford Group, isn't it ? " said Peter. " Confessing your sins and so on. That's what they do, isn't it ? "

Patricia said, " Have another potato, Peter."

" Thanks very much," said Peter. " Mind you, I think

those Oxford Group people are a bad influence. Conchies in the war, weren't they?"

When Barbara and Pat had gone, Peter said, "I'm glad we've got a few minutes alone. I've got a thing I want to ask your advice about."

Milne waited. Peter lit his cigarette and wriggled rather restlessly in his chair.

"This stuff you do," he said. "Of course it's not much in my line, that sort of thing. But I can quite see that there might be something in it, y'know."

"Yes?" said Milne politely.

"Oh, yes. After all, people have these things—funny ideas and so on."

"They certainly do," said Milne.

"And there ought to be some way of curing them. After all, nature always provides remedies, doesn't it?"

Milne said, "Well . . ."

"Of course I know a lot of people say it's all bunkum. But I'm not so sure. You're an intelligent man, Felix. I don't believe you'd be in the job if there wasn't something in it."

Milne said, "What was it you wanted my advice about?"

"Well," said Peter hesitatingly, "it's about Barbara."

"Barbara?"

"Yes. Of course I'd never say so to any one else, but Barbara's a queer girl, y'know. Very queer in some ways."

"What sort of ways?" said Milne cruelly.

"Oh, all sorts of ways." Peter took his cigarette out of his mouth and looked at it carefully. "For one thing," he said in a low voice, looking up, "I think she's got a bit of a sex complex."

"What do you mean by that exactly?"

"I don't want to go into details now," said Peter hastily. "But I've got a certain amount of reason to think so. Now you might think that if she's got a sex complex already, the last thing for her would be this stuff you do. But I'm not so sure. It might be just the thing. That's what I wanted to ask you about." He smoothed his hands down over the marked bulge of his waistcoat and looked at Milne inquiringly.

Milne hesitated. " Well, of course I can't really advise you without knowing a bit more about it," he said lamely. The whole conversation had altogether too many funny and exciting and terrifying possibilities.

" I can quite see that," said Peter. " But I thought maybe if you had a talk with her . . . ? That's why I led the conversation round that way at dinner. I wanted to see her reactions. I know Barbara pretty well, of course. I think she trusts you, Felix. She'd confide in you."

Milne pulled himself together with an effort.

" I rather doubt there's much the matter, you know," he said. " At least anything that I could put right." Remembering Barbara's sleek black hair he added weakly, " I don't know, of course."

" I wouldn't be so sure," said Peter, shaking his head. " I tell you, she a very queer girl is Barbara."

Milne's mind flew back to an incident of fifteen years before. He had been twenty-one. He had said to himself, " What I am now going to do is very silly, will cause endless trouble, and won't be worth it. But I'm going to do it." He looked at Peter and saw that his neck formed a fold over the side of his collar.

He said, " Well, of course if you really want me to see her I'd be pleased to."

" I'd be glad if you would," said Peter gratefully. "After all, it can't do any harm, can it ? "

" No," said Milne untruthfully.

* * * * *

" I've never heard such bunkum in my life," said Patricia. " What in God's name does he think's the matter with her anyway ? "

" Darling, he says she's got a sex complex," said Milne lightly. " I asked him what that was, but he went vague."

" I should darned well think she has, if she's married to him. After all, a girl must have something."

" Oh quite," said Milne. " Not much doubt what's wrong with that party."

"I should have thought the best thing was to tell him," said Patricia rather coldly.

Milne said, "I did my best."

"But wasn't it rather dumb of you to say you'd see her?" said Patricia. "After all, there's obviously nothing to do. Isn't it exactly the sort of thing you were complaining about this evening?"

"One can't be sure, of course," said Milne slowly.

Patricia said, "I should think Bab will laugh her head off."

"Oh, she probably won't mind."

"Mind? Of course she won't. She'll love it. You won't have much trouble in getting Bab to tell you all—and she's probably got quite a lot of all to tell. But I don't see that it'll get any one anywhere."

"Look—you don't *mind* about this, do you?" said Milne, as though it had just occurred to him.

"Mind?" said Patricia bluntly. "Of course I mind. And if you get going with her and Bab starts falling in love with you or something, I shall be livid." She gave him a slightly pathetic grin.

"You know I don't like you to have female patients under forty-five unless they wear thick glasses. Particularly in the present state of trade. Anyhow," she added morosely, "Bab will take advantage of the situation. She always takes advantage of situations. And she's always had an eye for you anyhow. Oh damn. You are a low lifer, Felix."

"Come, come!" said Milne. "You are imputing to me conduct infamous in the professional sense, my girl. Anyhow, *I* didn't suggest it."

"No. But you could have told that ass Peter not to be a fool. When's she coming?"

"Thursday afternoon."

"Then that settles it," said Patricia without conviction, "because you've got Mrs. Whatsername—Lucian. The one I booked you."

"That's at three. Barbara isn't coming till half-past four."

"Tea tête-à-tête," said Patricia. "I don't like it at all.

The more I look at it the less I like it." She shook her head despondently. " Felix darling, do be careful. Bab's awful, you know. She'll come after you with her teeth bared if you give her a chance." She paused, and added suddenly, " You don't *want* her to, do you ? "

" Yes, darling," said Milne promptly. " Of course I do. You know I always make passes at my female patients, don't you ? "

" Most of your female patients are impossibly passée." She looked at him thoughtfully. " I wouldn't put it beyond you to have fixed the whole thing."

" Spit me death—I didn't," said Milne. " I never thought of it. Otherwise I might have."

" I've never liked the way you looked at her anyhow. Oh hell ! "

Milne said, " I like making the Rhinoceros jealous."

" Well, you ought to be careful. Everybody knows the Rhinoceros is a very dangerous animal when its eyes go green." Patricia shook her head. " What you don't realise," she said, " is that I've been being jealous of Barbara for nearly twenty years about pretty nearly everything except husbands. So you see . . ."

" What in the name of Pete have you got to be jealous of Barbara about ? " said Milne. " The trouble is that the Rhinoceros has a very little brain and is very stupid."

" Well, she's got black hair and I've always wanted black hair ; and she's got blue eyes which is nicer than just nondescript ; and she's a lovely shape and has nice legs . . ."

" Well, so have you."

" Yes," said Patricia reasonably. " I'm not *very* jealous about legs really. But anyhow she's got lots of nerve and knows how to be attractive."

Milne said, " And as a result she's married to an Apollo like Peter Edge, while you have to put up with me."

" Oh yes," said Patricia. " It's all right as long as it *stays* like that."

It was nearly midnight. Patricia put down her book and said nonchalantly, " Sleepy. I'm going to bed."

Milne looked at the clock and nodded. There was just

a moment's questioning silence. Patricia got up and came over to him. " Good-night, honey," she said, kissing the top of his head.

He said, " Good-night, Rhino," and picked up her hand and kissed it and put it down again.

Patricia went towards the door and then turned.

She said, " Felix."

" Yes ? "

" You're not in love with Bab by any chance, are you ? "

Milne closed his eyes rapturously and said, " I worship the ground she treads on."

Patricia said, " That's all right then. At least I think so."

" Go to bed, sap. See you in the morning."

Patricia said, " Yes. Good-night."

II

On Wednesday and Saturday afternoons Milne travelled from Highgate to a large house in Belgravia. An elderly lady had left it to Dr. Norris Pile in gratitude for his charming efforts to cure her of claustrophobia. After a ding-dong, twice-weekly battle which had lasted for nearly twenty years, the old woman had died triumphant, as claustrophobic as ever. But if she died uncured, she died a believer ; and 47 Laston Square, together with the furnishings thereof, to Dr. Norris Pile, to form a clinic for free psychological treatment.

The only trouble about the Norris Pile Clinic was that while the old lady had left it a house, she had not left it any money ; and since No. 47, even with the furnishings thereof, could not cure the poor of London of anything by itself, the free treatment side of the idea was left to Dr. Norris Pile to arrange. He arranged it with the help of his own private income, plenty of good intentions and the services of anybody who was prepared to work for nothing.

" The greatest tribute you can have to the value of this stuff," as Milne had once remarked to Patricia, " is that even a bogus, muddle-headed, badly run, unorganised dump like the N.P. Clinic does more good than harm."

Norris Pile greeted Felix warmly. He always greeted everybody warmly, being a warm man. But he reserved a special warmth for the medically unqualified consultants who gave time to the clinic. The warmth was a tribute not only to their unselfishness, but to his own breadth of mind in employing people (even unpaid) whom the medical profession regarded as quacks.

"What have you got on the stocks now, Felix?" he said in his eager voice. It was his standard question, but it was always asked with bubbling enthusiasm and keenness.

Milne said, "To-day I've got that girl I told you about. Chronic anxiety state. No idea what it's all about yet. I've only seen her once. A conversion hysteria—not very bad but rather interesting. Chap tends to fall downstairs."

"Downstairs?" said Pile, leaning forward and peering through his horn-rimmed spectacles with his head on one side. "That's very interesting."

"Apart from that I've got a case of bed-wetting."

"Ah," said Pile. "Enuresis." He shook his head doubtfully. "You know, Felix, I'm never happy that we get to the bottom of these enuresis cases. They improve, of course. The symptom disappears. But I often wonder whether we really get to the root of the matter."

Milne said, "Well, this kid's father is a large navvy who thinks the kid wants it thrashed out of him. He came along a fortnight ago and kicked up hell because his wife had brought the boy here. I've spent my time so far trying to get the kid Charlie to realise that I shan't clump his head if he speaks. So maybe the difficulty isn't so very far down. He's only twelve."

Pile said, "You dealt with the navvy all right?"

"Oh yes. He was just a great ox of a man who didn't mean any harm. He just thought children ought to be hit good and hard and often. He seemed quite put out when I told him the kid was scared out of his wits of him."

"By the way," said Pile, bubbling, "did I tell you I'd got a couple of thousand out of the Marchand Trust?"

" Really ? "

" Yes. I went along and saw Freethorne—he's the chairman of the Trustees. He said, ' This Trust is for medical research.' I said, ' My dear Sir George, if what we're doing isn't medical research, I'd like to know what it is.' In the end I talked him round. He's starchy, of course. Give a medical man a title and he always thinks he's God Almighty. But I talked him round."

" What are you going to do with it ? Pay off some of the overdraft ? "

" I don't think we can. I think we shall have to use it *positively*. For one thing, I think we certainly ought to have an encephalograph."

Milne said, " For the love of Pete ! "

" Why not, Felix ? "

" I should have thought it'd be better to spend the money on some decent training courses or in ordinary research grants."

" Well yes. But you know my views there. There's no training and no research like clinical work, you know."

" Maybe," said Milne. " But I don't like this work-it-out-as-we-go-along stuff. It's too like a surgical operation in the dark. "

" Well, well ! " said Pile, heaving his fifteen stone on to his feet. " You may be operating in the dark, Felix, but you seem to get your results. How about your man Gonderton ? I looked at him and I said to myself, ' There's nothing to be done here. That's man's finished.' And look at him when he left you."

" Gonderton," said Felix slowly, " was a beautiful example of the confidence trick, pure and unalloyed."

" Oh come ! " said Pile, beaming. " Surely we all know that the whole job is a confidence trick ? The point is whether it comes off."

" Maybe," said Felix, shrugging. " But personally I'll wait to see what Gonderton's like in two years' time before I start throwing my hat up."

" Well," said Pile briskly, " the follow-up ought to give you that. I'm glad the follow-up is organised now. It's been a bad flaw in the past, not having it. Freethorne was very impressed when I told him about it." He glanced at his watch. " My first patient's about due."

" And mine," said Milne. " See you later."

No. 47, though a fine house, was most unsuitable as a clinic, since it contained a small number of large rooms instead of a large number of small ones. Milne worked in what had once been one of the principal bedrooms, looking out on the quiet square.

His patient had arrived. She was a girl of about twenty-seven, with rather large projecting front teeth. Her sallow face had dark sleepless marks under the eyes, and as they shook hands Milne could see that she was trembling violently.

" Well, Miss Lucas," he said cheerfully, " how are you ? "

The girl's lips trembled and her eyes filled with tears.

" Oh, I've been much better," she said quickly. " Better than I've been for months."

" That's good," said Milne, sitting down.

The tears welled out and rolled down the girl's cheeks. She fumbled shakily in her handbag for a handkerchief and put it to her eyes.

" Oh, I knew I should do this ! " she wailed suddenly. " And I didn't want to because I have been better and I thought you'd be p-pleased. . . ."

" Well, that doesn't matter," said Milne with a smile. " Why shouldn't you cry if you feel like it ? Come and sit over here on the couch and just let go of things for a bit."

She rose obediently and sat down on the couch.

" That's right," said Milne. " Shove your feet up and make yourself comfortable."

" I can't think *why* I feel like this," she said in a low voice.

" Well, that's what we'll try and get at," said Milne. " Comfortable ? "

" Yes, thank you."

" Right. Now relax all your muscles. Breathe deeply. You'll find that'll help."

She shut her eyes and her underdeveloped chest rose and fell slowly.

" Now—have you let go ? "

" Yes," she murmured.

Milne put a finger under her hand, slightly raised her arm and let it go. It returned slowly to her side.

" Now you see you haven't *quite* let go," said Milne gently. " I want to see that arm just flop down when I let go of it." He tried again. " That's better."

He picked up his notebook. " Now—where were we . . .?"

By six o'clock the boy Charlie had smiled twice, but that was all. Milne sent him home and went downstairs to the common room for the usual tea and bun.

Pile had dashed away to his inevitable committee meeting (he represented the psychiatric point of view on a large number of committees dealing with everything from architecture to philately). But the rest were still there. Milne thought, as he had often thought before, that they were an odd-looking bunch—Tautz, about five feet two and completely round, Phyllis Snow, a school-teacher with a secret sorrow, and Paston, sitting by himself, looking like a commercial traveller for something rather shady. They made Garsten look almost comically big and handsome and capable. But even Garsten had to have that ridiculously unexpected silver hair.

Garsten said, " Hallo, Felix. Just in time for the last bun."

" God, what a fug in here," said Milne.

" Expulsion of hot air. Have some tea."

" I've had that kid Charlie Oakes," said Milne wearily. " I can't get a word out of him."

" There you are, you see," said Tautz excitedly. " A perfect example of what I tell you. He won't talk. Felix waits. He waits. Nothing happens. So what ? " He peered up at Garsten through his abnormally thick spectacles.

" Well, so what ? " said Milne.

" Active technique," said Tautz, throwing out a hand. " The only solution. If you cannot follow, you must lead. How many times have I said that ? "

" Hundreds," said Garsten cheerfully, lighting one cigarette from the stub of another. " And it's still bunkum."

"Why you say it's bunkum?" said Tautz, turning on him angrily.

"How the hell can you lead when you don't know the way?"

Phyllis Snow said in her quiet voice, "Felix, do you remember a case of Adler's where he got a strong negative transference and found that it was something to do with a pun on his name?"

Milne said, "I don't remember it happening to Adler. You couldn't have a pun on his name, could you?"

"I can't remember," said Miss Snow with a sigh. "I can't remember anything nowadays. My memory's going to bits." She turned back to her notebook, slowly adjusting her spectacles.

"Ah ha!" said Paston, with a giggle, coming over to him. "Very significant that, Phyllis."

Miss Snow looked up at him for a moment and then lowered her head again without comment.

"You know what the 'Psychopathology of Everyday Life' says about memory failure, don't you?" said Paston, grinning.

Nobody said anything. Paston did not seem to mind. He turned to Felix and said, "Well—and how's my brother quack, Felix?"

"Have you got a brother named Felix?" said Garsten icily.

"No, I meant this one," said Paston, poking Felix in the ribs.

"But *why* you say active technique is bunkum?" said Tautz to Garsten. "You're old-fashioned, see? That's your trouble. Old-fashioned, see? I get results, don't I? I always use active technique."

"What exactly do you mean by active technique?" said Milne.

"I mean get *on*," said Tautz, bouncing excitedly at the knees. "Don't let the session stagnate."

"Hear, hear!" said Paston.

"You agree?" said Tautz, turning sharply. Then, seeing it was Paston, he added quickly, "It must be done properly, of course."

Garsten said, " I had a patient who went to sleep on the couch the other day. I don't blame him, poor devil. I expect he was just bored. Would you have woken him up ? "

" Didn't you ? " said Tautz.

" No. I was brought up to believe that that meant he wasn't ready."

" But you *should* have ! " said Tautz explosively. " You wake him. You tell him he has gone to sleep as a resistance. You explain. You keep going."

" Good heavens, it was Freud himself," said Phyllis Snow suddenly. " Of course it was. ' Freud and Friend.' That was the pun. My memory's just getting funny."

" I didn't think you meant that case," said Milne. " There's another classical one. What's the point anyhow ? "

" I've got a pun association on ' Snow ' and ' Cold ' from one of my patients. Very reasonable too. She bores me stiff and I just can't get her going at all."

Milne said aloud, " Has Norris told anybody about his two thousand pounds ? "

" You bet he has," said Garsten. " We're going to have an electrocephalograph and a convulsion machine. And God knows what gadgets." He turned to Milne. " Have you ever convulsed anybody, Felix ? "

" No," said Milne. " And I don't think I propose to begin now."

" But why not ? " said Tautz eagerly. " That is what I cannot understand. You are so stodgy—so set in your ways. Excellent results have been obtained. Why you will not use convulsion technique ? " He blew through his nose disgustedly. " You want only to sit and listen always. Just—sit—and—listen."

Garsten said, " Whereas what we ought to do is throw people into convulsions all the time ? "

" You sit," said Tautz sarcastically, " and you listen. You listen and you sit. After a very long while you say ' Ah ! We know what is the matter with him. It has taken a long time but we have it now.' " He jack-knifed up and down at the knees excitedly. " But the patient is no *better*. You have diagnosed but you have not cured."

" Well hell, we haven't made him any worse anyhow," said Garsten cynically. " Or not much."

" You're very disillusioned, Garsten," said Paston. " I've noticed it before. I think it's a bad thing not to have faith in your work, y'know. It's no use crying stinking fish, is it ? "

Garsten said, " And it's no use crying good fish if you haven't got any."

" Speak for yourself, old boy."

" I am speaking for myself," said Garsten. " If I were you I should have boundless faith in my ability to cure anybody of anything using charm convulsions, surgical interference, ice-packs and the whole bag of tricks. Being only me, I have my doubts."

Phyllis Snow shut her notebook and got up. " I'm going home," she said. " Good-night."

When she had left the room Paston said, " I think I'm off too. But I think I'll give La Snow a few minutes' start. Otherwise we might have to share a cab."

Milne said, " If you never share a cab with any one worse than Phyllis you'll be all right."

" Oh yes," said Paston rather awkwardly. " I've nothing against La Snow. It's just that I find her a bit inhuman. I think that's a big handicap in this work, y'know."

" Well, if you want someone to be human in a cab with," said Garsten, " you can probably pick it up on the way home."

" What a mind ! " said Paston, grinning. " Good-night, Felix. 'Night, Hans."

They watched him out. " Someone will have to tell Norris that that bird must go," said Garsten. " He just won't do, will he ? "

" He is an ignorant quack," said Tautz. " He knows nothing. He has no right here."

" Nor have I, if you don't like quacks," said Milne.

" No, no," said Tautz quickly. " It is quite different. You are a serious lay analyst. You have studied. You know more than any of us. But he—— ! "

Garsten said, " Norris always was a bad picker. But I will not work in a place with a chap who's still saying ' Ah, ah ! that's significant ! ' every time anybody speaks.

Paston's proper job is writing articles about Sex for the gutter Press."

" He is pretty terrible," said Milne. " Look here, there's one thing I think we ought to try to get going here and that's some group stuff."

" Yes, yes ! " said Tautz eagerly. " Of course we ought. I have always said so. It is folly that we always keep on in the same old ways. Activity ! Movement ! No stagnation ! "

As they walked towards the Underground, Milne said to Garsten, " You were very bitter to-night about everything."

Garsten threw his cigarette away violently. " Sometimes," he said, " I get so fed up with all the mumbo-jumbo and abracadabra and making of holy mysteries about simple things that I like to call a spade a shovel."

" I shouldn't have said we went in much for making a holy mystery of things."

" At the Clinic ? No, I don't think we do. But look at us. Norris—well, we all know about Norris. He sits on a pretty committee. Hans—a nice little man and takes his job seriously. But about as much judgement as a cockatoo. Phyllis Snow—a damn fine person in the wrong job. Paston—a fool and a bit of a crook. What a collection to deal with about the most difficult job on earth ! "

" You've left us out," said Milne with a grin.

" Oh, you're all right," said Garsten. " At least as far as I know. As for me——" he shrugged. " I never know whether I do more harm than good or more good than harm. Sometimes one and sometimes the other, I suppose." He kicked at a stone on the pavement. " I don't mind our being inadequate. What I mind is that we don't realise it."

" But don't we ? "

" Oh, when we're talking, yes. But can you lay your hand on your heart and say that when you get a strong positive transference, and a patient pretty nearly tells you you're God Almighty, you never get to the point of half believing him ? "

" Aren't you asking too much ? " said Milne.

Garsten said, " I'm not asking anything. It's the bloody

job that asks too much. That's the catch in the whole thing. It asks for people who're superhuman. And in fact what it gets is either fools or oddities. It's like being a parson. The only people who would make good parsons are the people who know too much about themselves to take the job on."

"Well, what do you think ought to be done about it?"

"God knows. I wasn't pretending to be constructive. Je n'impose rien. Je ne propose rien. J'expose."

It was nearly seven o'clock when Milne reached home. There was no light in the lounge. He knew that Patricia would be in her bedroom, and hesitated for a moment at the bottom of the stairs. But he felt tired and he was irritated and depressed by Garsten, and he knew from experience that the safer way was to sit down by himself for a while.

He went into the consulting room and flopped rather wearily into his chair, glancing automatically at his engagement pad. Patricia had put Mrs. Lucian down at three o'clock, but she had not made an entry for Barbara. For some reason he found this irritating. Patricia was usually very careful about his appointments. She was unlikely to have left Barbara out by accident. Milne took a pencil and scribbled, "4.30 Barbara." After a moment he altered it to "Mrs. Edge." He stared at the entry for some time and then, leaning back in his chair, closed his eyes.

Patricia walked along the upstairs corridor and started to come downstairs. Milne found himself reflecting that no one else in the world made quite so much noise as Patricia in moving about a house. Suddenly there was a scrabbling noise and a crash of glass, followed by silence. Milne went out into the hall. Patricia was standing a few steps up, looking at the fragments of broken glass.

She said, "Damn it! Hallo, darling."

Milne said, "Rhinoceros."

"It slipped off the tray," said Patricia.

"So it seems."

"It did it on purpose," she said childishly. "It didn't have to."

Milne hesitated for a moment, but she looked at him with a slightly nervous and ingratiating smile.

"Look, darling," he said acidly. "I don't mind your smashing glasses—even rather nice ones. But don't do a baby-mine about it, there's a pet."

Patricia's smile vanished and she looked quickly away. "Dust-pan and brush," she said briskly, vanishing in the direction of the kitchen.

When she came back to the lounge Milne was sitting gazing into the fire.

He said, "There we go again, you see."

"What?" said Patricia.

"I simply cannot keep my tongue off you."

Patricia fetched her work-box in silence. "It's my fault," she said at last. "I am irritating."

"Yes, by God you are. You're careless and clumsy and you forget things and you're altogether awful. But you're my personal Rhinoceros and there's no excuse for just being filthy to you all the time." He smiled rather crookedly. "If anybody else did it I should say he was an oral sadist and that something had better be done about it."

Patricia squinted at the eye of her needle. "No, it isn't very good," she said quietly. "Not that I mind—or not enough to matter anyhow. But it makes me worse. I get all nervous and jumpy and then I drop things and break things and forget and so on even more." She looked up at Milne with thoughtful grey eyes. "Of course that isn't really the point at all. If you wanted me, you wouldn't even notice that I crash about. But as you don't——" she shrugged.

Milne looked at her for a moment. It was on the tip of his tongue to say, "But I do want you," and grab her and kiss that look off her face, and let it all go to hell. But it would be a lie and he knew it, and she would know it.

He gave a sort of groan and said, "It's a bloody silly situation, Rhino."

"It isn't silly at all. You come in tired to death and wanting somebody and I just don't fill the bill. That's all."

Milne said, "You fill the bill a damn sight better than any one else in the world could," and put out his hand.

Patricia shook her head. "No," she said calmly. "No. That doesn't help. That's what we always do. We start to talk about this and then we get frightened and—and laugh it off. That doesn't get us anywhere, Felix."

Milne said, "Is there anything that would?"

"I don't know," she said helplessly. "I've rather given up for the moment. I just—take it as it comes. Sometimes it's all right. But I know there'll come a time when it isn't and you'll hate me and resent me and—and so on. One of these days it'll get so bad that it'll bust us up. I thought it had the other night."

Milne said harshly, "Why in God's name do you stand it?"

She shrugged slightly. "I'd rather have something than nothing."

He caught her hand and said incoherently, "But you do know it's all right really—basically all right? You know this is only a queer thing I've got and that I know about you and —and love you and that you're my person really? You do know?"

She smiled at him rather pathetically and said, "Yes, darling. I know. It's all right." But he knew that she didn't see—not all of it—any more than he did himself.

He dropped her hand and said drearily, "I'd give anything in the world to—to get this straight."

"I'll all come out in the wash, I expect," said Patricia.

Milne said, "What worries me is that here am I, trying to cope with other people's complications, and meanwhile there's this stupid mix-up inside me."

"Well, any stupid mix-up inside you at present," said Patricia briskly, "probably comes from wanting your dinner." She finished sewing on the button and snapped the thread. "Come on—let's go and eat."

She pushed her work-box aside. It hit a small vase of flowers and pushed it off the side table. Milne made a wild grab and caught the vase in mid-air.

"Golly—well taken, sir!" said Patricia rather breathlessly. They looked at one another for a moment and then broke into a simultaneous roar of laughter.

"Rhin-*o*!" said Milne, shaking his head.

"You know I'm not *safe*," said Patricia solemnly. "I shall set the place on fire or something."

III

MILNE had thought hard about how to conduct his interview with Barbara, but he had not given much thought to Mrs. Lucian. She would be fair, fat and forty-five, and the usual technique, as practised with success on Lady Maresfield and others would apply.

Mrs. Lucian was not fair, fat and forty-five. She was dark, thin and nearer twenty-five, and really remarkably small, being only about five feet high. She came in rather nervously and with as much dignity and solemnity as anything of that size can manage. But when Milne, slightly disconcerted, switched on his warm and friendly smile, she answered him at once with a broad grin from her big, bright scarlet gash of a mouth, and shook hands like a friendly street Arab.

She said, " How do you do, Dr. Milne. It's good of you to see me," with an American accent.

" Not 'doctor,' " said Milne. " I always have to get that straight at the outset."

" No—of course. I knew that really. Helen Rafer told me."

" Oh, you know Mrs. Rafer ? " said Milne. " Won't you take your hat and coat off and sit down ? "

He helped her off with the ridiculously small black coat and hung it in a cupboard. She pulled off her small black hat and gave a relieved shake to a bunch of jet black curls. The only result was to intensify the gamine effect. Milne took in the brown hands and dark eyes and guessed Italian or Southern French somewhere.

" Thanks v'ry much," she said, sitting down in one of his big chairs and looking smaller than ever.

" Well now ? " said Milne, sitting down also. " Did you say Mrs. Rafer suggested that you should come to me ? "

" Well no. Not exactly. But she was talking about you and I kind of suggested it to myself."

Milne said, " I see. What's the trouble ? "

She grinned the big-mouthed grin.

"It's not me. Maybe there's a lot the matter with me, but nobody's noticed it yet. It's my husband. Hereinafter referred to as Adam, because I get tired of saying 'my husband' all the time."

Milne nodded.

"I think maybe you could do something for him, Mr. Milne."

Milne hesitated for a moment.

"What makes you think he needs something done? You mustn't mind my asking that. I always do when people come to me about their husbands or wives."

"Well, he's had a couple of goes at murdering me," she said, looking at him with solemn dark eyes.

"Murdering you?"

"Yes." The momentary seriousness disappeared and the broad grin flashed out again, a shade pathetically this time. "Maybe you think that just shows he's normal. But you can't expect me to feel that way." He shook his head. "There are other things too," she said thoughtfully. "Quite a lot of other things."

Milne said, "But surely you've had some advice? Somebody will have seen him?"

"Well, that's the trouble," she said, wrinkling up her forehead and nose in a curious comprehensive frown. "Adam's nuts about doctors. He had quite a lot of them in the war, and he just hates the sight of them."

"That's why you came to me?"

"Partly. Mind, I don't know he'd play ball even with you. But I think he might if you'd take him on." She looked at Milne rather anxiously.

There was a moment's silence.

"Well, of course I will, if I think I can help," said Milne, smiling at her, and getting his reward at once in the reappearance of the grin. "Can you tell me more about it? When all this started and so on? Have a cigarette to start with." She took the cigarette and accepted a match with a quick upward glance at him.

"Well, it's like this," she said, crossing her legs and seizing herself firmly by the lobe of the ear. "I'm an American. I don't suppose I have to tell you that. I was over here in 1939 when the war started and I just stayed on to see what there was to see, doing this and that. I met Adam and we got married just at the beginning of 1940."

"How old is he?"

"Let's see—twenty-eight now. He was a pilot in the R.A.F.—flying officer then."

"Fighter or bomber?"

"Fighter. He just missed the Battle of Britain. He was on operations over here and he did very well and got a D.F.C. He was quite all right then." She smiled. "In fact I'll say he was more than all right."

"You were happy?"

"We certainly were, Mr. Milne. Well, he finished his tour of duty and instead of letting himself be grounded the old sap up and volunteered for another, just like that. He came through that all right, but it seemed to me he was pretty tired at the end of it, as who wouldn't be. Still, he was O.K. There was nothing funny."

"What made you think he was tired?"

"Oh, it wasn't anything. He just looked and acted like a boy who could do with a rest, that's all. Well, then, he did get a ground job. And the next thing was he was off out East, No flying, mind you. Just a nice quiet job on the ground organising and playing with a lot of paper." She shook her head. "Well, of course, the next thing I heard, Mr. Milne, was that he'd gone missing. He'd managed to get himself into the air, and he'd managed to get himself into a fight, and the last that had been seen of him he was going down on fire somewhere near Rangoon. Nobody had seen his crate hit the ground, but there was no doubt it was going to hit it pretty hard and pretty soon, and they told me in a nice sort of way that I'd better write one husband off my books."

She paused and stared thoughtfully into the fire.

"I never reckoned he was dead," she said with the queer wrinkled frown. "I suppose no woman ever does reckon her man's dead—not if she doesn't want him to be. I always had a kind of feeling he'd turn up. But I hadn't got any reason to think so, and I wasn't going to count on it. I figured the only thing to do was to keep pushing my chin at it. If he turned up, that would be fine. If not—well, that'd be too bad."

She gave the small ear a sharp tug. " Well, of course, you aren't holding on to your chair waiting for next week's instalment, Mr. Milne, because you know he *did* show up. After nearly a year. And what hadn't happened to that boy. He'd baled out and come down in a tree. He cracked his head against something, and the first thing he knew he was hanging head downwards in this tree in the middle of the jungle. He sorted himself out of that and started off to walk home, a few hundred miles. He had about ten days of it, and about the last two steps he could take fetched him up with some natives. They picked him up and kept him all nice and comfortable while they sent a guy along to trade him in to the Japs ; and there was the boy wonder, a P.O.W. The old Jap had his own troubles and he wasn't too fussy about what happened to prisoners. Among quite a lot of other things they were short of rope or guards or what-have-you, so they thought maybe the best way to keep Adam around was to break one of his legs. So they did that." She paused for a fraction of a second and swallowed.

" Christ ! " said Milne in a low voice.

" They did just that." She threw up her head and the invincible grin flashed out again. " But you can't keep a good guy down. This boy Adam wasn't in very good shape by then. But he took a dislike to the place and these people, and as soon as his leg was about a quarter mended he wrote off a Jap with a chunk of wood and lit out for home again."

" Alone ? "

" Oh yes. Quite alone." She stretched out a slightly shaking brown paw and knocked the ash off her cigarette. " Well, that wasn't so good either. He had a bit more jungle hiking, and I think what with his gammy leg and being pretty starved to begin with and one thing and another, this was the worst bit of the lot. But he came through somehow. He hit another lot of natives and this time the exchange rate for British prisoners was favourable, and he landed back with the Eleventh Army." She glanced suddenly at her watch. " Am I taking too long ? "

"Lord no!" said Milne. "Go as slow as you like. This is just what I want."

"You can get it all from him, of course—at least, you can try. Anyhow, the end of it was he got back to England, and of course I thought that was where they lived happily ever after. He'd weighed a hundred and sixty pounds when I leased him to your Air Force, and when I got him back he only weighed about a hundred and twelve; and his gammy leg wasn't right and probably never would be. But I'd got him back and I should worry." She paused and threw her cigarette end into the fire.

"Well, for a while it was all fine. He put on weight. His leg was better than they thought. They reckoned he ought to have ruined it for good, but it seems he hadn't. And—this is the bit you'll be interested in—he seemed all right in himself, Mr. Milne. He was a bit jumpy, of course—up and down and sideways. But in most ways it was amazing how little it had changed him. He didn't laugh much. But then he never had anyway. He could sleep and he could eat, and he still seemed to like the idea of having me around. And that went on right up till about six months ago. If you'd seen him when he first got back to England and then back again at the beginning of this year, you'd have said it had all gone fine. And then——" She spread out her hands helplessly.

Milne said, "It all began to happen quite suddenly?"

"Just like that." She snapped her fingers. "We'd been out dancing—for about the first time for five years. It was a try-out for his leg, and he was all lit up because it stood it all right. I've never seen him happier or more normal. We got home and were going to bed. I was in bed first, and being mighty tired I went to sleep before he came. Well, Mr. Milne, when I woke up this boy Adam had me by the throat and was he squeezing. He looked just crazy. I fought, like anybody would, but I can't give the weight away to a guy that size. I couldn't see much and I was beginning to think X marked the spot. I quit fighting and somehow I must have smiled—or at least so he thought. Anyhow he drops me as though I'm red hot and says, 'You smiled!' I coughed and choked and wheezed a bit and then I said, 'Did I hell! What have I got to smile about? And then he started to cry and that was the end of that time."

"He just stopped?"

"Yes. He just stopped. And he left me with some dandy bruises and a hell of a sore throat. But from that time it's never been very good for long. He seems all shot to pieces and he's getting worse. He isn't sleeping, and he's taking too many highballs, which he never used."

Milne said, "Has he ever actually attacked you again?"

"Not to say attack, Mr. Milne. But once when we were on a platform he grabbed me as a train was coming in, looking like he had the other time; and I thought I was going under the train. But of course I knew the form by then and I just smiled at him and said, 'Steady now, honey. Don't do anything you wouldn't like mother to know about.' He looked at me and started to laugh in a sort of ashamed way, and we laughed it off. But it wasn't really as funny as all that."

Milne said, "You say he's been different since the first time. In what ways?"

Mrs. Lucian wrinkled up her whole face thoughtfully. "Bit hard to say. He hasn't been well. Not sleeping, and eating too little, and drinking too much. But that isn't half of it really. He's taken to sitting quite quiet for a long time; and if you speak to him it's as though he isn't really there. He answers but—but *something* isn't there."

Milne looked up sharply. "You say you've had no advice?"

"No. The boy just won't play."

"But surely——?"

"Just will not play, Mr. Milne. And, mind you, he's all right most of the time. Apart from these goes with me, you have to know him pretty well to see there's anything wrong. It's just that it's not the same boy as before. See, his line is that he's quite O.K. and there's nothing to see a doctor about."

"How about the attacks on you?"

"Well, one I can't swear to. He didn't *do* anything that time. The other he just says he must have been crazy, and shies off it. It's my belief he doesn't remember a thing about it." She added slightly apologetically, " I haven't sort of kept on about it because I didn't see that could help." She paused and fumbled absently for a cigarette. " If you could do anything for him, Mr. Milne, I'd like to say you'd be doing it for a great guy." She smiled at him rather shakily.

Milne sat for a long while in silence.

" Look, Mrs. Lucian," he said at last. " I can tell you right away that of course I'll do anything I can to help. But I'm not a doctor, as you know. There are certain sorts of trouble that I can help with, and I'd be only too glad to see your husband and decide if there's anything I can do. But I can't take the responsibility for not warning you that you may be up against something outside my field."

" Such as what ? "

" There's no need to go into the technical details," said Milne evasively. " But the two pieces of advice I must give you are firstly, that you ought to get your husband to see another sort of specialist. I'll give you the name of a good man if you like. Secondly, you may be running a considerable risk in living with him, and you oughtn't to do it until someone's seen him and advised you."

The small woman uncrossed her legs and kicked thoughtfully at one foot with the other.

" Well, the answer to both those is easy, Mr. Milne. Is the other guy you want him to see a doctor ? "

" Yes."

" Then that's out. You won't get the boy Adam to see a doc without you use a tractor to pull him there. The other one's easier still. He may not be a very happy boy just now, but I reckon if he hadn't got me he'd be unhappier still. If he could go trekking round a jungle with a broken leg thumbing rides from elephants to get back to me, I reckon I won't walk out on him for the risk of a sore throat."

Milne said, " I don't think you realise——"

She suddenly grinned the expansive and cheeky grin.

" It won't go," she said gently. " The engine won't even start. Hell, if the boy's got to half-choke somebody it's got to be me, hasn't it ? "

She rose to her feet, looking absurdly childish in the short black frock, and carefully brushed a speck of tobacco ash from its skirt. Milne rose too.

"Well, Mr. Milne—there's my true confession. I reckon there's something there that the boy Adam's got to get out of his system. If you'll help, that's fine. If you won't——" She shrugged. "I don't know. But it's no good offering me doctors." She glanced at him anxiously. "Maybe if you could see him you'd know——?"

Milne hesitated.

"Yes," he said slowly, "I suppose that's the answer." He picked up his engagement book. "When could he come?"

"I wouldn't know whether he *will* come, Mr. Milne. But if you say a time I reckon I can probably make him. I can make that boy do most things if I go tough."

Milne looked down at her and smiled. "You do go tough, do you?"

She nodded solemnly. "If you're a vest pocket model like me, you have to go tough to keep your end up."

"Well, you certainly seem to keep it up all right," said Milne, smiling. "How about next Monday? Or would you rather it was sooner?"

It was nearly quarter-past four when Mrs. Lucian left. Milne glanced at his watch and realised that in a few minutes Barbara would arrive—if she came at all. It was quite possible, of course, that she wouldn't. He had left it to Peter to arrange, and had heard no more.

He found himself hoping, surprisingly but very definitely, that she wouldn't come. If she did, it would mean a complication one way or the other, and a distraction; and at the moment he did not want to be distracted. He tried to recapture some excitement at the prospect by raising his favourite vision of her—slightly mocking, consciously attractive, with the sleek black hair and Siamese cat eyes, pulling her skirt down over her knees with that careful modesty that no chaste woman can ever quite manage. But it would not fire, and with a little grunt he sat down at his desk and began to read through the notes of his talk with Mrs. Lucian.

Yet for all that, he found himself constantly glancing at the clock and waiting for the distant sound of the doorbell ; and from the moment it struck half-past four he was telling himself with altogether too much firmness that obviously she was not coming. He went so far as to ring the bell for his tea.

Barbara and the tea arrived almost simultaneously, and there were some moments of slightly formal confusion whilst Milne took Barbara's coat and Janet put down the tray.

" Just in time for tea," said Milne, as he hung up the big mink coat. Its bulk contrasted strangely with Mrs. Lucian's child's-size black cloth affair.

" This is marvellous," said Barbara. " A cup of tea is just what I want. It's gone uncommonly cold." She sat down and stretched out the long white fingers to the fire. Milne noticed the classical plainness of the black frock and reflected that if Peter Edge didn't supply anything else, he did at least supply the money.

When Janet had gone, there was a moment's silence. Milne picked up the teapot. " I'll give you some tea," he said. " And thereafter grab. Then we needn't keep interrupting to be polite."

" I won't eat, thanks," said Barbara.

" Not even a bit of toast ? "

" No. If I eat at tea-time at all I find myself eating a disgraceful amount. Just tea."

" Right," said Milne. He gave her the cup and settled back in his chair. " Well now, Barbara——"

She looked back at him with the slow mocking smile. " Well now, Felix——? ".

" I suppose Peter told you about our talk ? "

" Well, yes and no," said Barbara meekly. " You see, Felix, I don't suppose Peter's ever explained anything to you when he's embarrassed. But if he had, you'd realise that he's a bit difficult to follow, poor lamb."

" He was very keen that I should have a talk to you. Professionally, so to speak."

" Yes. He said something about a ' preliminary examination.' I think an 'examination' sounds rather awful, Felix. Do I have to take my clothes off or anything?" She looked at him with gentle inquiry.

Milne hesitated. "You can if you'd feel more comfortable without them," he said shortly. "But there's no need from my point of view."

"Oh," said Barbara. "Snubbed. Made to feel forward or worse. Oh dear. This is going to be rather awful. I don't think I like your being professional."

Milne handed her his cigarette box and took a cigarette himself.

"Now look, Bab," he said firmly. "No old horse."

"Certainly not," said Barbara, with equal firmness. "No old horse whatever."

"I told Peter that he was almost certainly talking nonsense and that there was no point in my seeing you. But he was so keen on it that I couldn't very well get out of it."

"I'm very sorry," said Barbara gravely. "I wouldn't have come if I'd known——"

"Don't fool," said Milne irritably. "You know what I mean, don't you?"

She did not answer, but merely gave him a quick smile.

"Now is there anything in what Peter said?"

"But Felix dear," she said helplessly. "How can I possibly tell you? I don't know what Peter *did* say. He just told me he thought it would be nice for you to examine me."

"Well," said Milne, glancing at his cigarette. "He seemed to think there was a certain amount of sexual difficulty between you."

"Difficulty?" said Barbara. She shook her head. "I'd hardly call it *difficulty*."

"Well, anyhow, he thought things were less satisfactory than they might be. And being Peter he assumed that this must be because there was something odd about you. I may say that husbands always think that about their wives. People in my job nearly always get sent the wrong half of a marriage."

Barbara considered. "Of course," she said meekly, "it's hardly for me to say. But I've never had any complaints before."

Milne said, "You are a bad little slut, aren't you? I can't think why Pat likes you."

"No, but seriously," said Barbara, "what does he think's the matter with me, Felix?"

"He thinks you're over-sexed, whatever that means."

"I see. And is that one of the things you cure?"

"Not in people like you," said Milne firmly.

"Then why did you let me come?"

"I tell you I couldn't get out of it. Anyhow, it was just possible that there was something wrong. But I take it that it's all bunkum, of course?"

"Wait a minute," said Barbara, shaking her head. "I'd like notice of that. What happens if it *isn't* all bunkum?" She crossed her legs and pulled the black frock carefully into position. "What I mean is, supposing you make a preliminary examination and find that I have got something? What happens then?"

"Then," said Milne, with a grim smile, "I go and see Peter and recommend him to send you to an excellent man I know who is five feet two in height, wears thick glasses, and takes his profession very seriously."

"But would that be a friendly action?"

Milne swallowed. "Yes. A very friendly one."

"There doesn't seem to be a lot in this for me, whichever way you look at it," she said, shaking her head despondently. "I don't think I could confess to a little man in thick glasses. Pearls before swine."

Milne said, "The joke is, my girl, that whereas Peter may be talking bunkum, he isn't talking *complete* bunkum. You're a thorough-going exhibitionist. And people aren't exhibitionists for nothing."

"What's an exhibitionist?"

"In your case it's a person who loves to parade her sins."

"But Felix, surely that's the idea? I mean, I thought that's what you wanted people to do? It's good for them, isn't it?"

"In certain circumstances, yes. But not as an amusing game for a wet afternoon. More tea?"

Barbara took her cup and lit another cigarette. "Seriously though, Felix, what do you *do* to people? I've always wanted to know."

"Well, it's like this," said Milne slowly. "The theory of the thing, very roughly, is that in most of us there are two people. One is the natural person, that has various desires and instincts; and the other is the conventional person that believes in the law, and morality and religion and so on. So there tends to be a scrap between what we want to do and what we know we *ought* to do."

"Fair enough," said Barbara. "Like wanting to buy a hat you can't really afford?"

"More or less."

"Of course you always do buy it. At least I do."

"I'll bet you do. Well, since the sexual instinct is the one where there tends to be the biggest scrap between nature and convention, sexual desires of one sort and another tend to get squashed down—repressed—by the conventional person. The conventional bit of you not only won't let the natural person do what it wants to. It won't even allow the things to be thought of. It shoves them down into a pill-box in the mind and stands on the lid."

"I don't think my conventional person does that," said Barbara. "Not much, anyhow."

"Maybe not. Though I wouldn't be too sure about it. Don't forget that sex here means something much wider than just sleeping with people. Anyhow, these things which have been shoved out of sight haven't really gone. They've merely been pushed out of your conscious mind into your sub-conscious mind. You never consciously think about them, but they're there all the time underneath. And unfortunately they have a habit of making trouble."

"How?"

"Well, they set up a sort of pressure—raise a sort of mental blister. It may take all sorts of forms—hysterical paralysis, or headaches, or hatred of being in a confined space—all sorts of oddities. Those are the things people come to chaps like me with."

"And what do you do about it?"

"Dig out what the repressed stuff is. If you can bring it into the conscious mind so that people remember it and think about it, the blister goes. There's no longer any pressure, because it's been released."

"But how do you?"

"Get them to talk quite frankly. Give the natural person a chance to say what it really thinks. It will probably take a long time, but if a person just goes on saying whatever comes into his head when he's quite relaxed and doesn't care any longer about the conventions or what anybody will think, it will probably come out in the end."

"And then he gets better?"

"That's the idea."

"And it really works?"

"More or less. The snag is that very often the root of the trouble is something which happened when he was a small kid and which he literally hasn't thought of since. Stuff like that takes a lot of time and patience to dig out."

"But I don't think I can remember *anything* that happened when I was small. Hardly anything, anyhow."

"You'd find you could after a bit of practice. One doesn't really lose things, you know. They're only mislaid and overlaid."

Barbara frowned. "But have small kids anything to repress? Sexual things?"

"Like hell they have. If you've ever watched a baby at the breast you'll know if children have sexual desires."

"Oh yes. But that isn't *really* sexual."

"I tell you, you mustn't think of sex as just going to bed with people. That's why the layman doesn't believe in this stuff. Someone has told him that trouble may arise because a kid of three was in love with its mother, and he thinks it's bunkum. So it is in the sense he means. I always remember a time when old Loewe, who taught me, was lecturing in England. He'd been talking about a case and at the end a very distinguished old philosopher who's dead now got up and said, 'Do I understand you to say, sir, that this child of four was jealous of his father's sexual relations with his mother?' Old Loewe hesitated and then just said 'Yes.' The old boy looked at him for a moment and then said, very politely, 'I find that very difficult to believe' and sat down. You see, they were talking about entirely different things."

There was a long pause.

" It all sounds rather fun," said Barbara. " And that's all you do? Just make people remember? "

" Not make them. Let them. Arrange for them to. At one time people used to hypnotise patients and get things out of them like that. But there are a lot of snags about using hypnosis, and it isn't much used now."

" Can people really be hypnotised? "

" Oh yes. If they want to. Not otherwise."

" Oh well, that hardly counts," said Barbara, disappointed. " The sort of hypnotism I like is when somebody stares into your eyes and makes you go and murder your aunt."

" No. That sort only happens in films."

" Could you hypnotise me, Felix? "

" I dare say."

" Rather fun. What could you make me do? "

" Well, what I *couldn't* make you do," said Milne pointedly, " is anything which you found morally repugnant as the books say. There's a classical case of that."

" But you could make me do something I want to but thought I oughtn't to? "

Milne said, " I could probably do that without bothering with hypnosis." He smiled at her confidentially. " You are awful, aren't you, Bab? "

She smiled and then looked away, the smile vanishing quickly.

" Well, Felix my dear, so would you be if——" She stopped.

" Yes, I know," said Milne gently.

" I doubt you do."

" You're not happy with Peter? "

" What do you think? " she said bitterly.

" Why did you marry him, Bab? "

Barbara shrugged. " Why does one do these things? "

" Were you in love with him? "

" Good God no! "

" Well then, what did you think you could get out of it? "

Barbara thought for a while. " I wanted to get away from home. I wanted to be married to somebody. And I wanted to be—safe. I mean—to have money and clothes and so on and somebody to rely on."

"Well, from that point of view it hasn't been a bad bargain, has it?" said Milne bluntly.

"Oh, Lord no. Excellent. Don't think I'm complaining. The person who's got a grouse is Peter—if anybody has. That's why he sent me to you. He thinks I don't fulfil my side of the bargain."

"And do you?"

"I try," said Barbara slowly. "In fact I sometimes try rather surprisingly hard. But you can't get over the fact that poor old Pete's a sap, and rather a nasty one in some ways." She looked up. "Is this what a preliminary examination ought to be like, Felix?"

"It's certainly very normal," said Milne.

There was a long pause. Then Barbara said, "Well, I think the answer's obvious. I'm very ill indeed and you'd better take me on." She looked at him with the quick secret smile.

Milne said, "Oh, you do, do you?"

"Yes. It would do me all the good in the world to be able to talk to someone sane occasionally."

"Unfortunately I can hardly charge your husband fees for that."

"Well, who knows? I might become less over-sexed."

"I doubt you would," said Milne expressionlessly. He glanced at his cigarette and was annoyed to see that his hand was shaking.

Barbara's smile vanished. "I see," she said coldly. "Then——"

Milne pushed his chair back and got up. "Listen," he said rather breathlessly, "I wouldn't take you on as a patient if it was all that stood between me and the work-house. Do you understand?"

Barbara stared at him steadily. "Of course I understand. What could be clearer?" she said calmly.

"And do you also understand why?"

Her eyes fluttered. "Presumably you're not interested."

Milne said, "You know quite well that it's because

I'm a damn sight too interested." He sat down on the broad arm of her chair and seized her by the wrist. "See?"

Barbara looked down at the hand grasping her wrist and smiled secretly and silently.

"I didn't know that psychologists suffered from these human weaknesses," she said, after a moment's silence.

"Liar!" said Milne.

"I don't mean it isn't very nice to find they do." She threw her head back and gazed up at him mockingly. "Well, now what, Felix?"

Milne hesitated for a moment and then dropped her wrist and rose quickly to his feet.

"Now," he said curtly, "you go away. I then report to Peter that there's damn all the matter with you."

"But he'd be so disappointed, Felix."

"I can't help that."

"——and anyhow, it's very disappointing for me. I was looking forward to being hypnotised and being made undersexed and so on."

"I'll be pleased to arrange that—in my private capacity," said Milne grimly. "Now come on, Bab—stop it and go away, there's a dear."

Barbara hesitated for a moment, and then with a little shrug rose to her feet.

"All right." She patted at the sleek black head and walked over to the mirror. "But I think you're rather a cad and rather a prig. There's nothing worse than a man who makes you take off your self-respect and keep your clothes on."

Milne said, "Don't be a mutt. You know it isn't like that at all, don't you?"

"My God, how livid I should be if I thought it was," she said with a grin. "Dear Felix. Now give me my coat and let me shake off the dust of this dutiful, disappointing place."

At eleven o'clock that night Milne finally became tired of waiting and said, "You haven't asked me what happened with Barbara."

Patricia said, " Oh yes, of course—you were seeing her to-day. I'd forgotten."

" I've been sitting here all the evening watching you having forgotten," said Milne. " You've been like a cat on hot bricks."

Patricia grinned. " Well, you know I'm far too well trained to ask you about what happens with a patient. Anyhow," she added frankly, " I know nothing did—or nothing much."

" How do you ? "

" Because if it had, you would have been being much nicer to me. You're always nice to me if you've done me dirt."

Milne said, " Anybody'd think I did you dirt on Monday, Wednesdays and Saturdays."

" No, ass ! But you *are* always particularly nice when guilty. When you've resisted temptation you tend to be a bit fed up with me."

Milne said, " You're a disconcerting cuss at times, honey."

" Did you just tell her there was nothing the matter with her ? "

" Of course. As a matter of fact, it isn't true. There's plenty the matter with her. But nothing I want to mess about with."

" Did Bab come at you with bared teeth ? "

" More or less."

" What did you do about it ? "

" Told her to can it. She's very good-tempered about that sort of thing."

" Oh Lord yes. So now what ? "

" Now nothing. I shall just tell Peter there's nothing I can do."

" Poor Felix," said Patricia suddenly.

" What d'you mean ? "

" Well, it would have been fun for you. I can see Bab would be fun to play with." She looked at Milne with wide-open, thoughtful eyes. " Honestly, though, darling, I think it's a good thing—even from your own point of view. Of course I *should* think so. But it would have been so complicated, and there might have been such a mess."

IV

LUCIAN'S appointment was for eleven o'clock, but at eleven-fifteen there was still no sign of him. Milne was not surprised. He would have been more surprised if Lucian had arrived punctually. He went on working at his notes on Miss Lucas.

At eleven-thirty, glancing out of his window, Milne saw a big man with a slight limp walk slowly past the garden gate. He was dressed in a sports jacket and old flannel trousers. His bare head was bent, and he was kicking a stone aimlessly in front of him. He did not look at the house, but walked on slowly out of sight.

Milne gave it two minutes and then went out to the garden gate. The big man was leaning against the wall about twenty yards away, staring down at the pebble at his feet.

Milne said, " Hallo. Are you Lucian ? "

" Yes," said the big man, looking at him without marked interest.

Milne said, " I'm Milne. How about coming in ? "

Lucian seemed to consider for a moment. " All right," he said at last. He stooped, picked up the pebble, put it carefully into his pocket and followed Milne into the house.

As they went up the path, Milne said, " Is that a special pebble or just *a* pebble ? "

" I've kicked it all the way from Camden Town," said Lucian. " So it seemed a pity to leave it now."

" Oh, you walked up ? "

" Yes. They say it's good for my leg."

" How's your leg getting on ? "

" Oh, it's better," said Lucian vaguely.

They went into the consulting room. " Sit down," said Milne. " Cigarette ? "

" No, thanks, doc."

" No," said Milne. " *Not* doc. That's a thing I always have to put right. I'm not a doctor."

Lucian smiled for the first time, quietly and inwardly. " Oh yes, Doctor."

" No. I'm not qualified."

" Doctor from my point of view," said Lucian with gentle obstinacy.

" Maybe. But not legally."

" I shall call you doc," said Lucian with finality.

" All right," said Milne with a grin. " It's a bit of an insult, but still——"

" Insult ? " said Lucian with sudden energy. " I'll say it is. The bastards." He looked at Milne thoughtfully. " Molly says she came to see you."

" Yes."

" And you said you could cure me of all sorts of things, whether I'd got them or not."

" Oh come. She didn't tell you I said that."

" Well, maybe not quite. Anyhow she liked the look of you."

Milne said, " I'm glad of that." He lit a cigarette and added brusquely, " What have you got anyhow ? "

" Nothing," said Lucian. " Not a bloody thing. But she thinks I have."

" You're quite all right really ? "

Lucian's eyes were wandering slowly round the room. " Quite all right," he said uninterestedly. " Except for my leg and one or two oddments like that. I had rather a sticky time in the war." His eyes suddenly came back to Milne. " Maybe she told you about that ? " he said sharply. " About being a prisoner and escaping and so on ? "

" Yes. She told me a little about it."

Lucian nodded. " Well, when that happens it's bound to upset you a bit. Bound to," he repeated emphatically, passing a hand quickly over his forehead. Milne noticed that just where his fair hair joined the brown skin of his forehead, there were sudden little beads of sweat.

" Of course," said Milne. He smiled. " I must say it seems to have affected you very little really."

" Oh, I'm fairly tough," said Lucian. " If I weren't I

shouldn't be here." He lowered his eyes to the floor and sat still and silent.

"What's your wife worrying about? Any idea?" said Milne.

"Moll? Oh, she always worries. She thinks I'm not well. You know how it is."

"Just doesn't think you're well? Nothing in particular?" Milne grinned. "Usually wives know exactly what's the matter with their husbands. Or think they do. Mine always does."

"Well, if she had any ideas about that she'd have told you," said Lucian with a quick glance.

"But anyhow, you yourself don't feel there's anything to be done?"

"Not unless you can tell me what the hell's the use of being alive," said Lucian promptly. He smiled derisively. "Is that up your street, doc?"

"Oh yes," said Milne calmly. "Very much so. I can't tell you, but I might be able to help you find out for yourself."

"How the hell could you?" said Lucian contemptuously.

"Well, if people find life's not worth living, it's because something's messing life up for them. Get rid of that, and it *will* be worth living. Getting rid of these things is what I'm for."

Lucian gave a non-committal grunt. His eyes had gone back to their restless, uninterested wandering.

"Do you want to get things right?" said Milne.

"Oh yes," said Lucian politely.

"No, you don't. You don't care a damn whether they're right or not. Do you?"

Lucian looked at him for a moment and then shrugged his shoulders indifferently.

Milne said, "Quite. But how about your wife?"

"What about her?"

"If you don't care about it, she does."

"She's a bloody little marvel, is Moll," said Lucian with sudden energy. "Just let me tell you what that kid's done——"

Ten minutes later Lucian leant back in his chair. His eyes were shining and he was breathing quickly. He looked at Milne with a proud, triumphant smile.

Milne nodded slowly. " You're lucky," he said. " There aren't many women like that about."

" There aren't any," said Lucian. " Not like Moll."

" And then you tell me that life isn't worth living ! " said Milne, with a smile.

" Oh, Moll's nothing to do with that."

" How d'you mean ? "

Lucian said, " Nothing to do with life."

" Isn't that taking rather a limited view of life ? "

The excited look faded from Lucian's face. " Maybe," he said indifferently, and went back to his dispassionate glancing round the room.

" Well, I should have said that if you feel like that about her there was a good deal that was worth living for," said Milne gently.

Lucian made no reply.

Milne said, " By the way, you said that you'd given her a hell of a time. I take it you mean by being away and so on ? A lot to worry about ? "

" What else could I mean ? " said Lucian with the sudden suspicious glance.

" You're not conscious of ever having treated her badly ? Been unkind to her and so on ? " As Lucian hesitated, he added quickly, " I only ask that because though I'm very much in love with *my* wife, I know I'm often unkind to her."

Lucian was staring at him fixedly now. " Did she say I'd treated her badly ? "

" Of course not."

" Everything I've done has been for the best," said Lucian in a curious, almost pleading, voice. " It hasn't always worked out, of course. But it's been done for the best."

" You really feel that ? "

Lucian's face flushed. " Of course I do," he said angrily. " What the hell d'you mean by asking me that ? I shouldn't say it if I didn't feel it, should I ? "

" Oh, people do sometimes say things without feeling them," said Milne, with a smile.

"Well, I don't," said Lucian sullenly. He threw himself back in his chair and closed his eyes. "Well, are you going to treat me?" he said wearily.

"I don't know," said Milne thoughtfully. "D'you think it would be a good idea?"

"Moll seems very keen on it. I don't much see that you can do anything. But you're welcome to try, if she wants you to."

"We might try for a bit and see how we get along. I think that's what your wife wanted."

"All right," said Lucian indifferently.

"But if we're going to try," said Milne, "you've got to help. The whole thing depends on you, not on me, don't forget. You know what your wife wants far better than I do. You can give it her. I can only help you to get things straight for yourself."

Lucian nodded in his curious, abstracted way.

"That means you'll have to be frank," said Milne. "Particularly with yourself."

"What d'you want me to do?" said Lucian curtly. "I'll do anything you say. Hell, of course I will, if Moll wants it."

"Well, it'll mean your coming here three times a week for an hour."

"How long for?"

"I don't know yet. We shall have to see how it goes."

"And if I do that for a bit, Moll will be happy?"

"If she thinks you're getting any good out of it"

"All right," said Lucian resignedly. "Whatever you say. How much will it cost? Did Moll tell you we hadn't a bean?"

Milne said, "We'll come on to that when I see whether there's anything I can do. We'll take one another on approval for the moment."

"That's an advance on most docs anyhow," said Lucian bitterly. "O.K. When do we begin?"

Milne opened his engagement book. "Can you make Monday, Wednesday and Friday. Say at eleven?"

"I can make any time," said Lucian. "They won't let me work yet anyhow. God knows why."

" All right then. Monday, Wednesday and Friday at eleven." Milne wrote it down and stood up briskly. " Fine. Then that's all fixed." He saw a shadow pass over Lucian's face.

Lucian got up. " That all for to-day then, doc ? "

" I think so," said Milne casually. " Unless there's anything else you've got to tell me—— ? "

There was a moment's silence. Milne turned aside and picked up a cigarette.

" I don't think so," said Lucian indifferently.

" All right then," said Milne. " Cheerio."

" Cheerio," said Lucian. He hesitated a moment and added with a derisive smile, " Doctor."

From his window Milne watched Lucian limp slowly down the path. His head was sunk forward, as it had been when Milne had first seen him. At the gate he paused, as though uncertain which way to go. After a moment he fumbled in his pocket, and producing the pebble, dropped it on the pavement. Milne heard the rasp of his shoe on the ground as he kicked it, and the rattle of the pebble on the pavement. Lucian limped slowly after it out of sight.

Milne sat for a moment in thought. Then, rising, he walked quickly to the front door and carefully propped it slightly open. Going back to his desk he picked up a pencil and began to scribble some notes.

It was twenty minutes before Lucian returned. He walked straight in and said, " What you don't know is that I nearly murdered her once."

Milne said, " Oh yes ? "

" Tried to strangle her after we'd been dancing. That's what she's worried about. She thinks I might do it next time and be hanged." He smiled crookedly.

" Any idea why you did ? " said Milne.

" No."

" Why didn't you actually kill her ? "

Lucian frowned. " I'm damned if I know. Something happened that interrupted and then I didn't want to." He shook his head. " The whole thing was pretty silly, and I can't remember a lot about it. We'd been out and I was damned tired."

Milne said, " I see."

" I thought you ought to know about that, but it slipped my mind."

" Oh yes," said Milne. " I think that's important. It'll give us something to go at."

Lucian nodded. His eyes had begun to travel listlessly round the room again. For a moment Milne hesitated. Then he made up his mind.

" Thanks very much," he said. " That'll give me something to think about before our next meeting."

Lucian nodded again. " I thought you ought to know," he said dully. He turned towards the door.

" Can you find your way out ? " said Milne.

" Sure."

" Right. Cheerio."

" Cheerio," said Lucian. He hesitated for a moment and turning his head, looked at Milne.

" Cheerio," he repeated, and went out.

Milne's room at the Clinic was large, but it had once been larger still. It was separated on one side from Tautz's room by a thin partition. It was impossible to hear what was being said next door, but Milne could usually hear the faint mutter of the patient's voice and occasionally the louder, brisker voice of Tautz himself.

Miss Lucas was getting on. She no longer cried all the time, her hands shook less, and she was beginning to talk fairly freely about her everyday life. Milne was not hurrying her. He stuck rigidly to the principle of " through the present to the past " and distrusted short cuts. He sat listening patiently while she rambled on, telling him about the life of a twenty-eight-year-old spinster typist—at least, about some of it. Soon there would come a time to lay a firm and inquiring finger on the gaps and omissions and the revealing dodging of issues. But not yet. Meanwhile there was nothing much to do, except for an occasional quiet prompting; and even that was becoming less and less necessary. For all practical purposes, Miss

Lucas could have managed this part of the treatment by herself.

But if it was dull and quiet in Milne's room, it was neither next door, where Tautz was applying active technique to a demure, red-haired, eighteen-year-old who had shocked her parents by stealing like a jackdaw. Tautz was rather always a noisy performer, and his patient's demureness vanished as soon as she lay down on the couch. This afternoon matters were obviously coming to a climax. Milne could hear the drone of the girl's voice gradually rising in pitch and intensity. Now and again there would be a sharp bark from Tautz and it would sink again into a murmur, only to begin the gradual crescendo again in a few moments. Milne could not repress a grim smile. He had an idea that the lid might come off the pot at any moment.

With a conscientious effort he returned to Miss Lucas. She had turned her head away from him and was speaking in a low mutter, so that it was difficult to catch her words. Her eyes were closed. She was talking of her aunt in that queer, half-hypnotised monotone—" never seen why Mummy felt like that about her she's always been so nice that locket she gave me lockets have pictures in them one of Mummy's it had a picture of her father he had a big beard." There was a tiny pause. " It was on a chain gold it was golden slumbers kiss your eyes piano tuner one day he came when we were all out I came back and found him at the door Patch was inside and he was barking. Patch——" She stopped for a moment. " Patch," she said again. There was a long pause. Then she heaved a deep sigh and lay silent. Her eyes opened and stared blankly up at the ceiling.

Milne leant forward. " Try not to stop," he said gently. " It's much better. You're getting the knack of it now. But try not to control it at all. Just go straight on with whatever comes into your head."

" I thought I was," said Miss Lucas.

" You are most of the time. But every now and again you switch a bit."

" I'm sorry, Mr. Milne."

" That's all right. It's coming. Who's Patch ? "

" My terrier."

" All right. Well, start from him."

Miss Lucas closed her eyes. " Patch," she said tentatively. There was a long pause.

" Go on," said Milne quickly.

" Dog," she said at length. " Cat. Phyllis said Marian was a cat. Marian new blue frock had a split under the arm——"

There was a sudden terrific uproar in the next room. The demure red-haired girl had suddenly started to scream and shout hysterically. Tautz seemed to be shouting too. Miss Lucas stopped and sat up, startled.

" What's happening ? " she said anxiously.

" Just somebody getting excited."

There was a loud crash and a tinkle of glass. The shouting stopped for a moment. Then Tautz barked something and there was another crash.

" They're throwing things ! " said Miss Lucas in an awed voice.

" It's nothing," said Milne. " They're only playing the fool. Listen."

The red-haired girl had begun to laugh heartily, and so had Tautz. He said something, and the conversation lapsed into an audible mutter.

" It sounds as though they were having rather a nice time," said Miss Lucas rather wistfully.

" Why ? " said Milne, with a smile. " Do you like throwing things about ? "

" Sometimes I'd like to," said Miss Lucas unexpectedly. " Sometimes I'd give *anything* to throw things." Her lips trembled slightly.

" There's a great deal to be said for it," said Milne. " That's why those booths in fairs are so attractive—you know, the ones where you pay sixpence and throw wooden balls at crockery."

" Do people do that ? " said Miss Lucas. " I've never been to a fair." She thought for a moment or two and then leaned back, closed her eyes and sighed.

" Let's go on," said Milne. " Start from ' locket.' "

" Locket," said Miss Lucas obediently. " Mummy's. The picture of her father. He had a big beard." A fractional pause. " Beaver. Beaver fur. Beavers build dams. It sounds like a swear word." A long pause.

" Try not to stop," said Milne patiently.

" What on earth were you up to this afternoon ? " said Milne, as he and Tautz were drinking their tea. " I very nearly came in to separate you once."

" Oh, it was nothing," said Tautz casually. " She started to be excited and shout. She said, ' I shall throw at you.' I said, ' O.K. go ahead, throw.' So she threw."

" What did she throw ? "

" A little stool. It was only a little one."

Milne said, " Well, I'm glad it was only a little one. It broke something, didn't it ? "

" Oh yes. It broke a vase. Then I threw a cushion at her and that knocked down some books and then we laugh."

" What fun you have."

Tautz shrugged his shoulders and poked at his thick spectacles. " Only she is acting out a bit. There is a lot of aggression there. She will have to act it out more yet." He thought for a moment. " I think she will hit me soon," he added with quiet satisfaction.

Milne said, " Why did you throw the cushion back at her ? Isn't that rather playing along with it ? "

" Yes, yes," said Tautz. " I know they always say that. But what else can I do, Felix ? She say ' I throw.' I say ' O.K. Throw.' You agree that's right, eh ? "

" Can't tell without being there," said Milne. " But I can see it might be."

" Right. Then she throw. Now what ? If I just interpret and say, ' This is your aggression ' then I stand away from her. I am wisdom. God. Super-ego. Censor. She will not trust later. Nobody ever trusts God." He began to bounce a little at the knees. " But if I throw back a cushion—— ! *Then* I say, ' That is *our* aggression. It is nice to throw. You like it. I like it. Now why ? ' " He bounced violently. " You see, Felix ? We are together. See ? "

" Yes," said Milne. " And very nice too. But I still think it's playing along for all that."

"Ah, playing along," said Tautz impatiently. "You get these phrases and they restrict your technique. I know what I do." He pounded himself on the chest. "I was there. The man who write books about not playing along, he was not there!"

"Oh quite," said Milne. "I was only thinking of the general principle."

"There are no general principle," said Tautz, bouncing excitedly. "Not a damn one. See?"

"Well, one of these days you'll get a nymphomaniac," said Milne grimly. "And then you'll see."

"I think I got one now," said Tautz calmly. "But we shall see."

Once a month Dr. Pile stopped expressing the psychiatric point of view to architects and advertising agents and held a meeting of the Clinic workers to "discuss policy and exchange views." Nobody but Dr. Pile enjoyed it much. Garsten had once said, "After a day's work I haven't got any views. And if I had, I'm damned if I'd exchange them for any of Norris's—not without a sizable cash adjustment."

As they settled down Garsten said to Milne, "I give this exactly twenty minutes and then I'm off. Coming?"

Milne said, "Yes. But don't go until I've seen you. There's a thing I want to ask you about."

"Well now, fellow labourers in the vineyard," said Pile, beaming fatly round him. "What's doing?"

"Hans has been doing some active technique and it's broken a vase," said Milne. Tautz aimed a good-natured kick at his ankle.

"A vase?" said Pile jovially. "Has he started hitting people over the head?"

"Rather significant, isn't it?" said Paston with a giggle. "Shattering of the receptacle for flowers?"

"Was that the little red-haired girl?" said Phyllis Snow.

"Yes," said Tautz. "She acts out a bit. It is all right. She's getting on."

"Good," said Pile. There was a moment's pause. "Look, unless anybody's got anything of particular interest, I'd like to spend a few minutes on policy."

" A very few minutes, Norris," said Garsten. " The other labourers in the vineyard have had a hard day. You're the chap who turned up at the seventh hour."

" And still got the full day's rate," said Milne.

Pile joined in the general laugh. " Yes. All right. Five minutes and no more. It's about this money from the Marchand Trust. I think we may have to put up with a visitation from Sir George."

" What, Freethorne ? " said Garsten. " Good God ! "

" I know," said Pile apologetically. " But it's quite reasonable. After all, he's chairman of the Marchand Trustees. If they're going to give us money, he naturally wants to take a look at what we're doing."

" Well, we'd better not let him come when Hans is acting out aggression with his red-head," said Garsten. " I doubt he'd quite understand."

" Will he understand anything ? " said Milne. " I always think of him as about the dumbest dumb pill-doctor in England."

" Oh, I wouldn't say *that*," said Pile reasonably. " He's a bit sticky, of course. Definitely sticky. But he's on the way to conversion. Otherwise we shouldn't have a chance of this money."

" What you mean," said Garsten, " is that he's prepared to pay a few thousand of somebody else's money to hedge on the Psychiatric Stakes."

" Put it like that if you like," said Pile, shrugging. " But there it is. He's got control of the money and we want some. All I'm saying is that it's perfectly reasonable for him to come."

There was a slightly hostile silence.

" What's he going to do if he does come ? " said Milne.

" We should have to put on some sort of show for him."

" Show ? " said Garsten. " Looks as though we shall want Hans and his red-head after all."

" Do you mean he'll want to—to sit in on a case ? " said Phyllis Snow nervously. " Because really——"

" No, no ! " said Pile. " Nothing like that, of course."

" I could do a demonstration of hypnotism if you like," said Paston helpfully.

"Not so easy in view of what it's done to him. He's a war case."

Garsten said, "Oh, one of those?" He shook his head. "Well, of course if we arrange the real world so that some people get hell on earth, we shall always get plenty who'll think up a better one for themselves. And then people like you and me haven't got much of an argument."

V

PATRICIA said, "Hey you—it's ten o'clock. If you don't get up soon you'll be cursing me because the whole morning's gone."

She came and sat on the side of the bed and prodded Milne gently in the stomach and said, "Ten o'clock" again.

"Golly—is it really?" said Milne sleepily. He put out a hand, took hers, and closed his eyes again. "I feel as though I could sleep for a week."

Patricia kissed him lightly on the top of his head and went towards the door.

"Don't go, for Pete's sake, Rhino," said Milne, sitting up hurriedly. "I shall never get up if you do."

"Well, there's no earthly reason why you should. It's Sunday. I only woke you because you kick up such a fuss if I don't."

"No, no," said Milne firmly. "Must get up." He put out a hand. Patricia hesitated and then came back and sat on the bed again.

"Look, I can't stay. Come on, I'll see you out of bed and then I must go."

"What's the rush?" said Milne lazily.

"Well, this is Janet's Sunday off, and if we're going out I've got to iron myself and one thing and another."

"Going out?" said Milne vaguely.

"Yes. To Barbara and Peter. We fixed it when they came."

"Oh, that's to-night?"

"Yes. Don't you want to go?"

Milne said, " I don't mind. I'd just forgotten." He threw back the bedclothes and swung his legs out of bed.

" We needn't go if—if it'll be awkward for you," said Patricia casually.

" Awkward ? Why should it be ? "

" I just thought it might after your last encounter with Bab."

" Oh, Lord, no ! " said Milne shortly. He yawned and stretched himself.

Patricia smiled at him rather uncertainly and said, " You're all rumpled. I always like it when you're rumpled." She jumped up quickly before he could reply and said briskly, " Now the eternal Sunday problem. Big breakfast which will be nice and spoil your lunch, or just toast which will be beastly and not spoil your lunch ? "

Milne looked at her for a moment. She looked absurdly young in her bright cotton overall. " Come here, awful," he said, with a grin.

Patricia hesitated and then came one step nearer.

" You mustn't look at me too closely," she said in awkward defensiveness. " I'm not made up."

Milne said, " I know. Your nose is shiny."

" Well, I'm getting old ; and if you're going to look at me I need to be warned."

" You look about seventeen." He stretched out a hand. She took it but did not come any closer.

" You'll catch cold sitting there," she said, a trifle unsteadily. " It's bitter to-day."

Milne said, " Listen. I've just had a 'phone call from my brokers." He pulled her down so that she was sitting beside him. " He tells me that Rhino Proprietary shares are very weak. There has been heavy selling. They now stand at threepence nominal." He put an arm round her waist and squeezed hard.

Patricia said, " Threepence ? They were sixpence only a day or two ago. Anyhow, I thought you were going to sell out."

Milne said, " I'm seriously considering it. But I doubt any one would take them off me."

" No," said Patricia sadly. " The property is now of little value."

The silly game came out pat enough, but she was still sitting away from him, despite his encircling arm, and he could feel that she was trembling.

He said foolishly, " Are you cold ? " but he knew that wasn't it. He turned and put both arms round her and kissed her, and waited for that quick, hungry response that he knew so well and half dreaded. It did not come. He said, " Darling Rhino," and kissed her again. She was looking at him with the grey eyes. Then she made a small movement to escape and said, " Yes. But I must get on."

He let her go at once. She put her hand up to her hair and it was trembling violently. She got up and said, " I'll run your bath. The water's beautifully hot."

Milne said, " Damn the bath and damn the water. Come back, Rhino."

She stood there and said, " No. I—I can't."

" Oh, all right," he said, with childish anger. " If that's how you feel."

Patricia said drearily, " Oh God—can't you see ? I'm on the wrong foot—and—and frightened and——"

He looked at her standing there and hated himself. He said gently, " Yes. Of course I see. I'm sorry, pet." She did not reply but went out quickly.

Milne suddenly realised that he was cold. He put on his dressing-gown and went slowly along to the bathroom. As usual, having slept for ten hours instead of eight, he felt tired and his head ached slightly. He turned on the bath taps and moved over to get his razor. As he did so he caught sight of his face in the mirror, and saw the queer, childish, peevish expression that narrowed his cheeks, tightened his full lips into a thin line, and seemed to sink the light blue eyes deeper into their sockets. The expression startled him. That was because she hadn't come to his casual whistle. He had badgered her and bullied her and threatened to leave her, and then because he felt warm and sleepy and she had looked pretty he had clicked his fingers. And because she had hesitated and hadn't rushed at him like a spaniel bitch, he had been surprised and angry. Yes, surprised. The steam from the bath clouded the mirror. But he stood for some moments gazing with puzzled horror at the blurred image of his face. There were Lady Maresfield and Mrs. Betts and Miss Lucas and Mrs. Sears and all of them, and he was kind and patient and understanding. But Patricia was unhappy and frightened—frightened of him. And that face was his reply. Just that.

The Edges lived in an appallingly ugly and very comfortable house near Finchley Road. Peter, who had no eyes to speak of, defended it on the ground that he never personally stood in the Finchley Road and studied the architecture of his house. What he wanted was to get inside and find a fire, a comfortable chair, a drink and a decent meal. He dealt with this side of life very lavishly, and left the rest to Barbara. As Milne accepted his first drink he felt again that whilst Peter's house was a standing joke, it was rather a cheerful and pleasant place to visit.

It was nearly nine when Milne and Patricia arrived, and the party was in the full of its limited swing. The big drawing-room was full of people, smoke, and a gabble of talk.

Peter said, " I've got a chap I particularly want you to meet." He took Milne by the arm and piloted him through the crowd. " Extraordinarily capable man. Head of Fenshaws in Mincing Lane. Very big man in the commodity market——" He seized a tall, thin man who was passing. " Hey—Phil. Want you to meet Felix Milne,—Phil Fenshaw."

Milne and the tall man shook hands. " Felix is a psychoanalyst," said Peter. " Sees right through people."

" Golly ! " said the thin man, recoiling slightly with a grin. " I don't know that I want to talk to him ! "

" That's right, Felix, isn't it ? " said Peter. He was flushed and sweating a good deal. " You just look at them and see right through them ? "

" Depends what they're made of," said Milne.

" Talking about seeing through things," said the thin man. " D'you know the story about the window cleaner ? "

" No," said Milne politely.

" Tell him that," said Peter, clapping the thin man on

the shoulder. " He ought to know that. Go on—you can't shock him. It's nothing to what his patients tell him every day. Is it, Felix? *Hallo*, honey——!" He drifted away.

" It's an old one," said the thin man, " so stop me if you *have* heard it. But it appears there was a chap married a widow——"

Barbara was talking to a burly man in a double-breasted suit, with a neat round bald patch like a tonsure in the middle of his thick, curly iron-grey hair. He was leaning towards Barbara, talking confidentially, with a knowing smile. She was looking up at him with the sardonic blue cat's eyes, and smiling back. Milne reflected that if you thought you were making a hit with Barbara, there was nothing more sobering than to see her talk to anything else in trousers, even if it was seventy and had a wooden leg.

" How about another drink?" said the thin man. " Come on, you're behind the party. Have another of Peter's whiskies before the old devil drinks it all himself."

Milne took the glass and lit a cigarette. The thin man turned to a small, rather battered looking blonde woman who was in the act of pouring out a drink. " Now, Susie—how many's that? By the way—my wife—Dr. Milne."

" Not doctor," said Milne.

" Oh, you're not a doctor? Mr. Milne then. He's a psycho-analyst, Susie. That'll teach you."

" Isn't that something rude?" said the little blonde woman owlishly. She seemed a trifle drunk.

" I wish you could psycho-analyse *her*, Mr. Milne," said the thin man, putting an arm round her. " I've never seen such a girl for whisky. Love it, don't you, Sue?"

" I adore it," said the blonde woman soberly. " Don't you?"

" Not much," said Milne, with a smile. " Gives me a head."

" Only if you don't drink enough of it," she said firmly. " Drink enough of it, you haven't *got* a head." She turned to her husband. " You say he's a psycho—psycho-analyst?"

" That's right."

" All about sex, isn't it?" she said accusingly to Milne.

"Not *quite* all," said Milne.

"Aha!" said the small woman, waving a hand vaguely. "You can't tell *me*." She prodded her husband in the waistcoat. "I know his type. Don't I, darling? *I* know them." She shook her head at Milne and walked rather unsteadily away.

"I never knew such a girl as that," said the thin man proudly. "Always full of beans. She's always been like that."

"Remarkable," said Milne.

At about half-past nine the thin man went in search of another drink, and Milne seized the opportunity to edge over towards Barbara. She was talking again to the man with the tonsure.

Barbara greeted him with correct hostess enthusiasm, but not, as far as he could see, with anything else. The tonsured man was introduced as Julian Briant.

Milne said, "You're looking very beautiful, Bab." She was. The close-fitting powder blue dress did exactly what it was intended to do.

"Like it?" said Barbara, looking down at herself.

"Oh, the frock?" said Milne, with a grin. "I hadn't noticed that."

The tonsured man made a gesture of comic fury. "There you are!" he said plaintively. "Here have I been at her all the evening and I never thought of saying that." He shook his head sadly. "Slow. That's me. And getting slower."

"Oh, Felix is a model of tact," said Barbara, with a quick glance at Milne. "That's his profession."

"Oh, yes," said Briant. "So you were telling me. I know all about it, you see," he added to Milne.

"I wouldn't take too much notice of what Barbara tells you," said Milne, with a smile. "It's all guesswork."

"Doesn't she come and discuss all her—er—*problems* with you?" said the tonsured man, grinning.

"No," said Milne firmly. "She does not."

"Well, that's what she told me," said Briant. "And I was going to say if you wanted any help——"

" I soon should," said Milne. " Any analyst who took her on would soon need a fire brigade."

The tonsured man roared with laughter.

" There you are, you see," said Barbara. " Tact. Felix is noted for it. Look, Felix—where's Pat? I haven't seen her."

" Nor have I since we came. But she's here somewhere."

Barbara said, " My God, there she is—talking to Mrs. Fenshaw! I must go and rescue her."

She went quickly across the room. Patricia, in a weak tactical position in a corner, was being solemnly harangued by the little blonde woman. She was wearing a gallant smile, which Milne saw change to an expression of relief as Barbara arrived.

" It must be very interesting work, this of yours," said Briant. " I'm interested, because as a matter of fact, I'm a bit of a psychologist myself."

" We all are," said Milne, with a rather weary smile, " whether we like it or not."

" Oh yes. But it comes into my work—*practical* psychology. I'm in advertising."

" Oh yes."

" I know a lot of people say that the psycho-analysis is all sex. But what I say is, what about it? You've got to admit that sex is important."

" Very important indeed."

" Yes. People may not like it, but human nature is human nature. And there's nothing you can do will alter it."

" Have you ever noticed," said Milne suddenly, " that when we say a thing is ' human nature ' we always mean something bad? "

" I don't quite follow you," said the tonsured man.

" Well, you never hear anybody say that being kind, or gentle, or unselfish is ' just human nature ' do you? They only say that about lust, or selfishness, or laziness, or war or something deplorable."

" That's true," said the tonsured man. " That's very true. I'd never thought of that before." He paused for a moment, symbolically removed his hat and passed on. " Now you take my profession——"

Milne reached forward and picked up another whisky. " Yes ? " he said recklessly.

" In my profession," said Mr. Briant, " it's practically all psychology really. I always say you can have the best lay-out and art work in the world and it still won't get you across the street without psychology. Don't you agree ? "

" I do indeed," said Milne.

" Nothing vulgar, mind you," said Mr. Briant. " I don't believe in vulgar advertising. There are people who say that all you've got to do is to lay it on pretty thick. I'll never have that." He brushed vulgarity aside with a wave of the hand. " No. The way I look at it is this. There's got to be a sex angle. We're men of the world and we may as well face it. People will have it and we can't do without it. But it's got to be *subtle*, if you see what I mean ? "

" I see exactly what you mean."

" Of course it's easier with some things than others," said Mr. Briant pensively. " If you're selling stockings now, there's no difficulty at all in working in the psychological angle. Or with scent. Or even soap. But you come on to a line of cream cheese, and it gets more difficult."

Milne nodded profoundly. The last drink had been a marked success. A warm, comfortable glow was spreading through him, and he was beginning to enjoy himself.

The tonsured man said, " Mine isn't a big concern, of course. I don't handle any of these half a million pound accounts. Tell the truth, I wouldn't give a thank you for them. Lose one and you're bust. What I like is to take a small account and make it grow."

" Much more fun."

" Yes. But all the same, we're up-to-date. We like to feel that our clients get the most modern and scientific service there is going. Now this business of psychology is a science in itself."

" Part science, part art," said Milne. " Possibly part hokum at times even."

Mr. Briant laughed. " Well, you ought to know. But anyhow, I reckon it's a real science. Whenever I get an account, I always say to myself, ' Now what's the psychological angle on this ? ' "

" Well, with stockings, of course, the psychological angle will be looking slightly upwards from ground level," said Milne foolishly.

Mr. Briant roared with laughter. " Too true. Though mind you, I *have* heard people say that it isn't as easy to advertise stockings as you'd think. The men may look at your stuff, but it's the women who buy."

" Substitution," said Milne.

" Meaning what ? "

" Woman buying identifies herself with woman in the picture."

" Well, yes, that's true. But you take this cheese proposition."

" Cheese ? "

" Yes. Now I've got a line of cream cheese. Good stuff, mind you. But just ordinary cream cheese. Can't move it. Why ? Because we've never got the psychological angle on cheese."

" Because you don't know where to look," said Milne firmly. " Cheese. A milk product." He looked at Mr. Briant inquiringly. " Doesn't that give you a lead ? "

" I don't get it."

" My dear man," said Milne, shaking his head sadly. He was feeling very happy indeed now. " My dear man. Milk. Mother."

" The home and so on ? "

" The child at the breast."

" Well yes," said the tonsured man, scratching doubtfully at his bald patch. " We've run the home story, of course. But it's the psychological angle I was really after."

" You'll never find a more psychological angle than that," said Milne with conviction. " It goes right back to first principles." He finished his drink. " Take it from me, you can't go wrong with the milk appeal. Why have milk bars been such a success ? Why do people eat milk chocolate ? "

" I believe you may have got something there," said Mr. Briant. " That advertisement of Cadbury's now—— ? "

"Exactly."

There was a short pause.

"And you reckon that's the psychological angle?" said Mr. Briant, with a trace of disappointment.

"Yes."

"It seems a bit far-fetched," said Mr. Briant hesitantly.

"Far-fetched?" said Milne indignantly. "Of course it's far-fetched. You said you wanted something subtle, didn't you?"

"That's right. But of course we mustn't overdo it, Mr. Milne. It's got to be something our public will cotton on to. And there's not much it *will* cotton on to, you know."

"Not consciously," said Milne. "But I'm not sure that you want to spend your time fluttering round the Ego. Why not make an occasional pass at the Id?"

"What I had in mind," said Mr. Briant perseveringly, "was the psychological health angle. You know—it bucks you up. Makes you feel younger. Makes your wife more contented. Get me?"

"If you're going to sell aphrodisiacs," said Milne, "the first thing to realise is that they don't make people feel younger, they make them feel older."

"You mean they're no good?" said Mr. Briant, faintly puzzled.

"Broadly speaking," said Milne vaguely.

"Now a toothpaste," said Mr. Briant, "is a different proposition. The psychological angle's clear enough. It's more a matter of distribution."

"The psychological angle on toothpaste is that it cleans your mouth," said Milne, and stopped.

"That's right. White teeth are attractive."

"And so is a sweet breath." Milne felt suddenly tired and irritated. "Give me an ounce of civet, good apothecary, to sweeten my imagination." He laughed rather bitterly. "There ought to be a big enough market for toothpaste, God knows."

Mr. Briant said, "D'you reckon there's anything in the flavour?"

"There's something in damn nearly everything," said

Milne. "That's what makes life so complicated." He straightened himself and looked round the room. "I must go and find my wife."

"Half a minute," said Mr. Briant, laying a hand on his arm. "Just before you go——" He hesitated as though not sure how to go on.

"Yes?" said Milne impatiently.

"Mine isn't a big concern," said Mr. Briant. "I don't handle these big accounts. But all the same, we get these problems——"

"Yes?"

"And I like to feel we're giving the best possible service." Mr. Briant stared across the room. "Now I'd like to feel that there was somebody I could go to—somebody really first class—when there's a psychological angle in it." His eyes came back to Milne inquiringly. "Sort of consultant, if you understand."

Milne looked at him a little blankly.

"We're not a rich concern," said Mr. Briant modestly. "But we know that expert advice costs money. What we want is somebody we can put the problem to who'll give us the psychological angle on it—for ten or twenty guineas or whatever it might be. We mightn't use it, of course. But I reckon we ought to have it."

Milne slowly broke into a happy smile. "So do I," he said. "I'd say it was essential."

"Vital to our business."

"Essential. And I'll tell you exactly where you can get it. A chap I know named Paston."

"Paston?"

"Yes. He lives at 48 Bulteel Street, South Kensington. Just the man you want."

"I was hoping," said Mr. Briant, with a burst of frankness, "that you'd take it on yourself."

"I'm afraid I haven't got the time," said Milne regretfully. "Otherwise, of course—— But Paston's your man undoubtedly. Have you got the address?"

"I'll put it down," said Mr. Briant. "He's really good, I take it? It must be a first-class man, see."

"Good?" said Milne. "He's got the psychological

angle on everything on God's earth. B. R. E. Paston, 48 Bulteel Street, South Kensington. Got it?"

Patricia said, "It's nearly ten. Do you think we could go now?"

"In a minute, honey," said Milne. "No actual rush, is there?"

"Only that I'm very bored. Aren't you?"

"Moderately," said Milne. His eyes were roving round the room. He caught sight of the sleek black head and the pale blue frock over in a corner. "I shall make one more circuit of the room and have one more drink and then we'll go. That do?"

"All right," said Patricia without enthusiasm.

"You may remember," said Milne, "that when we last met I explained the difference between my private and professional capacities."

"I don't remember," said Barbara, "that you explained anything."

"Oh yes, you do. Well, I am here in my private capacity."

"Ah, but you see, Felix, *I* am now in my official capacity as hostess."

"Bunk!" said Milne. "You have only one capacity, Bab."

"Is that a dirty crack, Felix?"

"No. It's a compliment."

"Well, so what? Oh, by the way, how did you get on with Julian Briant?"

"Damn Juliant Briant. He offered me a job trying to put sex into cream cheese. You are lovely, aren't you?"

"I used to be quite nice. You couldn't have got away with that keep-your-distance professional stuff with me five or six years ago. But I'm getting old, Felix."

"We're all getting old. Hadn't we better do something about it before we actually reach the bath-chair stage?"

"What sort of thing?" she said, staring at him with the slanting blue eyes.

Milne swallowed. "We might take ourselves out one evening."

Barbara stared at him for a moment in silence and then looked away.

Milne said, "Would that be a good idea?"

After a moment her eyes came back, cool and unsmiling. "Yes, Felix. That might be a very good idea."

"Fine. Wednesday?"

"Can't do Wednesday."

"What night can you do?"

She hesitated. "I'm not really sure. Let's ring up."

"No. Thursday unless you ring me."

Barbara smiled a trifle grimly. "It sounds to me as though you've made this sort of appointment before." She heaved a tiny sigh. "All right. Thursday. Where?"

"Half-past seven at the Molyneux."

"Yes." She looked away again. "Felix—why do you want to take me out?"

Milne said, "I take pleasure in your conversation. Why d'you think?"

"You're a queer person, aren't you?"

"I don't see anything queer in wanting to take you out if you go round looking like that."

"I should have thought your job would have made you completely case-hardened."

"Well, it hasn't."

"So it seems."

Milne said, "Why should it, anyhow?"

"I don't know," said Barbara with a quick grin. "But a susceptible father confessor seems an odd idea."

"Haven't father confessors always been rather a notably susceptible race?"

"I suppose so."

"You can't think what an advantage it is in my job to know completely how people feel when they make fools of themselves," said Milne rather bitterly.

"Is taking me out making a fool of yourself?"

Milne said, "I don't think I can play that game, Bab."

"Well, my dear, it's up to you," said Barbara. "You

choose the exact degree of pat-hands you like and I'll try to fit in. Service is our motto—in my one capacity."

"Haughty like," said Milne. "I 'ates 'aught."

"I don't know what you hate," said Barbara. "But you pretty obviously hate something quite a lot at times."

"Chiefly me, if you want to know," said Milne curtly.

"Why?"

"That's a long story."

Barbara said, "It must be odd. I always seem to go on liking myself even when there isn't really a lot to like."

"So does any sensible person."

"And why all the complicated legal fiction about your professional capacity?"

"It isn't complicated and it isn't fiction. I don't let my job get mixed up with the bits of me I don't like, that's all."

"I suppose I bring out the worst in you?"

"Of course you do," said Milne, with a smile.

"I knew it," said Barbara resignedly. "If I've been told that once I've been told it a dozen times."

"Naturally. What people are trying to say is that they're really good and chaste and so forth, and that really it's all your fault."

"Well, I suppose it is in a way," said Barbara moodily. "Because it isn't a bit like that from me. I'm just plain awful all by myself, and the better everybody else is, the worse I become."

"Never mind, darling. Think how nice it is for us to have you to blame. Have another drink?"

VI

MILNE said, "Did you walk up again?"

Lucian nodded. "Oh yes. I walk everywhere. They say it's good for my leg."

"How's that going?"

"It's all right."

"Still got your pebble?" said Milne, opening a drawer and taking out a pad.

" It went down a drain. I've got another now."

" Why must you have a pebble ? " said Milne, with a smile.

" I like to see how long I can keep it on the pavement," said Lucian listlessly. " If it goes off the pavement I have to start again." He started to scrape the ash in the ash-tray into a pile with the glowing end of his cigarette.

" Well, let's get started," said Milne briskly. " I'd like to get down a few things about you first. I don't know why we always ask people these things but we do. I suppose it gives a professional touch to the thing. Now then—full name ? "

" Adam Lucian."

" Just that ? "

" Yes."

" Age ? "

" Twenty-eight."

" Parents living ? "

" No."

" Can you tell me anything about them ? Father's occupation and so on."

" My father was a barrister."

" Yes ? "

There was a moment's pause. Lucian leaned back in his chair and closed his eyes. " And my mother was his wife," he said, with a slight, far-away smile. " What sort of things do you want to know about them anyway ? "

A quarter of an hour later Milne shut his notebook and tossed it aside. " Right. That's that. Now next time you come I can look that up and I shall know that you're you and not Mrs. Talkinghorne. The next thing is this business you told me about last week—about trying to strangle your wife. I'd like to hear some more about that."

Lucian nodded. His eyes were fixed on a lamp in the side table.

Milne said, " What happened exactly ? "

" We'd been out dancing," said Lucian in his slow, listless voice. " We got back pretty late. Moll was wearing a green frock. When we got in, the clock in our bedroom had stopped. I wound it up and put it right by my watch. It was two minutes after one. I couldn't find my toothbrush so I went along and got a spare one out of my pack. It was in a cupboard in the spare room. Moll went out of the bathroom. The water was very hot. I turned it on and put my hand under it and it hurt me. My face was very rough. I've always noticed that if you stay up late your beard grows. Really if you stay up till one or two you need shaving." He paused and frowned.

"Yes?" said Milne quietly.

"I rubbed my face and it made a rasping noise."

Lucian closed his eyes. His forehead was puckered as though with a tremendous effort of concentration.

"Yes?" said Milne again.

"Then——" He paused again.

"Go on," said Milne inexorably.

"Then I came out of the bathroom——" There was a moment's silence. Then Lucian's face suddenly smoothed out like stretched indiarubber. "Then I tried to strangle Molly and she smiled and I stopped," he said with relief.

His eyes opened and he glanced at Milne with a queer, childish hopefulness.

Milne nodded. "I see. Can you tell me a bit more about what happened when you came out of the bathroom?"

"I said, 'You smiled.' And she said, 'Hell, what have I got to smile about?' or something like that. She croaked, because I'd hurt her throat with my hands. She's got all the guts on earth, that kid," he added, with sudden energy.

"I mean before that," said Milne gently. "You came out of the bathroom. Molly was lying in bed——?"

"Yes," said Lucian, looking at the table lamp.

"The bedside light was on?"

"There isn't a bedside light," said Lucian sullenly. "It's overhead with a switch on a cord."

"What colour is the quilt?"

"Blue," said Lucian, shutting his eyes. "It's blue."

"You came out of the bathroom and she was in bed with the overhead light on and the blue quilt over her."

A queer, cunning little smile played over Lucian's face. "The sheets and pillow-cases are blue too," he said.

"Oh, are they? And she has black hair, hasn't she?"

There was a long pause. The agonised frown of concentration had reappeared. "Yes," said Lucian, with a visible effort.

"You came out of the bathroom," said Milne in a low voice. "And she was lying in bed with the overhead light on. The bed was blue. Her hair was black. Did you stand and look at her?"

"No."

"You came straight into the room?"

"Yes."

"And then what did you do?"

There was dead silence for several seconds. Then once again Lucian's face cleared with the startling suddenness.

"I tried to strangle her," he said precisely. "And she smiled and I stopped." He opened his eyes and gazed at the table lamp. "You keep on asking me the same things," he said peevishly.

"Sorry," said Milne contritely. "Only it's rather important and I want to be sure I've got it into my head."

"That's all right, doc," said Lucian with a sigh. "That's a nice lamp," he added, nodding towards it.

"Yes," said Milne. "I can switch it on and off from here. Remote control."

"People don't understand about controls," said Lucian suddenly. "They gave us a crate once where the lever for controlling your undercarriage and the lever that works your flaps were exactly alike, side by side and under the seat. People were always coming in to land, trying to put their flaps down, getting the wrong lever and starting to pull the undercarriage up. Bloody silly piece of design."

Milne nodded. "Damn silly. From what I've seen of it, the controls on a modern plane are complicated enough without that sort of booby trap."

"That's what's the matter with me," said Lucian suddenly.

"Controls all over the place?" said Milne with a smile.

Lucian hesitated and then shook his head and looked away.

"How do you feel about flying as a whole?" said Milne.

" Had all you want of it, or would you like to fly again, or what ? "

Lucian shrugged.

" Don't care one way or the other ? "

" Not as long as I don't have to fly that bitch of a thing again," said Lucian with sullen anger.

" Which thing ? "

" That bitch of a Spitfire."

" Don't you like Spitfires ? "

" Oh, I like Spitfires all right. The old Spit was a grand machine. It was just that bitch. She's bust to bits. Bust to hell. And a damned good job too. She let me down." His eyes flashed with anger.

" How ? "

" Cracking up like that," said Lucian vaguely. " If she wasn't bust up I'd take a chopper to her, the——" He stopped short and gave the slow, listless shrug again.

" Look," said Milne. " Just before we go on—about that other business. There's still one bit I haven't got. When you came out of the bathroom, was she asleep ? "

" I don't know," said Lucian slowly.

" Were her eyes shut ? "

Lucian smiled a meaning smile at the table lamp. " If she was asleep they must have been," he said.

" But can you remember if they were ? "

Lucian's eyes closed and the painful frown appeared. " Were her eyes shut, you say ? "

" Yes."

There was a long silence. Then Lucian opened his eyes. " It's so long ago that I'm afraid I can't remember," he said politely. " I hope it doesn't matter, doc."

" It's only a detail," said Milne. " Perhaps it'll come back to you some time. I'd like to know if you do remember."

" Sure," said Lucian willingly. He looked down at his finger-nails. " I don't want to give you a wrong impression," he said. " I've nothing whatever against Spitfires. I was a Spit pilot and I'd rather fly a Spit than anything going."

" Oh, I quite see that," said Milne. " This was just a bad specimen ? "

" She hadn't been," said Lucian sombrely. " She'd been a honey. But——" He made a slight gesture of finality.

" You disliked her for—cracking up on you ? "

" Something like that," said Lucian vaguely. " Anyhow, don't let's talk about aeroplanes, doc. That's all washed up and finished."

" There's no particular significance about the lying down part of it," said Milne. " It's only to get you comfortable and because most people find they can talk better like that."

Lucian swung his legs on to the couch and lay back at full length. He looked very big.

" That comfortable ? "

" Very." He closed his eyes and crossed his hands on his chest. " Corpse," he said. " X marks the spot, as Moll says."

Milne said, " Now first of all I want you to get yourself completely relaxed. Try breathing deeply for a bit. You'll find that'll help you to let go." He raised Lucian's hand and let it fall. " Not bad. You're still holding on a bit though. Completely floppy so that when I let go, it just drops. That's better. Same thing with your legs."

" I shall never be able to think like this," said Lucian rather drowsily. " Far too comfortable."

" Nobody wants you to think. All I want you to do is just to talk. Remember—just whatever comes into your head. Never mind what it is. Just let go and let it come out anyhow." He glanced rapidly at Lucian's mask-like face and then sat down beside the head of the couch. " I'll give you something to start from and then just go on thinking aloud from there. Now—start from controls."

" Controls ? "

" Yes. Go right on."

There was a moment's pause. Then Lucian opened his eyes. " That doesn't make me think of anything."

" Oh yes, it does," said Milne gently. " You've thought quite a lot of things in those few seconds, but you haven't said them."

A slight smile played about Lucian's mouth. " The only

thing I did think was that this was all rather bloody nonsense."

" Then why did you say that? It's a perfectly good and reasonable thing to think. Try again. Start quickly, directly I give you the word. I'll give you another starting point this time—— Flying."

Lucian closed his eyes again. " What we were talking about a minute ago, I suppose," he said slowly.

" Straight on."

" Controls. Fire control. Food control." He stopped. " This is bloody nonsense if you want me to say it. Self control. Self reverence, self knowledge, self control—how on earth does that go on and what is it?" He stopped, opened his eyes and looked at Milne inquiringly.

" It's a bit of Tennyson's *Oenone*," said Milne quietly. " Try not to stop."

" But how does it go on?"

" ' These three alone lead life to sovereign power.' "

" That's right." Lucian closed his eyes. " It was the motto of my prep school." He sighed and relapsed into silence.

" Penny for your thoughts," said Milne suddenly.

" Haven't got any thoughts." He opened his eyes and frowned up at the ceiling. " This is bloody difficult, you know."

" It's a pure knack," said Milne. " Let me try and show you the sort of thing I want. You give me a word and I'll just think aloud from it." He shut his eyes.

" All right." Lucian glanced round the room. " Window."

" Window," said Milne, with the rapid yet careful dexterity of long practice. " Sash-cord sash book I've just been reading about the Japanese it's got a blue cover another book in a blue cover about chess cheese mousetrap marry it is called the mousetrap Hamlet his mother slut Barbara after which it all goes on about a young woman I feel rather lecherous about." He opened his eyes and smiled at Lucian's slightly startled face. " Get the idea?"

Lucian gave a little grunt and shook his head. " I don't think as fast as that."

"You think a damn sight faster. I switched three times even in those few seconds."

"No, I don't. I don't think at all. My mind just stays completely blank."

"Don't worry about your mind. It's your voice I want. Just start talking and keep talking." As Lucian closed his eyes, Milne hooked a finger under his wrist and raised the tell-tale hand again. It sank slowly. "You've tightened up a bit again. Slacken off. Breathe deeply. That's better. Now have another go. Start from 'doctor.'"

There was a long pause. "Doctor," said Lucian. "You. You say you're not a doctor. If you're not a doctor you must be a bloody quack." He opened his eyes. "Sorry," he said, with apparent concern, "I didn't mean to be rude. But you told me to say the first thing that came into my head."

"Of course," said Milne with a grin. "That was fine—except that it took rather a long time to work out."

Lucian suddenly flushed deeply. "What d'you mean?" he said sullenly.

"You're stopping to make it too polite. You want to punish me for badgering you and various other things, but instead of just letting yourself go and doing it properly, you're holding yourself in."

There was a moment's silence.

"Maybe," said Lucian indifferently. He shut his eyes and sighed deeply. "I shall go to sleep in a minute."

"No, I wouldn't go to sleep," said Milne with gentle urgency. "Going to sleep doesn't settle anything. You have to wake up again later."

"Can't help it," said Lucian drowsily. "Sorry, doc." His eyelids flickered for a moment and he sighed deeply again.

"Lucian!" said Milne sharply. "Open your eyes."

There was no reply. Milne leant forward and looked at him closely. Then with a quick glance at his watch he leant back and lit a cigarette.

"What you've got to realise," said Milne, "is that there's a part of you that doesn't like me, doesn't trust me, and is damned if it's going to talk to me. That's quite apart from anything you may think you feel. When I suggested that, the inside bit of you got a bit frightened, so it went to sleep so that we couldn't talk any more."

Lucian nodded. "Maybe," he said remotely.

"Now if you want to put yourself right, *you've* got to do the work. You may say what you like about me. I don't matter anyhow. But if you cheat—if you don't let go and let her rip—then I'm no good." He smiled at Lucian's sudden glance. "That sounds promising, doesn't it? There's a bit of you that would be very glad to find that I'm no good. But if so, what happens about your wife?"

He paused. Lucian's lips opened as though he was going to speak. Then he suddenly frowned, shook his head and looked listlessly away.

"What were you going to say?" said Milne quickly.

"Nothing," said Lucian dully.

"That's exactly what I mean. You were going to say something. Why didn't you say it?"

"It went out of my head."

"No. You see, you know perfectly well what it was. Don't you?" Lucian made no reply.

"Come on," said Milne with a grin. "I'll bet it's not complimentary."

A faint flicker of an answering smile showed for a moment on Lucian's face.

"Are we through for now?" he said wearily.

"Why? Tired?"

"I've got a bit of a headache."

"Bad luck," said Milne. "D'you get headaches often?"

"No."

"All right," said Milne. "We'll pack up now. Let's see—when do I see you again?"

Lucian made no reply. He was staring moodily out of the window. After a quick glance Milne picked up his engagement book and started to turn the leaves slowly.

There was silence for a moment. Then Lucian said, "I don't know whether I shall go on with this."

Milne waited.

"There's nothing the matter with me," said Lucian. "Or nothing that you can do anything about. It's a waste of time." He glanced at Milne. "Anyhow I shan't be able to afford it. We might go on like this for years." He turned restlessly in his chair. "Well, go on—say something," he said irritably. "Don't you agree?"

"Well, let's take item by item," said Milne quietly. "I don't agree that there's nothing the matter with you. I don't know whether I can do anything about it yet. I agree that it may go on like this for months. As for affording the fees, if I were you I'd wait till I was asked for some."

"I don't see what you think you can do," said Lucian wearily. He got up and passed a hand over his eyes.

Milne said, "Is that headache bad?"

"What headache?"

"You said you had a headache."

"It's nothing," said Lucian, going towards the door.

"Right-ho," said Milne. "Wednesday at 2.30 then."

"I shan't come," said Lucian childishly.

"Yes, you will, you old sap," said Milne, writing it down. "Look, you'd better not walk all the way home. You can get a bus just at the top of the road."

Lucian turned for a moment, sharply and angrily. Then his body slackened and he gave the listless shrug. "Cheerio," he said mechanically.

As he reached the gate, Milne noticed for the first time that he was using a stick. It was a thick ash-plant and there seemed to be something vaguely familiar about it. Milne went out into the hall and looked in the umbrella stand. His stick was gone. He nodded curtly to himself and went back into the consulting room.

Patricia was playing something which he vaguely recognised as Orlando Gibbons. Milne stood at the door and listened for a moment, wondering as he always did, why anybody who could play like that did so for a total of about half an hour a month, in spasms of not more than ten minutes. He went in and closed the door very quietly, but she heard it and stopped at once. She swung round hurriedly and said, "Oh—hallo."

Milne said, " Nice. Gibbons ? "

" Yes," said Patricia. " Mr. Sanders, His Delight. I've never quite seen why it should have delighted Mr. Sanders. But there——" She shut the book and got up.

" Don't stop," said Milne. " It's ages since you've played."

" It feels like it," said Patricia briefly. " And sounds like it, I should think. At present I feel as though I'm wearing boxing gloves." She shut the piano and walking over to the fireplace, lit a cigarette.

Milne said, "You are a mutt, you know, not to play more."

Patricia shrugged her shoulders. " How've you been going ? " she said shortly.

Milne sat down and shook his head.

" My God, I've bought a packet there," he said thoughtfully.

" Where ? "

" That boy Lucian. Most of the time I can't get near him at all. It's nearly hopeless. But every now and again there's a faint gleam. Everything turns on whether I can get it stronger. The trouble is that if you blow a fire that's burnt as low as that, you may blow it out." He leant back in his chair and stared thoughtfully up at the smoke from his cigarette. " The most hopeful thing is that he's beginning to dislike me quite a lot."

" Why ? "

" Never mind why. He's got plenty of reasons—or thinks he has. But as long as he'll feel *something*—anything —there's a chance for him. Several times he started off and I thought it was coming with a bang. But he just sank back into that queer not-really-there mood that schizos have."

Patricia nodded but said nothing. Milne was smiling up at the tobacco smoke.

" Anyhow he's pinched my stick," he said happily.

" Pinched your stick ? "

" Yes. Nice, isn't it ? "

" How d'you mean ? "

" Darling," said Milne patiently. " He comes here and

he's lame. In the house he finds my stick, and takes it away to help him walk."

Patricia still looked at him blankly.

Milne said, " Well, J.C., I'm not an enthusiastic symbolist, but——"

Patricia said, " Oh, yes. I see. The stick's you and his lameness is what's wrong."

" Correct," said Milne. " The penny took a hell of a time to drop though, didn't it ? "

" Sorry," said Patricia apologetically. " I'm always slow on that symbol stuff. I can never do dreams either."

" Talking of dreams," said Milne, " have a go at this. This boy was a fighter pilot. The other night he dreamed that he was coming in to land in his Spitfire. He landed, and his mechanic, a chap named Happy Martin, came forward to it. He doesn't know why, but it was very important that Martin shouldn't touch the plane. Lucian said ' No—keep away, you don't understand it. It's something down here '—pointing to the joy-stick." He cocked an inquiring eye at her. " All of which is very odd, he thinks. Because Martin was an absolutely first-class man, and what he didn't know about Spitfires isn't worth knowing."

There was a pause. Patricia was frowning down at the carpet. " Was Martin a real person ? " she said. " I mean —did he ever have a mechanic named Martin ? "

" Oh, yes. Happy Martin *was* his mechanic."

Patricia said, " Happy——" She looked up suddenly and said, " Oh, yes. I see. Felix—Happy. You're the mechanic and he's the Spitfire. He thinks you don't understand what's wrong with him."

" Yes. Or wants to think I don't. He's very emphatic that Martin was a first-rate mechanic and *would* know what was wrong, or would find out. It's just an ordinary resistance to analysis dream. But rather pretty."

" And the joy-stick ? Sexual symbol ? "

Milne shrugged. " Maybe. Not sure at present." He leaned back in his chair. " That's quite good, Rhino—to see that."

To his surprise she flushed and said hurriedly, " Well, it's a fairly simple one, isn't it ? Is he going to be all right ? "

Milne said, " I don't know yet. It's going quite well. But there's the very hell of a lot to do before we can get anywhere. First I've got to get him to talk at all. Then I've got to get him to talk about this business with his wife. Then there's whatever happened to him in Burma, which he's apparently very sticky about. And then when all that's done we're just about ready to start."

Patricia said, " By the way, Lady M. rang up this afternoon."

" Damn the woman. Wanting what ? "

" She wanted to speak to you. I said you had a patient. Was that right ? "

" It's always right to head off Lady M."

There was a long silence. Then Patricia said suddenly, " Look, I'm sorry about Sunday morning."

" That's all right," said Milne with a grin. " There's nothing to be sorry about—not for you anyhow."

" My God, isn't there ? " said Patricia bitterly. " For weeks I can't get near you, and then when you do come back a bit I go like that."

" Well darling, you can't be expected to hang around waiting for the five minutes a week when I'm civil to you."

Patricia got up and walked restlessly over to the window. " The trouble about this sort of thing is that it's a vicious circle. You don't like me and I get scared and can't play, and then you like me even less and want to go off with Bab or somebody." She hesitated and then said, " Have you fixed up anything with her ? "

" What sort of thing ? "

" To see her and so on ? "

" Why ? "

" Oh, for God's sake——" said Patricia irritably.

Milne said, " I've arranged to take her out on Thursday night."

Patricia nodded without speaking.

" You realise that it's nothing to do with Bab as Bab ? " said Milne.

" Oh, yes," said Patricia, her lips curling slightly. " It's nothing to do with Bab and it's no criticism of me and it doesn't make a hoot of difference to us and there we are."

" All of which is true, oddly enough."

" It damn nearly is," said Patricia bitterly. " It *doesn't* make much difference to us as we are nowadays."

There was a long silence.

Milne said quietly, " Do you want me to try to explain?"

" I want to—to know where I stand, Felix."

" All right," said Milne. " I don't know if I can, and I may only make it worse. But I'll try." He leant back in his chair and shut his eyes. " There's a bit of me," he said slowly, " that's never grown up. It stays at about mental age twelve. Most of the time I'm very grown up indeed. If I weren't, I couldn't do my job. But *outside* the job I come up against this thing. It takes all sorts of forms. You know most of them. I get fun—and not such very nice fun—out of teasing and bullying you. I sulk if a certain sort of thing happens that I don't like. All sorts of things like that. You know them, don't you ? "

" Some of them, I think."

" Yes. Well, this business about Barbara is a part of that thing. The thing that attracts me about Bab is that it's all so *obvious*—a sort of deliberate childish wantonness. When she throws herself at your head she does it like a naughty kid trying to get another kid to be naughty. I know that sounds awful, but I don't mean that there's anything charming about it at all—not to an adult. People always talk about a ' naughty child ' as if it were something too, too sweet. A naughty child isn't sweet at all. It's usually rather ugly and a nuisance. But it's often attractive to other children."

Patricia said, " And of course Bab does it very well. It's always been her technique."

" I don't know. In my saner moments it always seems too crude for anything. But it exactly rings the bell for my twelve year old bit."

He sat for a moment in silence.

" What I'm trying to show you is why it happens, and yet why I'm so sure it doesn't matter fundamentally. It happens because Barbara exactly appeals to a messy twelve year old, which is what I am in some ways. And it doesn't matter because there's nowhere it could possibly lead. It's simply a childish game whose whole point is that it's forbidden."

"And you can't play it with me?"

"Good God, no, honey."

"Why not?"

"Well, you're about the most completely adult person, sexually speaking, that I've ever met. You haven't the beginnings of any message for a twelve year old."

"Oh," said Patricia rather blankly.

"Of course you haven't. You're a grown up woman and you act like one. I don't mean you don't play. But it's a grown-up game with plenty that's real behind it—not just charades with 'bed' as the word you've got to act."

"You couldn't act bed," said Patricia. "It's only got one syllable."

"Well, Barbara never acts anything else."

"And what happens when you guess the word?"

"Oh, then *you* go out or come in, and act in another way, and she guesses. And so on. Then when you've tired of the game you go home."

"As long as it never goes any further than that," said Patricia doubtfully, "it doesn't seem very important."

"It isn't. Except that it makes me furious with myself and worries you."

"Of course it isn't really as simple as all that," said Patricia after a moment's pause. "Bab or no Bab, you're very bored with me, aren't you?" She looked at Milne thoughtfully. "Dull woman who doesn't attract you sexually and getting a bit long in the tooth. No fun for a man. And doesn't even produce children for him."

"There's no more reason why I should feel that than you. The fact that we haven't had kids may quite well be me."

"Do you think that would have made a difference?" said Patricia after a moment's silence. "Or is it just that I'm a dull female and would have bored you anyway?"

"Listen," said Milne. "When I want you to dance on the table in your underclothes with a bottle of champagne in one hand, I'll tell you so."

"No, you won't," said Patricia a trifle sadly. "That's

the trouble. You'll just look at me with quiet dislike and go away into the consulting room." She shook her head. "You know, I believe you underestimate me, darling. I think I should probably dance on the table quite nicely."

"Rhinotanze," said Milne. "It'd have to be a pretty solid table."

"Oh, well," said Patricia with a sigh. "I suppose it still may come right. I don't quite see how, and I don't know how to make it. But——"

"I don't think it does any good to go on chewing it over, honey," said Milne gently.

"I know. But if you're me it's difficult to stop. I think we ought to adopt a kid if we stay. At least, I think I think so. Thursday you say you're going out?"

"That's what we said."

"Then I shall go to the flicks. I'm never taken to the flicks, so I shall go while you're playing charades. If I could think of anything more dashing, I'd do it."

Milne said, "One of these days you'll walk out on me, and serve me damned well right."

She turned quickly. "I wish to God you really thought that," she said in a low voice, looking at him thoughtfully. "Because if I did, it would probably shake you quite a lot. You don't want me, but you've never quite faced up to not having me about. But the snag is that you know I never *should* clear out. Don't you?"

"No," said Milne after a moment's hesitation.

"Yes, you do," she said listlessly. "That's the devil of it. You know."

VII

CARLO knew about the consulting room. He did not come in but merely stood on the threshold and looked at Milne solemnly, giving a slight impression of the faithful but dutiful hound.

Milne looked up and said, "Hallo, dog. What d'*you* want?"

The whole of Carlo's rear section wagged. He came in,

put his forepaws out, lowered his head and made faint woofing noises.

Milne said, " No, that wasn't an invitation." He picked the spaniel up and went to the door, stroking its silky golden head. " Hey, Pat—come and take your hell-hound."

Patricia came and said, " Oh—has he come in with you ? Sorry."

" No. He stood outside quite good. But I spoke to him and that was too much. He knows enough not to come in, otherwise. It's about all he does know." He put Carlo in Patricia's arms. " Go on, you dumb blonde."

Patricia said, " Come on, beautiful."

" Beautiful but very dumb," said Milne. " It's about the silliest of God's creatures, that. By the way, have you got that licence yet ? "

" Damn ! " said Patricia. " I've forgotten again."

" Well, look here," said Milne seriously, " you must get it. We shall be run in. He ought to have had one weeks ago."

Patricia said, " I'll do it to-morrow. I really will. When's your patient due ? "

" He's been due half an hour now." Milne put a hand over Carlo's muzzle and waggled it. " Bye, sap." He went back into the consulting room and shut the door.

At half-past three the telephone rang. Milne was tired of waiting. He took the receiver off and said " Yes ? " rather curtly.

" Is that Mr. Milne ? " said the rather pleasantly American voice. " This is Mollie Lucian."

" Oh, hallo," said Milne. " How are you ? "

" I'm fine, thanks. Mr. Milne, have you got the boy Adam with you ? "

" No. I'm waiting for him now."

" Waiting for him ? " There was a slightly startled pause. " Why ? Hasn't he shown up yet ? "

" No. He was due at half-past two but he hasn't come."

" But say, he left me near two hours ago saying he was coming right along to you." She sounded slightly anxious.

" How was he coming ? " said Milne. " Not walking, a day like this ? "

" No. He was going to take a bus. I hope he hasn't gone and lost himself, or something."

" I don't think he can have," said Milne. He hesitated for a moment and said, " I expect he'll turn up in a minute. Shall I get him to ring you when he does ? "

" Yes. I'd be glad if you'd have him ring me, Mr. Milne. I wonder where the boy's taken himself ? "

" Met a friend, I expect. Anyhow I'll tell him."

At half-past six Milne came into the drawing-room and said, " Look, I think I'll have to go down and see Mrs. Lucian. He still hasn't shown up and he hasn't gone back there, and she's obviously pretty worried."

" D'you think something's happened to him ? " said Patricia.

" Oh, I shouldn't think so. But he left her five hours ago to come here, and he's in a pretty queer state. Might have gone off in a fugue or something. Anyhow I think I'll go. It won't take long, and she's a good little soul."

" All right, darling. Wrap up, though. It's a filthy night."

It was very dark and raining hard. As Milne went out of the gate and turned down the hill he caught a glimpse of a figure with a stick crossing the road. He stopped and said, " Lucian ! "

The figure approached, peered at him and said, " Oh, hallo."

Milne said, " I was just coming to look for you. Come in."

They went back into the house. Lucian hung his dripping coat in the hall in silence.

" You're a bit on the late side," said Milne, leading the way into the consulting room. " I'd better just ring your wife up and say you've arrived. She's been asking for you."

" I'll talk to her," said Lucian. He went to the telephone and dialled, standing with eyes closed, with the receiver to his ear. He said, " Hallo, Moll ? Adam. Yes. I'm here. With the doc. Just had a bit of business. Sure I will. O.K.

Good-bye. See you in a minute. 'Bye." He put the receiver down and smiled cunningly at Milne. "I'm late," he said.

"You certainly are."

"That's because I was busy. I haven't been wasting my time. There was something I wanted to get for you."

"For me?"

"Yes." Lucian fumbled in his pocket and pulled out a large gold cigarette case. "There you are," he said, holding it out. "For you."

Milne took the case and looked at it closely. It was of heavy, solid gold. Lucian sat down and lit a cigarette, looking at him with a curious insinuating smile.

"This is very lush," said Milne. "Where did it come from?"

"Shop in Regent Street."

"But why did you buy a thing like that?"

Lucian said, "I didn't buy it. I pinched it."

"Pinched it, eh? Why?"

"I thought it'd be nice to have," said Lucian off-handedly. "But I don't really want it any more. I'd rather have my old leather thing. You have it."

Milne put the case on his desk and sat down. "When did you get it?" he said casually. "This afternoon?"

"Yes. On my way here."

"But Regent Street isn't on your way."

"Near enough. I was cruising round."

"How did you manage it? I should have thought it was very difficult."

"Nothing in it at all," said Lucian. "I went in and asked to see some. They produced a lot together and one or two separately in boxes. I sent the man away to get some more, took one out of one of the boxes, put the box back under the others, and came away with the case."

"And nobody noticed?"

"Nobody noticed me steal it," said Lucian. He looked at Milne almost hopefully. "I just stole it and walked out."

"Amazing how careless these people are," said Milne. "You'd have thought they'd be on to you like a flash, handling stuff like that." He picked up the case. "Worth about two hundred and fifty, too."

"Two seventy five."

"I thought it was about that."

Lucian said, "You don't mind my having stolen it, doc?"

Milne shrugged. "Why should I? If you ask me, it was a silly thing to do—particularly as you didn't really want it much. But——"

"You didn't know I stole things though?"

"Oh, yes, I did," said Milne with a grin. "That stick you're walking about with is my ash-plant. You took it out of the hall."

"Did I really?" said Lucian, going red and looking very embarrassed. "Are you sure? I had one very like that, I'll swear."

"Well, anyhow it doesn't matter," said Milne. "Let's get on. It's late."

Lucian hesitated for a moment and then appeared to make up his mind.

"Look," he said. "If you like, I'll tell you exactly how I did it."

"What?"

"How I stole the case."

Milne said, "Oh, damn the case. What does it matter?"

"But I could be sent to gaol for it," said Lucian, looking rather hurt.

"Of course you could. In fact there's probably a detective outside now disguised as a lamp-post, waiting to nab you."

"And you don't care?" said Lucian bitterly.

"Not if you don't mind. Why should I? It's what you think about things that matters, not what I do."

Lucian considered for a long time and then made up his mind again.

"I tell you what," he said suddenly. "I'll tell you all about strangling Molly."

"All right," said Milne. "If you feel like it."

Lucian swung his legs on to the couch and lay down, folding his hands over his chest. "Corpse," he said.

"The bit I want is after you came out of the bathroom," said Milne in matter-of-fact tones.

"Yes," said Lucian. "My God, was that water hot." He paused for some seconds and lay with closed eyes. "I *saw* all this," he said quickly. "I sat in a chair and watched it, just like I did this afternoon. He came out of the bath-room. He had a dressing-gown on, but it was open in front and he looked pretty good. He looks glorious naked. The girl was asleep. The overhead light was on, and the counter-pane was blue and the sheets were blue and she was black. She was lying with her back to him. He could see the shape of her under the bedclothes."

He stopped for a moment and lay breathing quickly, his nostrils quivering slightly. "He stood and looked at her for a moment and said, 'Moll.' But she was asleep and didn't hear. That made him angry. *Bloody* angry."

"Why?" said Milne quietly.

"Because it did," said Lucian loudly. "Why the hell should she have been asleep? Anyhow, he thought, if she's asleep she might as well be dead. She'd be better dead anyhow. They all would."

His breathing was very rapid and shallow now, and he was shivering.

"Why would they?"

"It's no good asking me. All the good ones are dead anyhow. And better for them than to be married to me. Anyhow he came across the room very quietly so as not to wake her and went round to the other side of the bed. Then he took his dressing-gown off and stood there looking grand and magnificent and strong." Lucian's whole body was shaking convulsively, and beads of sweat were standing on his forehead. "And then he took her throat in his hands so that his fingers went right round it, and squeezed and squeezed. She woke up and struggled and thrashed about with her legs. She was strong, but nothing like as strong and big as he was. She had her eyes open and she looked silly with her eyes staring and her mouth open. I clapped. It was good. You know what I mean. It was the moment. And then——"

He stopped suddenly, heaved a deep sigh, and lay quiet for a long while. The shivering was gradually subsiding. "Well then, she smiled," he said at last in a dull tired voice.

"Just as though she thought it was a hell of a joke." He stirred restlessly. "I thought it best not to say any more about it," he said flatly. "What's done is done. Best forget it." He gave a last convulsive shiver. "That's the only way. Forget it. Like everything else. You don't know the half of it now. Nor do I." He paused. "Do you want me to tell you about the case?"

"Yes," said Milne gently.

"The case is a very valuable case," said Lucian slowly. "That's why it's made of gold."

"I see," said Milne quietly. "Is that why you brought it to me?"

"Yes." Lucian gave a sudden, almost feminine giggle. "You kept on asking me things about the case, so I offered to confess to you about it. But you stopped me."

"You want to talk about the wrong case, you see," said Milne.

Lucian opened his eyes. "Did you guess why I brought it?" he said.

"Oh, yes," said Milne simply. "It wasn't very difficult, was it?"

Lucian shook his head. "I don't think you can really have known," he said, "because I've just made it up."

"Oh no, you haven't. You've just thought of it, which is quite different." Milne smiled. "Do you know why you took my stick?"

"No," said Lucian, frowning.

"Well, have a think about it," said Milne. "That's quite simple too, really."

The shop in Regent Street seemed to deal entirely in things which cost a lot, without reference to their beauty, usefulness or any other quality. The only customer in it was a foreign-looking man in a camel-hair coat who was trying to make up his mind between a hideous writing set in gold and shagreen and a table-lamp held up by a nude young female made of silver. Milne decided that he must be buying a wedding present for an old enemy.

A young assistant, looking loutish in his formal clothes, came forward and flexed gently from the hips. Milne took the cigarette case out of his pocket and said, " One of my patients stole this from here yesterday. I thought you'd probably like to have it back."

The young man looked at Milne with his mouth slightly open, looked at the case, made a faint adenoidal noise and fled to the protection of a tougher and older specimen at the back of the shop.

The man in the camel coat switched the lamp on and off.

" Hand beaten," said the assistant. " Beautiful how the figure gleams up, isn't it ? "

" Yes," said the dark man. He seemed rather depressed.

The tougher-looking assistant came forward to Milne and said, " Yes, sir ? " briskly. He seemed prepared to forget the unfortunate misunderstanding with the adenoidal man.

Milne said, " My name's Milne. This cigarette case was stolen from here yesterday afternoon by one of my patients. I've brought it back."

" Stolen, sir ? " said the tougher man.

" Yes. This chap's slightly unbalanced mentally and he just put it in his pocket and walked off with it."

The assistant picked up the case, looked at it carefully and nodded to himself.

" Had you missed it ? " said Milne.

" Oh yes, sir," said the assistant with a knowing shake of the head. " We'd missed it all right. With the sort of stuff we've got here it stands to reason we have to be pretty careful."

" Well, you don't seem to have been very careful with this," said Milne shortly. " I shouldn't think this chap is a very good shop-lifter, and he got away with it easily enough."

" Ah, maybe he did for the *moment*," said the assistant. He shook his head. " Well, sir, I'm afraid I shall have to ask you to see the manager, if you'll be so good."

" All right," said Milne. " But I shall have to be quick. I've got an appointment."

" I'll see if he's there," said the assistant. He started off, hesitated, came back and picked up the case and started off again.

The manager was a small man with a rather red nose

who wrote things down. He said, " Well, well, Mr. Milne. This is an unfortunate business. Very unfortunate."

" Oh, I don't know," said Milne. " It might have been much worse. After all, you've got the thing back."

" Well, yes. There's that about it, of course. You say the man's er——? " he touched his head.

" Oh, I wouldn't say that. He's just unbalanced. He's a war case."

" Ah," said the manager, as though that made everything clear. " A *war case*." He wrote that down.

" He was a fighter pilot."

" Ah, a *fighter pilot*. One of the Few, eh? "

Milne said " No. One of the many. I'm afraid. There are a lot of these boys about who're only just showing what the war really did to them."

" Yes, yes. And you are his doctor, sir? "

" I'm a psychologist."

" Ah, a *psychologist*." This obviously made the thing as clear as crystal. The manager wrote it down. " It must be a fascinating profession, Mr. Milne."

Milne said, " It has its snags. This, for example."

" Oh, yes. I can see that. Responsibility. Yes." The manager jotted down a note at this point. Milne wondered vaguely what it was. " Well," said the little man after a moment's pause. " I can't promise anything, of course, Mr. Milne. The matter is not for me to decide. But I think that *probably* the company will decide to take no action. In the circumstances."

" You mean, not knowing who the man is or where to find him? " said Milne rather acidly.

" No, no. There is that, of course. But a war case. A man who is affected by his war experiences—— You know what I mean? "

" Good," said Milne briskly, getting up. " Well, you have my address. Perhaps you'll excuse me. I'm in rather a hurry."

As he went out, the foreign looking man was switching on the nude silver girl rather listlessly. The assistant was rooting in a cupboard for further atrocities. Somewhere in the gloom at the back of the shop Milne caught a glance of mingled horror and awe from the young man with adenoids.

At the clinic, Milne spent a rather exhausting hour with Charlie. The only thing that came out of it was that instead of wetting the bed every night, as had been his habit, Charlie was now wetting it only occasionally. His father, who had been persuaded by Milne and his own experience that bed-wetting every night could not be cured by strong arm methods, seemed to think that bed-wetting once a week was quite different, and had started in with the strap again.

Milne swore inaudibly, made a mental note to visit Kentish Town and carry the education of Charlie's father a step further, and went downstairs to coffee.

Paston said, " I had a call from a chap named Briant. You know him, don't you ? He said you put him on to me."

" Oh, yes," said Milne. " The cheese man."

" Cheese ? No. He's an advertising agent."

" I know. He advertises cheese though. Are you going to work for him ? "

" Oh, I don't know," said Paston casually. " I told him I'd think it over. Anyhow, thanks for the intro, old boy."

" You're welcome," said Milne.

" Mind you," said Paston, eyeing him rather doubtfully, " there's some interesting work to be done in that field. I often wonder whether one wouldn't be making as big a contribution to society there as anywhere."

" Probably a bigger one, when you reckon the Inland Revenue," said Milne. " Anyhow, what he wants is quite simple. Just the psychological angle. I told him you were the man for that."

" Well, I don't know," said Paston modestly. " I might be able to give him a few hints."

Norris Pile came up.

" Well, chaps," he said heartily. " It's all fixed. Freethorne's coming to have a look at us next week."

" What are you going to do with him ? " said Milne.

" Oh, nothing formal. Just show him round and introduce you all and let him chat to you. Nothing formal."

" You'd better not let him chat to me," said Garsten

from the other side of the table. " I've never spoken a polite word to him yet, and I'm too old to begin now."

" Get on with you," said Pile. " When I told him you were here he was quite impressed. He thinks you're good."

He turned back to Milne and Paston. " Look," he said in a low voice. " There's a thing I want to say to you two. The fact is that in spite of what Garsten says, he and the old boy know one another pretty well. You won't mind if I put him on to Garsten quite a bit? You know—make him our star turn?"

There was a moment's pause. Paston went rather red.

Milne said, " Good God, no! Why should we?"

" One has to do these things," said Pile. " You know how it is. Ah, there's little Phyllis." He hurried away.

" What the devil did he mean by that?" said Paston angrily.

" He meant," said Milne carefully, " that as Garsten is an old pupil of Freethorne's, he proposes to use him as Exhibit A. That's all."

" I don't think there ought to be an Exhibit A.," said Paston rather sulkily. " We all work here for nothing, don't we?"

" Think, think," said Milne with a grin. " The psychological angle in advertising, my dear man."

" These doctors make me sick," said Paston.

VIII

MRS. LUCIAN curled her legs up under her and sat in a small heap in the big chair.

" Of course this all sounds pretty queer to me, Mr. Milne," she said. " Because apart from being a bit dumb, the boy Adam just acts like he was normal—or nearly."

" Well anyhow he hasn't had a shot at strangling *me* yet," said Milne with a grin.

" Oh, I don't reckon that. That was just going plain hay-wire for a bit. But all this lifting cigarette cases and so on—that's new."

Milne said, "That's the whole point, of course. He's moving towards some sort of a relationship with me and this funny stuff is all part of it."

"But you reckon on the whole he's better?"

"No. I don't think he's better. But what I do think is that we're getting to a point where it may be possible to help him. The real difficulty about people like your husband is that you can't get *at* them. There's nothing to work on. They're completely withdrawn and unemotional. You can take them so far and then—bang! Down comes a sort of steel curtain, and you can't get beyond it."

She nodded. "Yes. I guess you're right there. That's Adam all right."

"Well, gradually I'm getting beyond it. As I've told you, he went over this strangling business for me. There still wasn't a lot of detail, but there was more than he'd ever given me before. And what matters is that he felt strongly about it—really strongly. Previously, he's never felt strongly about anything when he was talking to me. As soon as we got anywhere near a thing which he really minded about, down came the curtain."

She nodded thoughtfully.

"This business of the cigarette case was a sort of try-on. I wanted him to talk about the case—meaning himself. So he brought me another sort of case—a gold one—and tried very hard to get me to let him talk about that instead."

"Sort of joke? 'Case' and 'case'?"

"Yes. You're always getting puns of that sort in this job. What's more, he wanted to confess that he'd stolen it—that he'd done something wrong that would shock me. That's because he believed, subconsciously or consciously, that if he really talked frankly to me I should be shocked and disapproving. As soon as he found I wasn't interested in the cigarette case and didn't care a damn whether he'd stolen it or not, he threw his hand in and came out voluntarily with this stuff about strangling you which I'd never been able to get before."

"And you reckon he'll go on talking now?"

Milne said, "I don't know. I hope so. This is very much stage one of course. But at least it isn't hopeless."

Mrs. Lucian grinned her wide-mouthed grin. " Well, that's something anyhow."

" Yes." Milne picked up his notebook. " Now, there are two or three things I want to ask you, if I may."

" Sure. Go right ahead."

" Did you know either of his parents ? "

" No. I never did. His father died a while back—ten years or so. And his mother died just about six months before we met."

" Does he ever talk about them ? I mean—have you any idea what he felt about them ? "

She wrinkled up her whole face in a snubby frown.

" Not a lot. I guess he liked his mother a lot. But he never talks about her at all. His old man he has talked about sometimes. I reckon Adam and he didn't get on too well. Adam says he was a cold sort of guy who ran everybody around a lot. I think Adam was afraid of him when he was a kid."

" But he liked his mother ? "

" Sure. It seems she was pretty sweet. I've seen her picture and she looks swell. I think Adam reckons his dad gave her a bad time."

" He says that ? "

" He doesn't say anything much. That's just my guess."

Milne nodded. " The next thing is about his experiences in Burma. Does he ever talk about them ? "

She shook her head. " No, sir. Not ever."

" Have you ever tried to make him ? "

" A bit. But he won't talk at all. What I know about it mostly came second-hand."

" He never saw a service psychiatrist before he was discharged ? "

" No. He saw a heap of doctors, and though he won't have it I reckon they did a swell job. But it was his leg they were working on, not his mind. Of course he seemed quite O.K. there anyhow, right up till lately."

Milne nodded and lit a cigarette rather pensively. He said, " I'm afraid getting that stuff may be rather a snag. You see, it's like this—in a thing of this kind you've got to work backwards from the present to the past—from what's lying free in the memory to what's sunk down in it and become all silted over. The first thing was to get him to tell me about the strangling business. There was no doubt that he could remember most of it, and as it was the main reason why he came, there wasn't much point in going on until that had come out and been faced. The next stage is to get at what precipitated all this—which is probably the Burma business. But almost certainly the real root of the trouble lies a lot further back than that, and will be pretty difficult even if he does co-operate. I don't want to spend too much time breaking down a resistance to telling me what he really knows quite well, when we're probably going to need a lot of time later on digging up the earlier stuff that he genuinely doesn't know about."

Mrs. Lucian shook the curly black head. "I reckon you're going to need a sand-blaster to get that Burma stuff, Mr. Milne. He sure is very tight about it."

"More so than people usually are? Service people don't talk much about these things, you know."

"Well, this boy doesn't talk at all. He doesn't even answer questions so as you'd notice." She grinned rather ruefully.

Milne considered. "I think I may have to try something a bit different," he said at last. "During the war people had a lot of success with dopes that make chaps drowsy, when they wanted them to talk about what had happened to them. If he seems very sticky we might try that. Only I have to have help with it," he added with a smile.

"What sort of help, Mr. Milne?"

"Well, not being a doctor I can't go pushing drugs into people."

"You mean it's not allowed?"

"Yes. It's not a bad rule in a way, though it's often a nuisance. After all, there are some pretty odd people about who call themselves lay analysts. If they were all allowed to shove trick drugs into people there'd be liable to be casualties."

"But that's mighty awkward," she said with a frown.

"Oh, it doesn't matter. I've got a colleague who'll probably risk his professional reputation by helping a quack."

"Maybe. But Adam doesn't like doctors."

"Oh, Lord, no. I was forgetting that."

"He surely does *not.*"

"Of course it wouldn't amount to anything. I should only get Garsten to give him the actual injection. Nothing else."

Mrs. Lucian shook her head. "Won't play," she said decidedly.

"You think he won't?"

"I'm sure he won't. You show him a doctor and he'll be off like a shot."

"Hell!" said Milne.

"Don't you know about how they give injections yourself, Mr. Milne?"

Milne hesitated. "Oh, it isn't that. It's a perfectly simple job. In a hospital any sister does it—or any orderly. It's just that the stuff is only supposed to be given under medical supervision."

Mrs. Lucian grinned. "Well, I reckon that's O.K., Mr. Milne, as long as the medical supervision keeps out of sight or hangs round looking like a window-cleaner or something. But don't try showing the boy Adam anything with a stethescope and a bedside manner or you'll start big trouble."

Milne sighed. "Ah, well," he said. "It may not be necessary. Now—how are you?"

"Me?" said Mrs. Lucian with a cheerful grin. "Oh, I'm fine."

"He's been all right with you? No more funny business?"

"None at all. He's the gentlest thing really."

"Yes," said Milne absently. He was staring thoughtfully at the snubby face and the twinkling dark eyes. "Look," he said suddenly. "Is it any good suggesting that you should go away for—for a holiday while this is going on?"

"You mean and leave Adam?" She shook her head. "No, sir. No good at all. It doesn't start."

"All right," said Milne, after a moment's hesitation. "Then I want you to promise me three things."

"I could promise you anything, Mr. Milne," she said with mock solemnity. "Or most anything."

" Right," said Milne, smiling. " Then, first of all—don't go to bed first."

" I'd thought of that," she said cheerfully. " Won't do. It hurt too much last time."

" Second—if any funny business starts *don't* try to cope with him—get out and get out quickly."

" We-ll——" she said rather doubtfully.

" Seriously," said Milne. " This is important. I know you're not afraid and you'll think it's only Adam and you can handle him. You'll probably be right, but you might possibly not be. See ? "

Mrs. Lucian hesitated. " O.K.," she said at last. " If it ever gets really tough I'll beat it."

" And third, ring me up at once if anything happens that you don't understand or don't like."

" That one's easy," she said, smiling. " I'll certainly do that."

" Good," said Milne, getting up.

Mrs. Lucian uncoiled her legs and stood up to her full five feet of height.

" O.K. then, Mr. Milne. And you really don't want to talk fees yet ? "

" I do not," said Milne. He looked down at the small figure and something urged him to turn it round and give it a gentle and affectionate slap on the bottom with one hand as he picked up its coat with the other.

" Sure—I know you're busy. I'll beat it now," said Mrs. Lucian, grinning the urchin grin. " Good-bye, Mr. Milne—and thanks a lot."

On Thursday morning Milne woke up with a feeling that it was a special day in some way. It was some time before he remembered that he was taking Barbara out. He put a new blade in his razor, and it cut him four times. Moreover, there was a spot developing in a rather unsightly place on the side of his nose. Looking in the glass, he decided that if he was going to rely on anything it would have to be brilliant conversation.

Neither he nor Patricia said anything about it at breakfast, but there was no doubt that she had remembered too.

After they had finished, and Milne was smoking a cigarette with his last cup of tea, she looked at him in a worried way, and Milne thought it was coming. But she only said, "You're looking tired, honey."

"I'm not," said Milne, giving her a lead. "I'm looking particularly attractive. Four bits of cotton wool and a spot on my nose."

"Attractive but tired," said Patricia. "Can't you take a day off soon? You can't do this stuff six and seven days a week for long, you know."

"I'm all right."

"What have you got to-day?"

Milne thought. "I've got Beresford this morning and Lady M. this afternoon. And I must go down to Kentish Town and see that kid Charlie's father and tell him to stop mucking up all my work."

"Need you do that to-day? Why not stop after Lady M.? You're always fed up after her anyway."

"I must go and see papa. He's taken to licking the kid with a strap again." Milne grinned. "Anyhow I can go there on my way to my childish amusements." As Patricia did not reply he added, "It's this evening that I'm going on the tiles with Bab."

"I know," said Patricia abstractedly. "But I wish you'd cut the work down a bit. There's a damned sight too much of it to be good for you at the moment."

"What are you going to do this evening?" said Milne, anxious to get some reaction.

"I shall stay in, I think," said Patricia calmly, "and send Janet out. It seems a good opportunity. Then I shall be free on Saturday." She looked at him with a worried frown. "I think you ought to try to arrange to have one day in the middle of the week completely clear."

Ever since he could remember, Milne had hated the time just before treats and holidays and nice things in general. It always took the form of wishing, almost violently, that he needn't go or needn't do it. Several times during the day he nearly rang Barbara up and put the dinner off. At lunch, after a long silence, Patricia suddenly grinned at him and said, " It's all right, honey. You'll probably like it when you get there."

" Like what ? " said Milne feebly.

Patricia just went on grinning.

" Oh, all right," said Milne with a wry smile. " You think I shall ? "

" I hope not," said Patricia frankly. " I hope you'll be bored stiff and think you'd far rather have taken me. But in common honesty I had to say that, because I know about you and playing."

" You're an odd young woman," said Milne thoughtfully.

" I expect I need psychiatric treatment," said Patricia. " Go and see someone and tell him your wife acts peculiarly."

" Fair enough," said Milne. " You can have that one. What I propose to do this evening——"

" No," said Patricia firmly. " You can come and tell me all about it *afterwards*—in fact I shall be rather hurt if you don't. But not beforehand, Felix. It isn't decent." She smuggled an illicit lump of sugar down to Carlo.

Milne said, " Have you got that hound its licence yet ? "

" Yes," said Patricia, looking down at the sleek and scrumping Carlo. " Amazingly enough, I have."

Lady Maresfield was in a trying mood. She cried rather a lot and said that her life was a failure and that if it weren't for Milne she would commit suicide. Milne spent an hour and a half gently pointing out that this, though flattering for him, wasn't a very satisfactory basis for existence, and that she really must stop ringing him up twice a day and try to find some other *raison d'être*. But little progress was made. It is hard to convince non-swimmers like Lady Maresfield that they will be far better off without a life-belt.

At half-past six Milne went to Kentish Town. Charlie's father had just reached home and was sitting in his shirt-sleeves having tea. He received Milne with a mixture of cordiality and suspicion. Milne sipped a large cup of very strong tea and said, " He's quite a lot better, I think."

" That's what my wife says," said Mr. Oakes. " You reckon he's a lot better, don't you ? "

" Oh, yes," said the little, yellow-faced woman in her hushed voice. " It's nearly all right now. And he's a lot brighter in himself too."

" I reckon it's done him a lot of good," said Mr. Oakes. " 'Course I don't know anything about these things. But the proof of the pudding's in the eating. Mind you, sir, his master at the school says he's bright enough. Got plenty in his 'ead."

" Oh, Lord, yes," said Milne. " He's bright enough."

" I mean the boy isn't feeble-minded or anything."

" Nothing like that at all."

" Only when you came here first, I thought that was what you was after, see. I know it isn't now. I reckon it's done him good," said Mr. Oakes, with the air of a man pronouncing a reasoned judgment.

Milne sipped his tea and gently approached the point of the meeting.

" Of course," he said, " it'll take a little time before it clears up completely. The bed-wetting may start again if he's upset about anything. Or if he gets frightened or nervous about it."

" Ah," said Mr. Oakes, looking at his plate a trifle guiltily.

" He's still a trifle scared of you, of course," said Milne with a smile.

" Of *me*? " said Mr. Oakes in amazement. He turned and looked at Milne with his rather fiery eyes. The movement pulled his unbuttoned shirt away from his huge hairy chest. " Scared of *me*? "

" A bit."

" But——"

" There's nothing surprising in that. You must remember that to him you're power—authority. If there's any punishing to be done, you're his father and you do it. So it tends to be you he's a bit nervous of."

" He's never had no cause to be frightened of *me*," said Mr. Oakes rather sulkily.

" Of course not. But he's naturally a bit jumpy about all this business—afraid he'll be punished and so on."

" Mind you," said Mr. Oakes, counter-attacking, " I

reckon you can be *too* soft with a boy." He looked accusingly at the little yellow woman. "I don't believe in being 'arsh. But I believe in being *firm*."

"I quite agree with you," said Milne. "Too much softness is a bad thing. But too much firmness is a bad thing too. You remember I suggested that over this business, for example, punishment wouldn't help much."

Mr. Oakes nodded rather grudgingly. "You reckon we ought to go on 'umouring him?"

"I don't know about that. But I wouldn't actually punish him for bed-wetting. It'll only put him back to where he was before."

"I thought now it was nearly right, if we could just make him *try* a bit more——?" said Mr. Oakes. "'Cause that's all it is now, see. He don't *try*."

"No," said Milne firmly. "I'm afraid that won't work. It isn't quite a matter of trying. It'll come right if we're patient for a little while longer."

"It means a lot of trouble for the wife," said Mr. Oakes. "That's what *I'm* worried about." He shook his head righteously.

"I think probably Mrs. Oakes would rather have a bit more trouble now and get it right, than go on having trouble indefinitely," said Milne, smiling at the little woman.

She said, "Oh, yes, sir. It's nothing to what it was. I don't mind it at all now."

There was a moment's silence. Mr. Oakes put down his knife and fork. "All right, sir," he said at last, pushing his plate away from him rather angrily. "He's better. The proof of the pudding's in the eating. If that's what you say's got to be done, then that's it. Just let him alone and no scolding or anything, eh?" He looked across at his wife as if commanding her not to beat Charlie with a strap in future.

"I think you'll find that's the quickest way," said Milne.

"Ah, well," said Mr. Oakes. "'Course I don't know anything about these things. But I'm always ready to learn."

The little woman saw Milne to the door. As he went out he said quietly, "Will that be all right?"

" Oh, yes, thank you, sir," she said in her hushed voice. " Oh, yes. It'll be all right. He'll do it now he's said so. Otherwise he'd just tell you straight. It'll be all right now."

You could never be sure with the Molyneux. Either it was full of beautiful women and distinguished-looking men, or else the complete staff of a raree show seemed to have come along. Milne looked round at a man in dark spectacles, a woman with a very small head at the end of a very long neck, and a pair who must have weighed nearly forty stone between them, and decided that it was a raree night. Checking them over, he could identify the whole troupe except for the strong man and the spotted lady.

He made sure that the table was booked, came back to the lounge and ordered himself another pink gin rather moodily. Soon—say ten minutes after Barbara arrived—it would be all right. But for the moment he was still wishing that he was comfortably at home. He had drunk his second drink before he realised that it was only ten-past eight. On normal form, Barbara might easily not arrive for another twenty minutes, which left him the alternatives of sitting drinkless or getting somewhat ahead of the party. He compromised by buying another drink and leaving it untouched before him.

Barbara actually arrived at eight fifteen. She said, " Sorry, Felix. I thought I might as well strip for action before I came in. I hate sitting around in a coat." She was wearing a pale-blue-grey frock that fitted closely from her neck to her hip bones and then became confused and broke into protestations of modesty.

Milne ordered her a drink and said, " My God, what a garment ! "

" Like it ? "

" Oh, yes, I *like* it. But it's a screaming hypocrite, isn't it ? "

" I have trouble about clothes. I'm awkward colours to dress."

He looked at the black hair and the blue cat's eyes. " In Pete's name, why ? I thought every one wanted dark hair and blue eyes ? "

" Maybe. But it's a tricky combination. You can wear black and you can wear blue. But apart from that, it always feels as though there was something wrong somewhere." She took a cigarette. " How's Pat ? "

" Very well, thank you," said Milne politely. " How's Peter ? "

" Peter," said Barbara, " is very well. He's gone into his long woolly pants, and as long as he keeps up with his gargling I see no reason why he shouldn't get through the winter."

" Is he a gargler ? "

" A gargler ? " said Barbara. " My dear, he's the biggest gargler in the North-Western Postal District. He's got stamina, if you understand me. He's the sort of gargler who never throws away the drop in the bottom of the glass. He sees the thing through. It shakes the bathroom when he's really firing on both tonsils."

" And does it stop him from having colds and things ? "

" There's no means of telling. You see, I don't know how many he'd have if he *didn't* gargle. It couldn't be any more. But anyhow," she added quickly, " I didn't come here to be bitchy about poor old Pete. Who's the female with the long neck ? "

" The human giraffe," said Milne. " The man in dark spectacles is Hi Flung Dung the magician. He's trying to take her away from the lion tamer—the chap over there with the handle-bar moustache and the double whisky."

Barbara closed her eyes and sighed. " Go on," she said. " That's nice. And very good for me. I haven't been really silly and childish for weeks."

At nine o'clock they were still sitting over their drinks.

Milne said, " We shall have to go and eat soon."

" I suppose so," said Barbara. " It's a queer thing, but as soon as you're really comfortable, there's always some reason why you've got to stop."

" Don't you like eating ? "

" Yes, but people come and make you order and choose *hors d'œuvres* and generally interrupt."

"Well, we don't have to dine if you'd rather not."

"Nonsense," said Barbara, getting up. "Of course we must. I was only complaining. I like to complain a bit sometimes when I'm sure nobody will take any notice. Come on. Food. You're probably starving."

As they were eating their sweet it was gradually borne in upon Milne that it was half-past nine; that it would go on getting later with great rapidity; and that though there had been a number of very pleasant local engagements, there had so far been no major advance. "Look" he said as the waiter went away to fetch coffee. "This is all very well."

"It is, indeed," said Barbara. "I feel at peace with all the world. Aren't you very happy, Felix?"

"Yes. But I didn't bring you out to feel happy or to make you feel at peace with all the world. I brought you out to make love to you and seduce you and so on."

"But couldn't that be some other time when everything wasn't so nice? I mean, one can always make passes at people when everything's lousy, which it usually is. But it seems a shame to spend time on it when you're happy and warm and comfortable." She looked at him solemnly. "Dear Felix. You can't think how warmly I feel towards you this evening. Just like an affectionate sister."

Milne said, "I don't believe you've ever in your life felt like a sister to any male creature."

"Well, perhaps not *quite* a sister. But *very* gentle, Felix. And affectionate. Don't *you* feel gentle and affectionate?"

"No," said Milne untruthfully. "I feel distinctly rough. And anyhow, to come out to dinner with a man in that frock and then do a sister-act is getting food and drink under false pretences."

"There you are," said Barbara tragically. "If I have a decent impulse, it's dragged in the mud. Ah, world. Ah, life. Ah, time."

Milne said, "Look, darling—you've eaten too much. It must be that, because you've hardly drunk anything."

"Anyhow," said Barbara "I resent your attitude about this frock. I particularly chose it as being suitable to a serious dinner party with my medical adviser. It is a discreet frock. It may imply, but it never *says* anything."

"I should have thought it said quite enough."

"Yes, Felix. But there's nothing on paper. And anyhow you may quite well have misunderstood it."

"But to get back to the object of this dinner——" said Milne rather restlessly, The waiter arrived with the coffee.

The band launched tirelessly into the third encore of a waltz.

"Listen, Bab," said Milne as they circled the crowded floor, "I'm an old man now and I like to know where I am. If you want to keep me at arm's length you've only got to say so."

"Well, if I get much closer to you, my dear, we shall be turned off the floor."

"*No*," said Milne impatiently. "Not that stuff. I'm not fooling now and it's not fair for you to."

Barbara turned her head and looked moodily away over his shoulder without speaking.

"Don't *want* a sister?" she said at last.

"No. Won't have a sister, what's more."

She sighed. "I was afraid you weren't really a family type," she said wearily.

"Well, damn it all, Bab, I never pretended——"

"Oh, no. You never pretended anything, Felix. I know that."

They danced on until they were near the door and then stopped by tacit consent.

"Come along," said Milne quietly. They went out into the foyer. "Get your things."

"Where are we going, Felix?"

"To Jimmy Douglas's flat."

"Is he there?"

"No. He's in Ireland."

She hesitated for a moment, looking at him with an unusual worried look in the slanting eyes.

"All right," she said at last, with a tiny shrug, and turned away to the cloakroom.

It was a long time before she emerged from the cloakroom

in the big fur coat. Milne slipped a hand inside her arm and they went out to the taxi in silence.

"Look," said Barbara as Milne was about to give the address. "Not Jimmy's. Let's go home."

"No," said Milne in a low voice. "Jimmy's."

"But look, Felix—you don't see what I mean. Peter's away."

"Away?"

"Yes. We can go in—and—and talk."

They looked at one another for a moment.

"Jimmy's," said Milne decisively, and turned to the driver.

As they drove, Milne said, "I don't understand about wanting to go home, Bab."

"I do," she said almost viciously. "I understand only too bloody well."

He put his arms round her and kissed her vigorously. She responded without hesitation.

"Are you still feeling like a sister to me?" asked Milne rather breathlessly.

"No," said Barbara. "Nothing like it." She was silent for a moment and then kissed him again firmly and shamelessly.

They paid off the cab and went into the big block of flats. Jimmy Douglas's flat was on the third floor. Milne fumbled for a moment with the unfamiliar lock. The flat was pleasant but it had an unoccupied air.

Milne said, "The first thing we want is a drink. If I remember rightly, J. Douglas keeps his drinks in the other room."

"I don't want a drink," said Barbara abstractedly.

Milne hesitated. "What—no drink?" he said lightly.

"No, thanks. You have one."

"I shall."

Milne went into the other room and found a bottle of whisky. As he poured himself out a drink he came to a certain definite conclusion, and was uncertain whether he was glad or sorry. He went back with the glass. Barbara was still standing by the fireplace where he had left her.

He said, "This is a nice flat."

" Yes," said Barbara. She turned and stood looking at him for a moment in silence.

" Look, Felix," she said with a queer, rapid shyness. " I'd just like you to know that I'm now going to do something that I've never done before in my life."

" Oh, ho ! " said Milne quietly. " Are you now ? "

" Yes. If there's one thing in the world I hate it's women who play around with people and then——"

" Send them home to bed ? "

" Yes," she said desperately.

" And that's the idea now, is it ? "

" Yes."

Milne nodded. " I thought so," he said heavily. He dropped into a chair suddenly feeling very tired.

" You knew ? You mean I wasn't just leading you up the garden path in coming here ? "

" My dear Bab," said Milne bitterly, " I have the use of my senses." He shook his head. " You oughtn't to have let me kiss you, though."

" Well, hell's bells ! " said Barbara irritably. " I wanted you to kiss me. I tell you, I've never in my life been the steady partner in any firm before and I don't know how you do it. But——" she shook her head helplessly. " You see, it would be such a mess, and being just a bitch I don't know how to get out of it except by *being* a bitch."

" Why did you come at all if you felt like this about it ? " said Milne with quiet anger.

" Because I wanted to and hadn't the guts to say no, of course."

" You did want to ? "

" Of course."

" But not much ? "

" Well, why the hell did you pick on me ? " said Barbara with sudden anger. " It was bound to mean a bloody mix-up one way or the other. Now of course you're livid with me." Milne saw with surprise that her lips were trembling.

" No, I'm not," he said wearily. " Don't worry. Dear Bab." He put an arm round her and kissed her gently.

" I don't think either of us is very nice probably. But you're at least a better thing than me. Come on."

He hastily gulped down his drink and opened the door. Barbara hesitated and then went out. As they went down in the lift Milne said, " We shall probably have to manage with one cab. But I'll sit at the other end of the seat."

Patricia was lying in bed reading. He went in and said, " Hallo."

She said, " Well—good time had by all ? "

" Very," said Milne calmly. " We danced. An evening of innocent pleasure."

" Good God ! " said Patricia. " Was one of you taken ill or something ? "

" The trouble with you is that you're a pessimist, darling."

Patricia continued to look at him with interest.

" Was Bab awful ? "

" Not so that you'd notice."

" Didn't come at you with bared teeth ? "

" No. The Archbishop of Canterbury could have come with us and he wouldn't have felt out of place—at least, not very."

There was a moment's pause. Then Patricia said, " Felix ? "

" What, honey ? "

" You wouldn't—I mean, you would tell me if——? "

Milne bent down and kissed the end of her nose. " You know that the one advantage of me as a husband is that I *always* tell you the worst," he said. " It just didn't happen to be that sort of show. Good-night."

IX

WALKING down from Hyde Park Corner to the Clinic, Milne overtook Garsten.

Garsten said, " What-ho, Felix. Hope you've polished your buttons properly."

"Buttons?" said Milne.

"Yes. To-day's the big inspection, isn't it?"

"So it is. I'd forgotten."

"Bet you half a crown Norris is running around like a hen at a Sunday School treat."

"Why should I give you money?"

"All right. Then I'll bet you he's wearing sponge-bag trousers and a come-to-Jesus collar *and* running around, etcetera."

"Not half a crown," said Milne. "Sixpence. And even then it's giving money away. He asked me last week if I minded his making you the star turn."

"*Me!* In God's name why?"

"Seeing as how you know Freethorne."

"The man's mad. I've already told him that I hate the sight of the old bluffer."

Milne said, "Well, Norris hasn't a lot of choice, has he? Phyllis hasn't much of a stage presence and Hans is comedy."

"How about you and Paston?"

"Quack, quack!" said Milne derisively.

"God, yes. I'd forgotten. The old boy will hate that. He's the staunchest trades union doctor in England. Mind you rub it into him."

"If I do we probably shan't get the money."

"Oh, to hell with the money!" said Garsten impatiently. "What do we want money for, anyway? There are we and there are the patients, God help them. You can't just write a cheque for what's missing in this outfit."

"Look," said Milne as they turned into the square. "You remember my schizo? The one I told you I'd got?"

"Yes."

"Well, he's getting on a bit. Not much, but not impossible. But there's a lot of stuff about his war experiences that he's very sticky about. I was thinking of trying narcosynthesis."

"Sodium pentothal?"

"Or amytal."

"I'd be inclined to use pentothal. It's quicker acting and wears off quicker. You can go straight on when it wears off. We used it quite a bit in the war."

" I've seen it used, but I've never used it myself. You think it's a good egg ? "

" Oh, yes. For getting at recent stuff like battle experiences. It doesn't get you back to the root of things, of course."

" Oh, I know that. It's just that I want to get on with this chap, and I can't go any deeper without the battle stuff coming out."

Garsten nodded. " Be all right for that."

Milne hesitated. " Would you be willing to come and shoot it into him for me ? "

Garsten looked surprised. " Sure. If you want me to. But why ? It's quite straightforward. Ante-cubital. Put it in rather slowly—about point one of a gram a minute. Probably needs between a quarter and half a gram."

" Yes, yes, I know," said Milne impatiently.

" Then why not do it yourself ? "

" Dangerous drug," said Milne. " Qualified supervision and all that."

" Oh, bunkum ! " said Garsten.

" The snag is that this bird flies off the handle if he sees a doctor."

" Well, then, why worry ? Do it yourself. I'll supervise you from Welbeck Street. If he dies, just give me a ring and I'll come and hold the syringe while we collect some witnesses. Have you got any pentothal ? "

" No."

" I'll give you some."

" Seriously," said Milne. " You think it's all right for me to do it ? I know the technique backwards, of course."

" My dear old Felix," said Garsten. " When I think of the number of irresponsible dolts all over the country who'll shoot anything into their patients as soon as look at them, the thought of you giving somebody a spot of pentothal is a big relief."

As they reached the Clinic, Norris Pile came quickly out and dived into a large waiting car. " Hallo," he said through the window. " Just off to fetch the guest of honour."

" Fine," said Garsten. " What would you like the band to play when he arrives ? "

The car moved off. Milne fumbled in his pocket and handed Garsten sixpence in silence.

Garsten said, " Money for old rope."

" I hoped you might come down on the collar," said Milne. " The rest was a certainty."

Paston was in the hall. Garsten said, " Why didn't you go with Norris to help fetch Freethorne ? "

" He didn't ask me," said Paston, looking surprised.

Garsten shook his head. " There must be some mistake," he said. " He was looking all over the place for you. Now he's had to go by himself."

" But I've been here all the time," said Paston, obviously put out.

" Well, I should stay here until they come back," said Garsten, starting up the stairs. " After all, there must be somebody to open the door of the car."

" Pile said nothing to me."

" He's pulling your leg," said Milne gently.

As they reached their rooms, Garsten said, " What did you want to say that for ? He'd have stayed there and put his cloak down in the mud or something."

" That's what I was afraid of. It would have spoiled Norris's party."

" But it would have kept him away from his patients, wouldn't it ? You've got to take the large view in these things."

Miss Lucas was going much better now. Amongst other things, it appeared that she was, or had been the mistress of the junior partner of the firm for which she worked ; that this was by no means her first fall ; that she had been systematically deceiving her parents ; and that when the junior partner proved unfaithful she had tried a little amateur blackmail. Milne was not surprised. There was very little left now that surprised him about people's private lives. He merely noted, as he had often noted before, how the quiet preciseness of the mousey little typist remained as a sort of film over her account of even the least quiet and precise incidents.

He had nearly finished with her by four o'clock. She was off the couch and they were sitting opposite one another chatting. It was an important moment from Milne's point of view. Previously, even when she had talked freely on the couch, she had " frozen " as soon as they were face to face. To-day, for the first time, she was sitting talking quietly, yet quite easily and freely, about the junior partner and her feelings about him.

The doors of the consulting rooms were fitted with small glass peepholes, so that it was possible to see from the corridor whether a consultant was working or alone. Milne heard a step outside, and glancing up, caught a glimpse of a face outside. There was a low mutter and then a single knock. The door opened and Norris Pile stood in the doorway. Behind him was a very tall, thin figure

Milne jumped up and walked angrily over to the door. " Look, Norris——" he said protestingly.

" Ah, Felix ! " said Pile, beaming. He stepped aside. " Sir George—may I introduce Felix Milne. Sir George Freethorne."

Milne looked at the very tall, thin, lantern-jawed man with the bushy black eyebrows overhanging watery blue eyes with yellowish whites. Freethorne made a curious motion with his jaws, like a man chewing gum, nodded and said, " How d'you do ? "

" How do you do ? " said Milne, bowing slightly. He turned to Pile and said, " Look—I'm sorry, Norris, but I have a patient."

" Oh, I'm sorry, Felix. I thought you were just chatting, you know." He bowed and beamed past Felix to the girl. " Good-afternoon," he said brightly. " Sorry to interrupt." She nodded a timid greeting without saying anything audible.

" I shall be down in ten minutes or so," said Milne, beginning to shut the door.

" Oh, right-ho," said Pile. " Talk then, eh ? " He stepped back quickly to avoid the door. " Sorry, Sir George. Sorry. Didn't hurt you, did I ? "

Milne shut the door and went back to his chair. His hands were trembling slightly with anger.

" Now," he said, smiling with an effort. " Where were we? You were just telling me about the Sunday when you went out in the car."

There was a long silence.

" You went down to Virginia Water? "

" Yes," she said.

" And then——? "

She hesitated. " Oh, we just walked about," she said with finality. Milne sighed inwardly. It was obviously no good now for a while.

Usually everybody talked at once during tea. To-day there was comparative silence. Garsten was standing looking out of the window. Paston was sitting alone in a corner. Tautz and Phyllis Snow were talking in low voices in another. Tautz's fat little face was wrinkled up as though he was going to cry.

" If I go to talk," he was saying, " he look down at me and chew—chew—chew." He stood on extreme tiptoe, bent his neck and worked his jaws. " The more I talk the more he chew. And all the time he looks at me as though I am a liar."

" I think it's chiefly his manner," said Dr. Snow, comfortingly.

" Then he should not have such a manner. I wish I had chewing gum to give him."

Milne said, " Hallo. Where's the party? "

" No talking in the rear ranks," said Garsten, turning. " The inspection is due at any minute."

" Look," said Milne. " Did Norris come barging in on you with him? While you were working? "

" No. I'd just finished."

" Well, he did on me."

" He came in while you had a patient? " said Tautz in horror.

" What did you do, Felix? "

" I threw them out."

" Violently? " said Garsten hopefully.

" Violently enough to make Norris tread on the royal toe. I don't think it hurt much, unfortunately."

" He looks at me," said Tautz, rising on tiptoe, " and he chew—chew—chew. Bah ! "

" I thought he was quite all right," said Dr. Snow. " Quite polite and so on."

" Bloody nice of him," said Garsten. " You'd have expected him to rush up and insult you." He glanced at his watch. " Well, personally, I give Norris two minutes more and then I go home. What's he messing about at, anyhow ? "

Norris Pile came in, leading Freethorne like a genial elephant piloting a depressed giraffe. Milne judged that Freethorne was about six feet four with his stoop, and would have been quite six feet six without it. He looked round the room, chewed for a moment, smiled effortfully and said, " Well, well—everybody assembled for tea, eh ? "

" We always come down here to coffee-house and discuss the day's work," said Pile. " Let's see—you have met everybody now, haven't you, Sir George ? "

" I think so," said Freethorne, looking round without enthusiasm.

" Would you care for a cup of tea, sir ? " said Paston, coming forward with one.

" Thanks. Thanks. Very good of you." Freethorne took the tea.

" Always welcome after so much talking," said Paston conversationally.

Freethorne looked down at him for a moment, chewing vigorously. Then he nodded briefly.

" A bun ? " said Paston, passing the plate.

" Thanks. Thanks. Very good of you." Freethorne took the bun. Milne, watching fascinated as he opened his mouth and inserted it, noticed that he did so without missing a single beat of his rhythmically working jaws.

Pile looked round and said, "Have you had your tea, Garsten ? "

Garsten said, " Yes, thanks, Norris. I got here early and bagged the jammiest bun."

" By the way, Garsten," said Sir George, " wasn't a man named Haver a contemporary of yours ? "

" Bill Haver ? Yes."

"D'you know what's happened to him?"

"No idea."

"Thought you might. He was quite a good man."

"The only good man of my year," said Garsten curtly, "was Albury Clifford. And he was killed in the war."

There was a moment's pause. Sir George had turned slightly pink.

"Clifford?" said Pile tactlessly. "That wasn't the chap who——?"

Sir George made a little grunting noise and turned away.

"That's right," said Garsten calmly. "He was struck off the register for infamous conduct."

"I like his idea of a good man," said Pile, turning to Freethorne with a grin.

"He was an outstanding man," said Garsten. "Wasn't he, Sir George?"

Freethorne merely grunted and turned pointedly to Phyllis Snow.

"Why did you take up this work?" he said shortly. The bun was gone, but his jaws were still working steadily. Dr. Snow gazed at him like a rabbit looking at a weasel.

"I—I really hardly know," she murmured helplessly.

"You say you don't know, Phyllis?" said Tautz suddenly. "Well, *I* know. It was because you think him the most important work in the world." He glared up at Freethorne through his thick spectacles with a mixture of sullenness and defiance.

"H'm," said Freethorne, not looking at him

"She knew that," said Tautz, beginning to bounce a little at the knees. "An' so she——"

"What school were you?" said Freethorne, ignoring him.

"King's."

"Oh, yes. And you acquired this—this interest there?"

"Yes," said Dr Snow rather breathlessly.

Freethorne nodded ponderously. Pile gently edged Tautz away and engaged the remainder of the party in subdued conversation.

"And you had some sort of special training, I take it?" Freethorne was saying to the wretched Phyllis.

After about ten minutes, when Dr. Snow had been cross-questioned into a satisfactory pulp, Pile made another effort to deflect Sir George towards Garsten. But although Garsten lifted his eyebrows and smiled invitingly, Sir George did not seem to have much he wanted to say to Garsten. Instead, he turned to Tautz and said suddenly, " And you regard work of this kind as the most important in the world."

" Certainly," said Tautz defiantly.

" Well," said Freethorne drily, " I suppose we all think that about our job How long have you been in this country ? "

" I came over just before the war. At first there was opposition to Austrians working here."

" I know," said Freethorne with a grim smile " I opposed it for one."

" I know," said Tautz. They both laughed rather constrainedly. Norris Pile roared.

" You belong to the Viennese school, eh ? "

" Yes. I belong to the greatest school of analytical psychology in the world," said Tautz proudly.

" Well, I hope you don't hold to all the doctrine that has come out of Vienna," said Freethorne with thinly disguised contempt.

Tautz's eyes flashed behind his spectacles. " I am forced to hold to the doctrine which has come out of Vienna," he said quietly. " There is none come out of England for me to hold to."

" I'm afraid Hans is right there," said Pile " We haven't contributed much in the way of *original* work in England, though there's been some first-rate critical work." He was looking rather worried.

" Oh, nobody would deny the *originality* of much of what has been sent us," said Freethorne. He chewed thoughtfully down at Tautz and said, " Don't I remember a paper of yours on the future of psychosomatic medicine ? "

" That's right," said Tautz.

" Ah—so you *are* the man who says that by taking thought I am liable to ulcerate my duodenum ? "

Tautz gave a little bounce at the knees, like a boxer loosening his muscles for the fight.

"Yes," he said warily "You may."

"You know I think this is where I chuck my hand in," said Garsten quietly to Milne. "The whole thing's too bloody silly."

Milne said, "What was the point about Albury Clifford?"

"Oh, poor old Albury was cited in a divorce case. He'd known the woman for years. There was no question of his having just met her professionally. But the silly old ass treated her for some small thing, and some of these smug bastards went after him for professional misconduct and had him struck off the register."

"Freethorne didn't like what you said a bit."

"I knew he wouldn't. That's why I said it. He was at the bottom of the whole thing. He couldn't stick Albury at any price. The man was an absolutely brilliant person too. The whole thing was a complete scandal and he knows it."

"The trouble with you chaps," Freethorne was saying, "is that you always spoil your case by over-statement. We all know that these conditions are made worse by worry and overwork. There's nothing new in that. But then you must go and take a leap in the dark and ask us to believe that there's no other factor."

"I do not ask anybody to believe anything," said Tautz. "I say, 'Look at the figures and see for yourself.' But you will not look, because you have already made up your mind. So you say 'Ha. He is a liar. We know he is a liar because we do not agree.'"

Milne said, "Norris had better take him away from Hans or there's going to be a row."

"Fine," said Garsten. "It'll be damn good for him. He still thinks that people's bellies are test tubes."

"You've got Hans on to his hobby-horse now," said Pile to Freethorne with a deprecating smile.

"It's an interesting line," said Freethorne, champing. "I can't say I'm one of your converts, Dr. Tautz. I suppose I'm old-fashioned, but I can't help remembering that the body has its mechanical and chemical aspects as well as its mental ones."

"Of course it has," said Tautz with a violent bounce.

"And so has a motor car and a steam engine. But they all have also a driver and if they go wrong it is usually because the driver makes a mistake."

"Yes," said Freethorne vaguely. "It's an interesting line." He turned to Paston and said suddenly, "Let's see, you're——?"

"Paston, sir."

"Ah, yes. And your school was——?"

There was a moment's pause.

"The school of experience," said Paston.

There was another pause. Garsten turned quickly away and looked out of the window.

"Ah," said Freethorne, knitting the bushy eyebrows. "A lay brother, eh?"

"That's right, sir."

Freethorne nodded slowly and champed for a moment in silence.

"Of course," he said, turning and addressing the world in general, "I suppose you people, like all the rest of us, were given a tremendous opportunity by the war?" He looked inquiringly at Milne. He seemed to have forgotten Paston.

Milne said, "One of the few advantages of war. An endless supply of experimental rabbits."

"Exactly," said Freethorne. "In my own field of tropical medicine now. We learned more about the prevention and suppressing of malaria than we should have done in twenty years of peace."

"There were certainly enough malaria casualties to study," said Garsten acidly.

"Now there was a pretty problem for you people," said Sir George. "How to get men to take their suppressives—their mepacrine."

"The trouble was," said Milne, "that so many people who took mepacrine got malaria and so many people who didn't take it didn't get malaria."

"Let's see," said Freethorne. "You're a Cambridge man, aren't you?"

"Yes."

"What's the man's name—Field?"

"Yes. He's dead now. Died about a year ago."

"Really? You studied under him?"

"Yes. And then under Loewe in Vienna."

"Ah—*another* Viennese." He turned to Pile. "Vienna's well represented." He turned back to Milne. "You believe that there were a lot of cases—a *lot* of cases—where mepacrine suppression failed? Even when the drill was properly followed?"

"I always understood so. I was never in a position to go into it statistically."

"But you were in the war, I take it?"

"Yes. I was a gunner."

"A gunner?" said Freethorne, frowning.

"Yes."

"But how did you manage that? No doctor——"

Milne said, "I'm not a doctor."

"You mean——?"

"I did first and second M.B. and then went to Vienna instead of doing hospitals."

"I see," said Freethorne. He chewed slowly for a moment, staring at Milne with his watery blue eyes. Then he looked away. "Had you any particular reason for doing that?" he said without great interest.

"I was proposing to do analytic work and I wanted some training in it," said Milne curtly.

"Oh, quite. But I should have thought that came after the normal process of qualification."

Milne said, "I had only a limited amount of time. I wanted to use it as practically as I could."

"Well," said Freethorne, shaking his head. "It's a matter of opinion. But I should have thought that any medical man—*whatever* he was going to do—would get more out of his hospitals than out of any sort of training with the Viennese gentlemen."

"It is, as you say, a matter of opinion," said Milne carefully.

"Oh, quite," said Freethorne. "Quite." He shrugged his shoulders.

"It's rather lucky for the rest of us that Milne did feel like that about it," said Garsten. He had gone rather white.

"Why?" said Freethorne.

"Because it means that we have got at least one man who knows the job from A to Z and isn't just a G.P. messing about with things he doesn't understand."

"Come, come," said Pile quickly. "You mustn't be too hard on your professional brothers. Of course," he said to Freethorne, "the whole question of training for this work is one that we've discussed many times. The whole thing badly needs straightening out."

"I should say it was quite fundamental," said Freethorne with a decided champ.

Pile muttered a question in his ear.

"I don't know," said Freethorne, looking round rather doubtfully.

"I think it would be appreciated," said Pile.

Freethorne nodded without enthusiasm. "Very well, as you like."

"Well, look, everybody," said Pile, turning and addressing the room at large. "I'm sure, before we part, you would wish me to tell Sir George, on your behalf as well as my own, how much we've appreciated his visit, and the chance to discuss the work of the Clinic with one of the great figures in the medical world."

There was a moment's pause.

"Hear, hear," said Garsten, leaving it just long enough.

"In this branch of medicine," said Pile, beaming round confidentially, "we sometimes feel that we are rather—how shall I put it?—out on a bough by ourselves." He turned to Freethorne. "We have even felt, sir, in our most depressed moments, that orthodox medicine is not wholly sympathetic towards us. Sir George has said that we all tend to think our own job the most important in the world. Well, we tend to think that. We should be no good if we didn't." He bubbled. "Enthusiasm," he said genially but a little vaguely, "that is what the world lacks. We have enthusiasm. We have faith in the value of our work and its future. We shall go on with renewed enthusiasm and renewed faith as the result of your visit to-day, sir."

There was another pause. Tautz was glowering steadily

through his spectacles. Paston was sitting sulkily in his corner.

"Hear, hear," said Garsten, leaving it even longer this time. Milne looked quickly down at his feet and bit his lower lip hard.

"Would you care to say a word, Sir George?" said Pile.

Freethorne gave a few meditative champs and raised his bushy eyebrows a really surprising distance.

"Well, ladies and gentlemen," he said sonorously. "I haven't much to say, except that I have been most interested by what I have seen and heard from you. I am, of course, a mere child in these matters—these very difficult and delicate matters in which you—er—deal. But even an orthodox physician of my type if he has, as I have, some experience of the whole field of medical practice, must have more conception than perhaps some of you believe, of the importance of mental things. That is not new. Many of us have been considering the body-mind relationship throughout our thirty or forty years' experience." He glanced across at Tautz. "I was advising patients with dyspeptic tendencies to avoid nervous strain, for example, forty years before Dr. Tautz published his interesting and provocative paper. So you see, there is nothing *new* in the phenomena you are studying. What is new is the elevation of these matters into a science—the founding of schools and the propagation of doctrine—sometimes almost of dogma. And here, as a physician of some small experience, I might perhaps be allowed to offer one word of advice and warning." He paused and chewed his way slowly round the room as though surveying an Albert Hall audience. "There is no reason, in my considered view, why work of this kind should not take a place—even an important place—in the body of orthodox medical practice. Whether it does so or not—or at least the speed with which it does so—depends entirely upon its ability to dispel the suspicions which it has aroused—and I say quite frankly that these suspicions have sometimes been reasonably founded—by the unwise attitude of some of its adherents in the past. Medicine——" he chewed reflectively for a moment and gazed up at the ceiling, "Medicine, dealing as it does with the well-being of mankind, has a great responsibility. It cannot lightly accept views and theories, however attractive, which are not fully and scientifically established. Nor can it give its approval to any superficial approach. I agree entirely with Dr. Pile's view that some systematization of training and qualification for this work, and research in it, are urgently required. Without them, your subject cannot achieve the general acceptance you seek for it."

He paused, looked round the Albert Hall, and did the trick with his eyebrows again.

"This then, must be my advice to you, and to all workers in this field. I state it quite frankly. I believe in frankness. Put your house in order. Apply the strict rules which your responsibilities demand to the charlatan and the dilettante. Systematize your training. Pursue objective research. Restrain what I might call your wild men. You will forgive me, but Dr. Pile has said that you feel that the body of orthodox medicine looks askance. I may claim some slight knowledge of the medical profession, and I can tell you that the only way to be taken seriously by the medical profession is to give undoubted evidence of your own seriousness."

He glanced at each of them in turn. "I need hardly say that no criticism I have made or suggested applies to any of you in this room. I have been most impressed by the seriousness, the enthusiasm and the sense of responsibility apparent in this Clinic. I think Dr. Pile is to be congratulated on the—the faith and energy with which he has brought this Clinic into being. Most valuable work is being done. Much more remains to do. What I have tried to suggest is some of the ways by which your work can attain that general recognition which I am sure it deserves, and take its rightful place in the corpus of medical practice."

He nodded and took a step backwards. There was a moment's silence. Garsten glanced round the room. Then with a bright smile and a little nod, he raised his hands level with his chin and began to clap loudly and very slowly.

It was nearly seven o'clock when Milne reached home. Patricia had heard his key in the lock and came out into the hall to meet him. There was no light in the hall and he did not see her face. He said, " Hallo, darling," and went to hang up his coat. Patricia said, "Hallo " in a low voice. Milne switched on the light. When he turned she was standing looking at him, her face very white.

Milne said quickly, " Hey—what's up ? " and came across to her. She still did not say anything. He was startled and took her by the arm and said, " What's the matter ? "

Patricia said, " That damned dog. It's bitten the postman."

It came as an anti-climax after her white face. Milne laughed. " Bitten the postman ? Badly ? "

" No, I don't think so. I don't think Carlo did more than snap at him really. He's afraid of dogs."

" I thought from how you were looking that somebody was dead." He started towards the lounge.

Patricia said quickly, " No—don't go in there for a moment. In here." She went into the consulting room.

Milne followed her. " Look here," he said, puzzled, " what *is* this ? "

She said, " There's a policeman in there. He's come about Carlo."

" D'you mean they want you to have him destroyed or something ? Because—— ? "

" Oh, no," said Patricia flatly. " He's only come to tell us to keep him under control. They always do if the Post Office complains. But of course the first thing he asked for was Carlo's licence."

She looked at him miserably. Milne saw a great light. With a mighty effort he didn't laugh. " Oh, ho," he said solemnly. " Did he ? Lucky you remembered to get it the other day, wasn't it ? "

Patricia's lips trembled. He said quickly, " All right. I know. You forgot."

" I went out to get it," said Patricia furiously. " I actually went out specially for that. And even then I forgot the bloody thing." Her eyes filled with tears.

" Well now, you'll be run in and fined seven and six-pence," said Milne cheerfully, " which is a serious matter but not fatal. Cheer up."

" But you don't understand. I've told *him* I've got one."

"Oh," said Milne rather blankly. He frowned. "That was a bit dumb of you, wasn't it? What on earth did you do that for?"

"I don't know," said Patricia helplessly. "I had a conscience about the whole thing, and as soon as he asked for it I just panicked and lied again. I had a wild idea that I could rush out and buy one and pretend I'd had it all the time."

"But, good God, surely it was hardly worth while to do all that for the sake of a seven and sixpenny fine?" said Milne irritably. "You say he's still here?"

"Yes. In the lounge."

Milne hesitated. "All right," he said curtly. "Stay here, and I'll go and fix it."

The large, smooth-faced, clean young constable was standing by the window with his helmet in his hand.

Milne said, "Good-afternoon. My name's Milne. What's this about that dog of mine taking bits out of the postman?"

The policeman said, "Well, we've had a complaint from the Post Office, sir. I don't think it's anything much, to tell you the truth. I think the dog just nipped him. Didn't break the skin or tear his clothes or anything. But they always report it, see, because it's not very nice if they're gone for when they're only doing their work."

"Of course it isn't. I'm very sorry. I'll see it doesn't happen again."

"That's right, sir. If you'll see the dog's kept under control. Because if there was another complaint, see——"

"Yes. I'll see to it." Milne grinned. "Now of course you want to see my dog licence. And now we find we haven't got one."

"Oh," said the constable. "You *haven't* got one?"

"No. It's a fair cop on that, I'm afraid. My wife thought I'd bought it and I thought she had. And now we find nobody has."

The policeman looked at him for a moment and then nodded expressionlessly. "I see."

"You know how these things happen."

"Oh, yes." He shook his head. "Well, I'm afraid I shall have to report it, sir," he said with firm regret.

" I suppose so."

" The lady seemed to think you *had* got one and mislaid it."

" Well she was wrong," said Milne curtly. " We haven't."

He saw the policeman out and went back to the consulting room. He said calmly, " That wasn't a very good show, was it ? "

" No," she said stonily.

" What on earth made you tell him that ? It really is too damn childish to tell lies to a bobby—particularly when he's bound to find out."

Patricia turned away and said shakily, " I was afraid you'd be cross."

Milne said, " Oh, come—I'm not such a brute as all that, my dear."

" Not now. Before. When you asked me at breakfast. You'd told me about it twice before—and—and—I thought everything seemed a bit better and I didn't want you to be irritated again so I said I'd done it. And then of course when this happened I was caught."

He was touched, and put an arm round her, but she said, " Oh, for God's sake don't be nice about it."

Milne looked at her for a moment and then said gently, " Look, honey—this just won't do at all. I'd never realised you felt—like that about it."

" Hadn't you ?" she said bitterly.

" Well—I knew you were a bit nervous and jumpy about us and—and one thing and another but I didn't realise——" he stopped rather helplessly and said, " Oh, hell ! " and took her in his arms. This time she did not resist. But she said quietly, " You'll remember this."

" Don't be an ass."

" Oh, yes, you will. It's all right now because I've fussed and you're sorry for me. But you'll remember it—when you want something to hate me for." She said it quietly and she was not crying. Milne held her tight to him and kissed her.

" Look—you're being a sap," he said gently, automatically, and without conviction.

X

"It's entirely up to you," said Milne. "I only suggest it because I think it may save us both a lot of time and effort."

Lucian looked at him with the veiled, slightly hostile eyes. "All right," he said at last, with a shrug. "Whatever you say. I'm used to having stuff pumped into me anyway."

"Fine," said Milne. "Let's try it then."

He rose and got out the hypodermic from the cupboard. Lucian sat still and silent, but following his movements with an unusual wariness.

"Supposing I do talk?" he said suddenly. "How are you going to know what's true and what isn't? People talk all sorts of rot under anæsthetics."

"What is truth, said jesting Pilate?" said Milne, looking up for a moment with a smile. "All I want is to get you to talk. I'll worry over what to believe later." He examined the syringe with care. "This isn't exactly an anæsthetic. I mean I'm not going to put you right to sleep. It'll just make you drowsy."

"What is it?"

"Sodium pentothal." He eyed Lucian thoughtfully. "I think you're what we might call 'a large subject,' so you may need a spot more than usual."

"How d'you judge it?"

"Just go on putting it in slowly until you're satisfactorily sleepy. Right. Now then, we want it half dark——" He went across and adjusted the curtains.

"Jacket off and shirt sleeve up, so that I can get at your arm. And then just on the couch as usual."

Lucian slowly took off his jacket and rolled up his right sleeve. His hands were trembling slightly. "I loathe these damned needles," he said savagely.

"It won't hurt, of course," said Milne.

"I know that. But I loathe them all the same." He lay down on the couch and flung out his bare right arm. It was thick and heavily muscled, with a covering of soft, fair down.

Lucian lay with his head turned away, staring sullenly into vacancy.

"When I say 'count,'" said Milne, "I want you just to start counting slowly. About like this. One—two—three—four—— Just go on counting steadily. Got it?"

Lucian nodded slightly without turning his head. His bare arm was shaking a little. Milne steadied it, swabbed the skin quickly with alcohol, and slipped the needle into the vein. It was a good needle and it went in easily.

"Now count," he said, pressing very gently on the plunger and glancing at his watch.

Milne had aimed at putting on 0.1 of a gram a minute, but he got it a little fast at first, and Lucian was less resistant than he had expected. By the time he had counted as far as fifty he was beginning to cough a little, and his voice was becoming husky and thick. At seventy it was little more than a mumble. Milne noted that he had had just over a quarter of a gram, glanced quickly at his closed eyelids, and withdrew the needle.

"Lucian," he said quietly. There was a pause and then a vague mumble. Milne put the syringe carefully on the table beside him, and leaned forward.

"You're in your Spit on that last trip," he said in a quiet matter-of-fact voice. "Now then—what's happening?"

There was a pause. Lucian stirred slightly and made a noise between a snore and a groan. His lips opened for a moment and then closed again. A frown flickered over his face and vanished.

"Come on," said Milne still quietly but more urgently. "You're flying the Spit that last time. You're over jungle. The Nips are down below there. What's happening? There's flak coming up at you, isn't there?"

Lucian's face suddenly seemed to crumple. His lips opened again.

"Christ!" he said in a low, horrified voice. "Christ!"

"What's the matter?" said Milne quickly and urgently. "What the hell's happening?"

"She's on fire!" said Lucian in a queer, high-pitched voice. "Christ, she's on fire. Christ, she's on fire." His hands suddenly thrust convulsively forward. " Steady the Buffs," he said breathlessly. " Steady." There was a long silence, broken only by Lucian's rapid breathing. Milne leaned forward and then hesitated.

Lucian suddenly said calmly, though breathlessly, " It wouldn't dive out so I pulled her up. It was too quick and I blacked. I put the lid back and rolled. I hung for a moment as though it caught on something." He made a sudden convulsive movement of his head. " Christ ! " he said sharply and lapsed into silence. There was a long pause. His breathing gradually became slower and quieter. When he spoke again it was calmly and with a detached, half-amused interest.

" What the hell's happened to him now ? " he said very slowly. He smiled slightly. " Alive and kicking. Alive and kicking. Caterpillar Club. But how the hell—— ? "

The breathing was becoming more rapid again. " I don't know how long I was in the tree. Not long. It was quite easy to get down. There was a branch I could reach. Difficult getting the harness off in that position. I nearly broke my neck dropping down. I didn't realise it was so far. It would have been damn funny to come down five thousand feet and then break his neck in the last twenty." He paused and groaned slightly. " I'm O.K. But I feel damn sick." He groaned again and was silent.

" Never mind," said Milne quietly. " You're out of it alive."

" Gentlemen in England now abed," said Lucian contemptuously. " God, I feel so sick. He had a compass, a map, a gun, some chocolate, some Horlicks, a torch, and no machete no machete no machete. It must have fallen out when he was arse upwards. This is going to be a long walk. London to Brighton and a chap on a bicycle feeding them. Well, Moll, here we come."

Milne was getting slight cramp. He silently shifted his position. Lucian's voice went calmly and monotonously on.

" I never thought about the Japs. I suppose they were there but it was so damned thick. There was a stream and

I filled my chargal and put the purifying tablets in it. I wished I had had the machete. As it was, I didn't make a hundred yards an hour. Compass point stuck a bit sometimes." He sighed. "I can't remember much," he said plaintively, "except the thorns. It was all the same. He sat down once and smoked a cigarette. What the hell—there's nothing to hurry for. There was a leech on my ankle." His face puckered with disgust. "I got it off with the cigarette. It had made the ankle swell." His body suddenly stiffened. "What was that about a snake?" he said sharply. There was a long silence. "That boy's far on," he said softly. "That boy will have to be careful. He just sat there. He just didn't move." A great shudder passed through his body and his voice rose hysterically. "He just sat there nearly touching the bloody thing. He was too lazy to move see? Just too lazy to move."

"Where was he?" said Milne quickly.

"In a sort of hole in the bank," said Lucian breathlessly. "He didn't see it. It had got dark on him. He never did see it. He was asleep and woke up and it moved. It was against him, right up against him." His face was convulsed and his whole body was rigid with terror. "He lay still and it stopped moving and he went to sleep," his voice rose almost to a shout. "He went to sleep with it there, and then it was light and there wasn't anything. Oh, Christ——!" He began to whimper quietly and cowered away into the far corner of the couch.

"It's all right," said Milne gently. "It was gone."

Lucian took a deep breath. "O.K., chief," he said calmly. "But this here is a long walk. Where's the bastard with the bicycle? My legs weren't working much and my tongue was swelling. I don't see why it should because there'd been plenty of water. But anyhow I was feeling all right. There wasn't anything when he got to the top. You could see for miles and there wasn't anything—not a bloody thing except more of it. He sat down and cried because of that. But hell, he'd been going a long time and he was fed up." He started and fell silent for a moment, and then shook his head. "The cartridges are wet anyhow. Everything's wet. It's a mystery what happened to that glove."

"Dr. Livingstone, I presume. And bloody well about time too. Here we come, Moll, if he doesn't cut my throat. They were all right. They were fine." Lucian shook his head and smiled bitterly. "It's no good asking me about that because I was asleep. They took me in and gave me some brown mess or other, but it tasted good to me. I don't know how long I was asleep. When I woke up and saw the Japs, I was still all mixed up. I couldn't think why we should have sent Japs to get me." His voice hardened. "That dirty bastard grinned at him," he said bitterly. "Grinned all over his ugly face. I said you dirty bastard. The big Jap hit me in the kidneys with his rifle butt and I fell down. My legs still weren't working much. That's all I can remember."

There was a long silence. Lucian lay with closed eyes, breathing deeply.

"What did the Japs do?" said Milne.

"No idea," said Lucian quickly and casually. "Can't remember a thing. No good asking me because I won't know."

"What did they do?" said Milne sharply.

"I don't know."

"What did they do? Come on—tell me."

Lucian's face puckered and his lips trembled. "I can't remember," he half whispered. "I swear to God I can't."

"What did the Japs do?" said Milne monotonously. "Come on—what did they do?"

There was a moment's silence. Then Lucian gave a queer, choking sob.

"I can't go any further," he said brokenly. "It's my legs. Legs, you little bastards. O.K., go on—I don't care. I'm through." He turned over and with a gesture of utter weariness and despair dropped his head on his arms. Suddenly he raised it again, and with eyes staring with terror shrank back into the corner. For a moment his mouth opened as though he were going to scream. Then with a great effort he seemed to control himself. He licked his lips and nodded slowly. "All right," he mumbled. "All right. But I'm tired, see? *Tired.*" He made a gesture of weariness with his hands. He lay back with a sigh and spoke more calmly. " They took away my water bottle. They wouldn't give me any water. I kept on asking for it and at last they gave it back to me." His voice broke a little. " When I went to drink it was empty. They'd poured the water out first. They stood round and looked at me and then laughed like hell. I don't know how far we went. We seemed to have been going for hours, but I don't suppose it was far really. If I didn't go fast enough the big Jap cracked me on the muscles at the back of my legs with the butt of his rifle. It got so that I couldn't stay on my feet. I wouldn't know I'd fallen down until I found myself on the ground and them kicking me. After a bit, I couldn't feel anything so it didn't matter. Only I was thirsty. The last time I remember I was lying on the ground. I think it must have been in a swamp or something. Anyhow it was cool. They'd stopped kicking me and were standing looking at me and jabbering. I just lay there. I didn't care any more. I thought they'd kill me now and that would be all right. Poor old Moll. They picked him up between two of them. There was a big thorn trailer and it scratched his face. Everything was green and dancing about. That's all. He must have passed out. I can't tell about it if he'd passed out, can I ? "

" Where was he when he woke up again ? " said Milne quickly.

" He didn't wake up again. He was dead."

" No, he wasn't. He woke up, didn't he ? "

" No," said Lucian pitifully. " He didn't. He *didn't.*"

" He woke up," said Milne inexorably. " Go on. Go *on*, Lucian."

Lucian began to sob quietly. " Oh, Christ ! " he said. " What the hell do they know about it ? Name, rank and number—finish. They were always telling us that. Whatever they do to you. Name, rank and number—finish. After that, don't say anything. Not anything. Not whatever they do to you. Just name, rank and number and that's all." He gave a convulsive shudder. " Christ, some fat bastard said that who——" He suddenly sat bolt upright and stared at Milne with terrified eyes. " He didn't talk," he said urgently. " He didn't tell them anything. Not anything but just name, rank and number and that's all right. That's all he told them——" He threw himself face downwards and began to sob convulsively.

"Did the interrogator speak English?" said Milne quickly.

Lucian raised his head. "Yes," he said in a whisper. "Yes. The little runt. And he grinned. He gave me a cigarette. He spoke English with a Cockney accent. He was very polite. I was polite back. He talked nineteen to the dozen to start with. He said he'd lived in London for five years after the last war. He was so friendly it nearly made you sick." He licked his lips. "Then after a bit he began to ask questions. Not anything that mattered. Just how old I was and whether I was married and so on." He licked his lips again. "It's all very well," he said hoarsely. "Maybe if you're taken back to a headquarters they're under control. I don't know. But right up forward like that they don't care what they do to you. Prisoners are a bloody nuisance anyway. Nobody knows if they kill you and nobody cares. He started off with name, rank and number and I gave him those and then—then I stopped." He stared at Milne pitifully. His whole body was trembling and the sweat was running down his forehead. "I could see it coming. There were three of them standing behind me. I said, 'I'm sorry but I can't tell you any more.' I heard them move. I heard them move behind me. I knew they were getting ready." He let out a long shuddering breath. "The little runt changed pretty quickly, too. He stopped grinning and chatting and started to squawk at me."

Lucian turned away. His head was shaking like an old man's.

"Yes?" said Milne gently.

"He started off again and asked how old I was. I started to say again that I couldn't tell him anything else, and one of them hit me a clip in the face with his fist. It split my lip. The runt asked me again and then one of them cracked me over the kidneys again with his rifle butt. I was all bruised there and I just went down and started to retch my heart out." He gave a convulsive sob. "It's all very well," he said brokenly. "But they haven't tried it. They

started to talk—even if it's only to tell them your age—then it all connects up. Your—your body knows as well as your mind. Not talking is the same as being hurt, and talking is the same as not being hurt. Your body gets to know that. And then you're done."

"How on earth you stuck it for three days I don't see," said Milne.

Lucian looked up sharply. "Why? It was—all right. I could have gone on longer but—oh, I don't know." He shook his head slowly. "Still. There it is. You know now. That bloody stuff of yours is a pretty low trick. But I'm glad somebody knows. In a way."

"I should bloody well think you are!" said Milne calmly. "Since you've been nearly driving yourself off your head for no good reason over it."

"It seems a pretty good reason to me," said Lucian. He met Milne's eyes and looked away.

Milne laughed. "Listen," he said. "That's damned nonsense and you know it. Don't you?"

"It was a bloody disgraceful business," said Lucian, without conviction.

"No, it wasn't. And what's more you don't even think so. Look—you've been making all this fuss inside yourself about it. Now you've told me. Do you care? Of course you don't."

Lucian hesitated for a long moment. Then a reluctant flicker of a smile played over his face. He said, "Well, as a matter of fact I don't care quite as much as I should have thought. Not at the moment, anyhow. But——"

"No," said Milne with a grin. "And you never will again."

"But *why* don't I?" said Lucian bemusedly. "This whole thing is a damned queer feeling. I don't——" He stopped and shook his head.

"Because now, having taken it out and looked at it, you can see that it's all in the past, and that there's nothing to be frightened about or ashamed of or anything. The whole thing's just a story now—like the things that happened to you at school. It's interesting, but that's all."

"It may feel like that now. But will it to-morrow?"

" Oh, yes. It won't go back now. Have you ever told your wife about it ? "

" Good God, no ! " said Lucian involuntarily.

" Well, why not ? You think. You could tell her now. Whether you want to or not is up to you. But it would be quite easy if you did want to. Wouldn't it ? "

Lucian considered. " You know you've got something here," he said at last, with a quizzical smile that Milne had not seen before. " I don't know whether it's your knock-out drops or what. But I just feel—well—what the hell ? "

" Quite," said Milne. " What indeed the hell."

" It would be a pretty good thing just to feel what the hell all the time."

" That's exactly what you're going to do."

" Now that certainly would be something," Lucian reflected. " I took you right through the story, did I ? " he said looking up.

" No. You told me about the interrogation business and then I thought you'd had enough."

" Oh, well, there's quite a bit more after that—and quite interesting." He hesitated. " Like to hear about it ? "

" Of course. If you're not tired."

" Oh, God, no. I'm fine." Lucian took a cigarette from the box and lit it. " Well, of course as soon as the Nips had got everything there was to be got out of me, I ceased to be a valuable property. They were right up in a forward area, and people in forward areas out there just find prisoners a bloody nuisance. It's the same on our side. It's difficult enough to get food and water and fuel up and generally to look after yourself, let alone looking after prisoners. Besides, these Nips were in a bad way. We were across their L. of C., and they were short of everything and having a hell of a time. I can't for the life of me see why they didn't just bump me off. They've no use for prisoners anyhow. They think a man who's taken prisoner a disgrace. That's why they won't surrender themselves and don't carry parachutes. And a man who lets himself be captured and then talks, like I did, they'd think was about the lowest thing that crawled. The only thing I can think of is that the little runt who spoke English wanted to take me back to show what a clever boy he was. Anyhow, instead of killing me they just compromised. They kept me around but didn't give me anything to eat or drink except every few days when someone happened to think of it."

He paused and shook his head. "Well, of course that was all right as long as I was in a state where you could put me down somewhere and be pretty sure I'd still be there when you came back—and I certainly was in that state after they'd finished asking me polite questions. But after a bit, even on a dish of rice every few days, I was beginning to be more mobile again. I wouldn't have cared to have to walk half a mile, but I could stand up anyway and that got them all worried." Lucian leaned forward and knocked the ash off his cigarette. His hands, which had been quite steady, were trembling again.

"I'm not going to like this," he said suddenly, looking up with a painful smile. "I know it's all just history now, but——"

Milne said, "Stop if you want to."

"Oh, no. I'm only fussing. What happened was that they came in one morning when I was lying in the hut. One of them was carrying a club. I was still pretty hazy, but I knew what was going on. I didn't think much of it. Maybe they'd come to finish me, but I was used to thinking that by then. One of them shoved a block of wood under my foot so that my leg was off the ground. I didn't quite get what all this was about and I just raised my head in a muzzy sort of way to see. And then——" He stopped for a moment. His lips were trembling and there was sweat on his forehead but he still grinned gallantly at Milne.

"Then before I saw what they were after, the other bastard just swung the club and cracked it down on my shin-bone with all his might. I heard a loud crack like somebody busting a thick stick, which must have been my leg going, and a hell of a scream, which must have been me, and then I suppose I passed out. For quite a long time too I think. Anyhow I can't remember anything clearly for a long time after, except lying being eaten to death by various sorts of insects, and sweating with terror that I might stir and move my leg. I suppose they must have gone on feeding me or I should have checked in. But why they did or how, or how I ate it, God knows. Anyhow it certainly settled the problem of seeing I didn't bolt for them." He squashed out his cigarette with trembling fingers and nodded to Milne with a smile. "There you are, you see. It's quite all right as long as I don't fuss about it. I still don't think it's a pretty story, but apart from that I don't give a damn now."

"How on earth did you ever get away?" said Milne.

"Oh—well now that *is* rather a pretty story—from my point of view anyhow. Apparently there's something rather queer about my bones, and they join up unusually quickly. That's what the docs say and I should think it's probably true for once, because I bust my collar-bone at rugger and it did heal very quickly. Anyhow, my leg certainly got usable quicker than the Nips expected. I don't know how long it was. Looking back, it seems as though it might have been several years that I was there. But it was quicker than they thought. It wasn't a very good leg of course. But I could stand up and hop around somehow when they still thought I was a static unit. Once I'd found it would hold, I spent about a week hopping about the hut whenever I got a chance to do it without being spotted, and then I began to think about getting back. I knew our lines weren't very far away. These Nips weren't fighting, but they acted as though they'd never be surprised if we showed up, and we saw planes quite often. There didn't seem to be a lot of chance, but I was tired of being around there. I had a pretty shrewd idea that they might decide they'd had me long enough, and just take the second pressure and write me off the books. So I thought well hell, I might just as well have a go."

"Could you walk at all?"

"Not sort of one foot after the other. But I could hobble. It hurt a bit, but not as much as you'd think. It ached more than hurt."

"What I don't quite see is why they didn't send you back to base."

"I don't think they could. We were across their L. of C.; and it would have meant carrying me anyhow. No. The puzzle is why they didn't kill me instead of keeping me there eating valuable food—even if I didn't eat much of it. The thing which gave me an outside chance was that they had got very careless about me. I suppose by that time I was just part of the scenery. Anyhow they didn't even know I could stand, let alone hop about. Whenever they saw me I was just lying there. Sometimes they just shoved my rice inside the hut and left it there. When they did that I never went and got it. I thought it might be a try-on to see whether I could move if I wanted to. That was one of the hardest bits of the lot really, because of course I was ravenous. I used to lie and look at the rice and slaver, and tell myself that if I got up and fetched it, I should be sunk. Anyhow, it worked. I didn't have a guard or anything like that from the time they bust my leg."

Lucian paused reflectively. "I thought it out very carefully. I had plenty of time for that. I didn't know the situation or where our chaps were, and of course they'd taken my map and compass and everything else. So what with one thing and another it wasn't going to be a very well-equipped expedition. But my guess, from the way they acted, was that there weren't any Jap troops between us and the British, and that though they weren't in contact, we weren't very far apart. I reckoned that if I could get clear of their perimeter, and keep going west for even a few miles, there was a chance of being picked up by one of our patrols. It wasn't much of a chance. But I'd got so that if I was going to pass out, I wanted to do it alone. Away from the smell of Jap. It gets you down after a bit, the smell of Jap.

"What I chiefly wanted was a stick. I reckoned that if I had a stick my leg would probably stand up long enough to get me clear. And after that I didn't care. From where I lay I could see through the door of the hut, and there was a sort of fence they'd made of sharpened stakes pointing outwards with wire mixed up amongst them. I could see six of the stakes, and I thought the third one from the left would do me nicely, if I could get it out. After that the only snag would be getting through the standing patrols round the perimeter. The Nips seemed to me in a pretty bad way—I think their morale was right down in the bottom of the jug. But it was too much to hope that they wouldn't have sentries posted anywhere that I wanted to go. I thought about it for a long time. At one time I thought of going out east instead of west, in the hope that there wouldn't be patrols that side. But that would have meant walking right round the perimeter before I got on my way and I didn't think my leg would stand that much. It was straight out or nothing." He shook his head with a slight smile. "That was as much of a plan as I could make, just lying there. But even after that I stayed two or three days trying to make up my mind to get on with it. I was in a queer state and I couldn't seem to take a decision. I still don't know why I finally started when I did. One moment I was just lying there and the next I was on my feet and moving out of the hut, just like that. It was as dark as it ever got, and I had to find my way over to my fence and get the stick first. It was a damned queer feeling hobbling about there in the open, and knowing you might tread on a Nip any time. What's more, I knew if one of the little bastards did see me he wouldn't just shout 'Hey!' or 'What's going on here?' He'd probably keep quite quiet and not move a muscle until he could jump me. I stopped and listened every now and again and I couldn't hear a sound. Not a bloody sound. I had a queer feeling that the Nips were all awake really, and just sitting round in the shadows looking at me and waiting. I could just see the entrances to the huts they'd built, but inside of course it was dark. I thought they were just squatting in there in the darkness, quite quiet, and taking it all in."

He gave a convulsive shrug of his shoulders, like a man who is cold. "But as it turned out, I had all the breaks on earth. My stake wouldn't come out, but the next one was loose and came away in my hand. It was about four feet long and very heavy for its size. Some of these jungle woods are like iron almost. It only made one twang coming out, and there was still dead silence after. By putting my weight on the stick I could get along quite well, though it tired my arm."

"I suddenly realised that I didn't know how far the wire and the stakes went, and that if they ran right round I was sunk and couldn't get out. The wire was too deep to get through. This panicked me a bit. But I had a feeling somehow that it didn't go far. I think I must have noticed it before when they were taking me about the camp. Anyhow I knew it stopped somewhere along to the right. I was moving very slowly, peering at it in the dark, and I must have been being damned quiet. Because suddenly I saw that it had stopped and that there was nothing but bushes. At least, that's what I thought for a moment. And then I saw one of the bushes move, and realised it was a Nip."

He drew a sharp breath. "The point was that the ground went away almost sheer there, both in front and to the right. That's why they hadn't wired any further, and this Nip was a sort of corner man. The only reason why I spotted him at all was because, being on the top of this slope, he was against the sky to me. I still think that if it hadn't been for my leg, and I'd been able to move properly, I should either have walked right into him or walked over the edge of the slope. It was only edging along the wire a foot at a time that brought me up to him like that without making a row. He was only about ten feet away."

"When I saw him I froze, and I must have stood there for half a minute. As long as I was standing still I suppose there wasn't much chance of his seeing me. I was against a dark background, and anyhow his job was to keep his eyes skinned forward. I was a bit short of breath and I was afraid he'd hear me breathing. But he just went on standing, with his back three-quarters turned to me. I put my weight on my good leg and very gradually shifted my grip on the stick so that I could use it like a club. Then I realised the snag—or rather two snags. First of all, he had a tin hat on. Imagine that. Miles from anywhere, and in the jungle, and just because I wanted to crack him over the head he had a tin hat on. I don't think I'd seen a man in Burma in a tin hat before, unless he was in action. Secondly, you can't hit a chap over the head at ten feet range when you're standing on one leg. It just isn't on. You try."

He paused and gave a curious giggle. "Well, this Jap must have realised that he wasn't co-operating properly, because as I stood there wondering what to do, he took his tin hat off."

"Good God!" said Milne.

"It certainly was good God. I don't see who else it could have been. He took it off and started to tap the top of it with his knuckles.

"Well, I knew he'd probably put it on again in a minute, so I had to work fast. I couldn't reach him in one hop, but I reckoned that two hops and a swipe would do it if only I could get it timed right. I just had to reckon that he'd be too surprised to be able to dodge or do anything." Lucian shook his head. "I've tried to do this again half a dozen times since, just for interest, and I've never got it right again. But that time it worked like a charm. I put my bad leg down at some point, because it hurt. But anyhow, the second hop brought me up to him and I got him over the head just as he turned. You know in stories if you crack anybody's skull it usually 'cracks like an eggshell?' Well, it doesn't. At least, not if he's a Jap. I caught this one right on the top, hitting as hard as I could, and instead of squashing his head the stick just bounced and stung my hands like hell. I had no sort of balance and I just went forward on my face and started to slide down the slope. I clawed at the ground and stopped myself. I thought for a moment that it wouldn't have knocked him out and that I was done. But it was all quite quiet, and after a moment I scrambled up again. He was lying there. I needn't have worried. I couldn't see so I had to feel. The whole top of his head was beaten down and there was a lot of mess." He looked up at Milne with sparkling eyes. "That probably sounds pretty ghastly to you. I suppose it was—beating a chap's brains out with a club. But I've never felt more triumphant in my life than when I realised that he was dead. I lay there for a moment and laughed like hell to myself over his having taken his tin hat off like that. I thought, 'I don't care now. Maybe I'm going to pass out but I don't care. I've scuppered that bastard.' I lay there for a moment and thought whether I'd take his rifle, so that if the worst came to the worst I could write off a few more and myself too. But it would have been too heavy to carry and I still had the stick. There was nothing in his pockets except some paper—probably letters I suppose—and I didn't want that. So I took his water bottle and got on my way."

Lucian paused and stretched out his legs.

"There was nothing to it after that," he said rather wearily. "Our chaps were further away than I thought. I should never have made it by myself. But I ran into some Burmans again and this time they happened to be pro-British—or anti-Jap anyhow—and they took me in. I'll tell you about that sometime if you like, but it's pretty dull. Cracking that Jap was my high spot." He glanced at his watch. "God, it's nearly five. Have I been boring you?"

"Good Lord, no!" said Milne. "But I suppose we'd better stop now." He rose and, opening a drawer, put away the syringe.

"You know, that's remarkable stuff of yours," said Lucian. "I feel a lot fresher after it."

XI

Two days before Patricia's birthday, Milne took the morning off and went down to the West End. Usually when Patricia had a birthday in sight, he would have started to prowl happily about the shops a fortnight beforehand with no idea what to buy. And then he would have found it and it would have cost seven pounds instead of the five he had intended. He was an expert present buyer; and Patricia, who was an expert present receiver, would have been genuinely surprised, and thrilled, and shocked at his extravagance.

But this time it was not like that. It would not take long. He knew what he meant to buy, and there would be no difficulty in finding it. The only difficulty would be in paying for it. He was not sure why it must cost every penny of his spare cash, but he knew that it must. And then he would give it to her, and she would not only be impressed and thrilled in the usual way but would see something that it was essential she should see—though quite what, he could not define.

He knew from experience that buying any present for

Patricia was one of the great events and should not be rushed. To spend this amount of money on it should be a thing to be taken slowly and savoured. He lingered for a while in the wine department, and then passed into pianos, noting with pleasure that there was a big Steinway grand to be had for the money he was about to spend. Then he went upstairs, and following the directions carefully, landed, as he always did, in a hopeless maze of suspender belts and underwear. There were ten entrances to the store, and in his experience they all led more or less directly into the underwear department.

As he approached the counter to ask his way, somebody in a fur coat looked up from a careful examination of some satin cami-knickers and said, " Hallo, Felix. Buying yourself a few pairs for the spring ? "

Milne said, " Oh, hallo, Bab. What are you doing here ? "

" Oddly enough, I'm trying to buy the woman your wife a birthday present."

" Me, too."

" Hell—you're not buying her pants too, are you ? "

" No. I just got in here by mistake. I always do. Where's the fur department ? "

" Through that arch and to the left. You mean to say you're buying that spoilt wench furs ? "

" Yes. I want a fur coat."

" Darling, they're the most fantastic prices."

" I know."

Barbara said, " D'you know what sort of fur ? "

" Yes. Ermine."

" Good God. It'll cost you the fillings out of your teeth. But you're dead right. Pat will look gorgeous in ermine. The *dark* sort, Felix. Not the red sort. And full length. Not a swagger. Swaggers are a compromise."

Milne hesitated. " You'd better come and help," he said.

Barbara looked at him eagerly. Then her face clouded slightly. " Oh, no. That would spoil it, wouldn't it ? "

Milne looked at the slanting eyes beneath the absurd hat. " Of course not. Come and be an expert. I don't know a thing about it."

" Well, nor do I really. You know her measurements, don't you ? "

" Does that matter with a thing you wrap up in ? "

" Oh, yes. If you're as good a shape as Pat you don't want it like a sack. Particularly in ermine."

" Well, she's five feet six, I think."

" Yes. And thirty-five, twenty-six, thirty-six."

" That's chest, waist and hips."

" Yes. I know, because she's almost the same as me except that there's a bit more in front and a bit less behind."

Milne said, " Well, look—come along, Bab. It'll be much better. You know what she likes anyway."

Barbara hesitated. " All right," she said at last. " But for God's sake don't let me interfere. It must be *your* thing. Let me just finish here." She held up the ice-blue satin cami-knickers. " Think she'd like these ? "

" I should think so. Very lush."

" Well, do *you* like them ? " said Barbara with a grin. " Because that's the main point of things like this."

Milne said, " They're nearly the colour of that frock you wore at the party."

" I think she'll look sweet in them," said Barbara. She turned to the assistant. " I'll have these, I think."

Barbara turned away from the mirror and faced him. " You've got to remember that it'll be miles nicer on Pat than on me because of the hair colour." She glanced over her shoulder at her reflection in the mirrors. " I think it's gorgeous." She put her head on one side and looked at herself appraisingly with the bright blue cat's eyes.

" Those are particularly fine pelts," said the white-haired assistant softly.

Milne stood for a moment in silence, looking at the ermine-clad figure. His eyes met Barbara's in the mirror and they both smiled.

" How much is that one ? " he said with an effort.

" That one's a hundred and seventy-five."

Milne nodded. A hundred and seventy-five was all right. Just. He looked again, trying, without success, to put another figure inside the coat. " You think it's right for her, Bab ? "

" Absolutely. She'll look marvellous."

" You certainly look pretty good in it yourself," said Milne, swallowing rather painfully.

" Not as nice as Pat will," said Barbara calmly. " Because it's not my colour. But it fits me perfectly and we're the same size."

Milne turned sharply away. " Right," he said curtly. " Let's make it that one."

" She'll adore that, Felix," said Barbara as they left the fur department. " God, what fun ! " She seemed genuinely pleased and excited.

" I wanted to get her one," said Milne. " She's got that old musquash, but it weighs about half a ton and she hates it." He hesitated. " How about a cup of coffee ? I think we've earned it, and it's only half-past eleven."

Barbara glanced at her watch. " All right. Thank you, Felix. I mustn't be long though."

As they drank their coffee Milne said, " That last expedition of ours was a funny do."

" Not so very funny," said Barbara, knocking the ash off her cigarette.

" It went wrong," said Milne. " Why did it go wrong ? "

" I expect we either drank too much or too little. Nothing mucks a party up like drinking the wrong amount."

" You had a rush of scruples to the head."

" I know. It's a thing that's never happened to me before. I think they must have put something in the food."

" Do you think it would ever happen to you again ? " said Milne quietly.

Barbara looked at him for a long moment in silence and then turned her head and gazed across the room.

" I—I don't know," she said uncertainly. " I expect so."

" Well, how about trying ? Scientific confirmatory experiment."

Barbara squashed her half-smoked cigarette out with unnecessary violence. " *No*," she said, " I don't think that would be at all a good idea."

"Why not?"

"You know perfectly well. I'm like Sadie in the story. 'Boss, I rape so easy.'"

"Well, last time you were like Penelope playing hard to get with the suitors."

"Yes. But I was aided and abetted by the fact that you knew damn well I was right."

As Milne was about to reply he caught the eye of a middle-aged woman at a table across the room. It was not a particularly disapproving eye, but it was interested and there was no doubt that it understood the situation. Milne suddenly realised that he was leaning forward in his chair and grinning foolishly. He sat back hurriedly and looked casually round the room.

"Well," he said, taking care not to use the fatuous grin, "when do we go out again, Bab?"

"We don't."

"What, not ever?"

Barbara hesitated. "I don't know about ever. Ever's a a hell of a time."

"Sometime, eh?"

Barbara looked at him for a moment. "All right," she said reluctantly. "Maybe. Sometime."

"Sometime soon."

"No. Just sometime." She gathered up her gloves and bag. "Now I must go. Don't you hurry."

Milne rose. "All right. I shall stay for a minute. 'Bye, Bab. And thanks for expert advice."

"Good-bye, Felix. She'll love it. And so she ought, the spoilt little so-and-so."

Milne watched her go with the quick, smooth step, and vanish through the swing doors. He turned back to his coffee rather moodily. It was only quarter to twelve, and there was no more present buying to do. It hadn't been a proper present buying expedition at all really. The thought of the coat cheered him a little. But not as much as it ought to have done.

Milne had smuggled the coat into Patricia's wardrobe after she had dressed and left her bedroom. He had carefully not wished her many happy returns of the day, and when he saw several parcels for her on the breakfast table, he started back in dramatic horror and said, " Oh, my God—it's your birthday ! "

This was in quite the right tradition. Patricia said, " Oh, Felix ! You oughtn't just to *forget* it," and went on calmly opening the parcels. They were a pleasant but not exciting collection. Even Patricia's eccentric aunt, who could usually be relied on for goldfish or a book of devotions, had sent a perfectly respectable handbag. There was no sign of the cami-knickers from Barbara. When everything had been opened and admired, they sat down to breakfast. Once or twice Patricia looked at Milne with an excited and expectant smile, but he stared back blankly, and went on with his egg.

It was only when he had finished breakfast and smoked a deliberately leisurely cigarette that he suddenly raised his head and began to sniff the air. Patricia jumped up with a gurgle of delight at this traditional signal for the treasure hunt to begin. Still sniffing, Milne followed what appeared to be a hot scent into the lounge, with Patricia close behind him. Once in the lounge, however, Milne's sniffing gradually died away. He looked round the room slowly and let out a howl of disappointment. Turning, he made the motion of scattering earth on the room and made for the consulting room, sniffing hopefully.

When they had been through every room in the house except her bedroom and were still empty-handed, Patricia said, " Hey—this is getting serious. Either scent's very bad or else you've got a cold. Or have you *really* forgotten ? "

Milne merely howled dismally and went sniffing off in the direction of the bedroom. This time he suddenly brightened perceptibly, and with excited barkings rushed over and began to scratch at the wardrobe door. With a loud yelp of excitement, Patricia pushed him out of the way and opened the door.

Half an hour later Patricia was saying, " Of course the only snag is that I shall never dare to wear it for fear I shall leave it in a cab, or upset ink on it or something."

" That's one of the things I wanted to tell you," said

Milne. " It's *not* to be that sort of thing. It's to wear, and to wear when you like and how you like. I wouldn't actually cook in it perhaps. But for God's sake don't fuss and worry over it. It isn't as though it was sable or anything like that."

" But I've never had one that cost as much as that, Felix. Suppose I lost it ? "

" Well, suppose you did ? It's insured. You could just buy another."

" Not as nice as that, I couldn't." She looked longingly at the coat lying on the sofa and said, " I must put it on again. I *must* ! "

" Well, why not ? "

Barbara had been quite right. It fitted perfectly, and the colour was dead right. Milne said involuntarily, " God, you do look rather gorgeous in it, Rhino."

Patricia turned suddenly away from the mirror. Her cheeks were flushed, her eyes were very bright. She said, " You're the nicest person in the world."

Milne put an arm round her tightly, without speaking.

" I don't mean just because it's gorgeous and cost a hell of a lot. But——"

She stopped and threw her arms round his neck. As he hugged her to him, he could feel the silky softness of the fur beneath his hands. It was nearly perfect. Nearly.

Barbara came in just before lunch and brought the cami-knickers. They all had to go up to Patricia's bedroom while she tried them on. It was only with difficulty that she was prevented from trying them on in the lounge. They were again an admirable fit. She said, " Bab, you're rather nice, aren't you ? They're simply lovely. Yes, you're quite a nice girl."

Milne noticed, as he had often noticed before, that they never kissed or touched one another.

Still wearing the cami-knickers, Patricia said, " Now, because you're nice I'm going to make you gnash. Just gnash. Look." She went to the wardrobe, took out the coat and put it on. " Felix gave it to me."

Barbara said triumphantly to Felix, " There you are. What did I tell you ? Fits her like a glove and the colour's dead right." About half a second too late she added, " I always told Felix ermine was your fur."

There was a moment's silence. Patricia had stopped smiling and was looking from one of them to the other with a queer blank expression.

Milne decided that it wouldn't do, and said, " Bab came and helped me buy it."

" We met in Gardner's when I was buying the pants," said Barbara brightly.

Patricia started to smile again differently. " Oh, *that's* how you got the fit so good ? I thought you'd been very clever, darling." She turned to Barbara. " It is nice, isn't it ? "

" It's absolutely perfect, Pat. You look a million dollars."

" Yes," said Patricia politely. " It's lovely." She took it off and hung it in the wardrobe.

Milne met Barbara's eyes. He thought for a moment she was going to cry. He looked quickly away.

" Are you going to keep those scandalous pants on ? " he said.

Milne said savagely, " She was there and there wasn't anything else I could do. It completely mucked the expedition up anyway."

" What a damn shame," said Patricia. " But, honey—it doesn't matter, does it ? "

Milne kicked the leg of the table with some violence. " Oh, for God's sake, Pat, don't be long-suffering. You know quite well it matters."

Patricia made no reply.

" It wouldn't have been so bad if I'd told you before. But I didn't because—well—you can see why I didn't."

" Of course." She grinned at him gallantly. " We're being awful fools, darling. It was just bad luck that she happened to be there—and then happened to say that."

There was a moment's silence. Then Patricia said, " Can I just ask you one thing and then I'll stop being silly ? "

" What ? "

" Did she put it on for you ? "

" Yes." Milne looked up. " She put it on," he said curtly. " And she looked very attractive in it. Now if you want to throw the bloody thing out of the window, I shall quite understand."

" Darling, it isn't like that at all. It doesn't matter a damn."

Garsten was in. As Milne rang the bell he could hear the radio going.

Garsten came to the door himself. He said, " Why, hallo, Felix. Come in."

" Are you busy ? " said Milne.

" No. Not a thing to do. I was just wishing somebody'd come in for a drink. Hang your things up."

Garsten was a rich bachelor. His flat looked like it. As they sat down, Milne said, " I always like this place. But why don't you have any rugs ? "

" Rugs ? "

" Yes. You've had a lot of fun with your pictures and your silver and your furniture and so on. But look at your floors."

" Nothing wrong with them," said Garsten defensively.

Milne said, " There's nothing wrong with the walls for that matter. But you put pictures on them."

" I was forgetting you were a rug fiend. What ought I to have in here ? "

" I don't know what you like. But I've got quite a nice Shirhazi that would be grand in front of the fire. I'll give it to you sometime. It's not valuable or anything, but it's rather beautiful. I only keep it rolled up anyway."

" That's remarkably civil of you, Felix, as naval blokes say."

" Not at all," said Milne with a grin. " Fee for the consultation. "

" Oh, this is a consultation, is it ? " said Garsten, raising his eyebrows. " Not just a drink ? "

" No. As a matter of fact it's two consultations. First of all—about my schizo."

" Oh, yes ? How did the pentathol go ? "

" Fine. It worked like a charm. I got all the war stuff I wanted."

" It's good for that."

" Yes. What's more, I got it good and strong and emotional. He really had a hell of a time telling me about it."

" They do, poor devils. But that's all to the good, of course."

" That's really what I wanted to get your view about. As you know, this bloke's very schizoid as a rule. He just isn't interested—isn't *there*. Now under pentothal all this stuff came out, and there was a very strong reaction and he was very distressed, which of course is as it should be. But part of what came out was stuff that there'd been a hell of a conflict about—stuff that he was afraid of and ashamed of and had been refusing to face up to with all his might. What are the chances that it was purely the comparatively recent stuff which he was consciously suppressing—that was making him act like a schizo ? "

" Oh, my God ! " said Garsten. " There's no answer to that one, old boy."

" Oh, I know you can't be sure. But do you think it's even a possibility ? "

Garsten thought for a moment.

" I should say it was *possible*. But not very probable."

" That's what I felt. There must have been some sort of pre-disposition."

" Sure."

" But what I'm wondering is whether he'll go back now to being pretty normal or whether now he's once become pretty obviously schizoid I shall have to get right down to the bottom of it before he's much better ? "

Garsten shook his head. " You simply can't tell in advance. He's got a pre-disposition and something touches it off. If you can remove the something, he may go back to what he was before, or he may stay schizoid, or he may be outwardly normal but with the pre-disposition increased."

" What happened to most of your battle neurosis cases ? "

" They varied. Usually I should say that they got back to being fairly normal outwardly, just on having the recent experience dug out. We hadn't time for long term analyses, of course. But I don't think most of them would have stood up to a new experience very well. They would have been more sensitive to it. They were all right if there was no strain. But I think they'd have come apart in your hand if they'd gone back into battle." Garsten lit a cigarette. "Anyhow, you've got to remember that we got our chaps *quickly*—immediately after the experience. I gather this all happened to your man some while ago?"

"Yes."

Garsten shook his head. "Well, these delayed fuse jobs are rather the devil as a rule."

"Yes. Well, I must wait and see. But I *think* he may be rather surprisingly better."

"Oh, that's very likely. All I'm saying is that you can't count on it, and that he's liable to relapse if anything goes wrong."

They sat for a while in silence.

"The other thing on which I want your help," said Milne slowly, "is me."

"You?" said Garsten inquiringly.

"Yes. There's a bit of my private life which is all over the place and I want an objective view of it."

"Well," said Garsten with a toothy grin and a caricature of a professional manner, "the first thing to realise is that there are two aspects of the mind. The *conscious*, which deals with realised and admitted thoughts, and——"

"No, don't fool," said Milne with a slight frown. "This matters." He paused and added briefly, "Pat and I are very near a break-up. In fact, not long ago we agreed to finish and then more or less changed our minds."

Garsten's grin vanished. He said, "I'm awfully sorry, Felix. What's the trouble?"

Milne stared at his cigarette.

"It's like this," he said slowly. "I give Pat a hell of a time. I don't know why. I love her. In fact I think I love her more than most men love their wives. But for some reason I'm unkind to her. I nag. I bully. Sometimes I almost hate her." He shook his head. "It isn't good enough."

Garsten said, " You must forgive this if it's a silly question—but does *she* think you're unkind to her ? "

" Oh, yes. I doubt if she'd say so if you asked her. But there's no doubt about it. I mean—I'm not just kidding myself."

" What sort of unkind are you ? "

Milne glanced down at the floor. " Well, here's a thing. It's a silly little example, but it's typical. I've got a rather nice rug in my room. It's a Kashan, and its colour depends on the way the light falls on it. I happen to prefer it one way round. Pat insists on looking after my room herself, and of course sometimes the thing gets round the wrong way. It sounds absurd, but I get absolutely furious about that."

Garsten frowned, opened his lips, closed them again without speaking and nodded.

" Then, not long ago, she left her mac in a taxi. It was the second time in six months she's done it. You know I could nearly have murdered her."

" It's all things like that ? "

" Oh, no. There are other things as well. But those are typical of the sort of attitude. The whole thing's completely fantastic. I know damn well that Pat's a grand person and the kindest and gentlest thing on God's earth. She puts up with more from me than anybody else would ever think of doing. And yet——" He broke off and shook his head again.

There was a long pause. Garsten was looking at his cigarette with a slight smile.

" Look," he said rather hesitantly. " It seems a bit odd to be saying this to you, Felix, but to coin a phrase in our profession, I can't help you unless you're frank with me."

" How d'you mean ? " said Milne.

" Well, you sit there telling me that Pat's perfect and you're impossible—which isn't quite what you really feel about it, you know."

" I wouldn't say she was *perfect*," said Milne defensively. " She's a bit slap-dash for an obsessional like me. But——"

" Better," said Garsten. " But it still won't do, will it ? " He looked up. " How many times has the rug in your room been wrong way round ? "

"God knows. Dozens of times."

"And you've asked her about it?"

"Asked her? I tell you, I've kicked up hell."

Garsten grinned. "Well, of course," he said gently, "it's very sadistic of you to kick up hell, Felix. But I think we shall get on faster if we admit that it's bloody careless of Pat to go on putting it the wrong way round."

Milne smiled rather constrainedly.

"Yes. I suppose there's something in that. But after all, it doesn't *matter*."

"Except that it makes you cross. You seem to think that matters." Garsten leaned back in his chair and looked at Milne solemnly. "And this ghastly affair of the missing mackintosh—you say it was the second one in six months?"

"Yes."

"And it was wet that night?"

"Yes."

Garsten shrugged. "Once again, Felix, there would appear to be faults on both sides."

Milne frowned. "It isn't as easy as that. What you don't see——"

"Look, Felix," said Garsten, leaning forward. "There's a whole lot that I don't see because you haven't told me about it. But there's one thing I *do* see—which is that you'll never get your feelings about Pat on a satisfactory basis unless you're prepared to take them out and look at them. Never mind whether they're just or fair or as you'd like them to be. What *are* they? Let's start from there and we may get somewhere. To start with, I gather that she's a bloody careless person who nearly drives you crazy with her carelessness. Well, why not say so?"

Milne sat silent for a moment. Then he looked up with a half smile. "Portrait of a patient exhibiting resistance to analysis. Yes. I suppose that's about the size of it. She's careless and she's got a memory like a sieve. Whether I ought to mind so much is another matter."

"Of course you 'oughtn't' to. You ought to be kind and good and as patient as Griselda. But you're not, so don't let's waste time on it." He broke off. "Look, old boy—I may be quite wrong but I don't believe you came all this way just to listen to me doing sales talk number one on repressed aggression. Did you ?"

Milne looked at his cigarette. "No," he said slowly. "There's the other side to it, of course. You'll be amazed to hear that it all begins in the bedroom." He paused. "Sexually, I have marked shop-girl tendencies."

"So have I," said Garsten promptly. "I'm a devil with tobacconists' lady assistants. Always have been."

"Yes, but you're not married to somebody very physically attractive."

Garsten wrinkled his forehead. "Not sure that it would make much difference if I were. I don't know, of course. Anyhow—go on and tell me about it. That side of it's no go, eh ?"

"No."

"Was it ever ? I mean—this is new ?"

"Yes. In some ways. It used to be quite all right." He hesitated. "I don't think perhaps Pat and I have ever been passionately in love exactly. I doubt if I'm capable of being passionately in love with anybody—for long, at least. But lately it's been much worse than that."

"How long is 'lately'?"

Milne considered. "A year. Longer. It's difficult to say. It's been gradual."

"Has the cooling-off been on both sides ?"

"It sounds a ghastly thing to say, but chiefly on mine."

"And this business of breaking up. Whose idea is that ?"

"Definitely mine. Pat would never leave anybody she liked unless she thought they wanted her to go."

"No children, have you ?"

"No."

"That deliberate ?"

"No. They just haven't arrived."

"Who's the unfertile party, you or Pat ?"

"Don't know. The medical wizards have never got as far as finding out for certain."

"Do you mind much ?"

"Not as much as Pat does. At least, I don't think so."

Garsten flicked the ash off his cigarette. "And you're

considering leaving her because you give her hell and think she'd be happier without you ? "

Milne smiled crookedly. " No," he said slowly. " Not even I can make that dog bark. If I left Pat it would be for the most purely selfish reasons."

" Is there anybody else ? Mistress or such-like ? "

Milne hesitated. " Vaguely such-like. I'd better tell you about that."

There was a long silence. Garsten got up and sat down again astride the arm of his chair, with his long legs sticking out stiffly.

" Well, what do you want me to say, Felix ? " he said almost brusquely.

" Anything you can think of that's helpful. I've known for a long time that things weren't very good. But this coat business was a bit too much. If I'm going to let this childish skirt-chasing muck up a thing like that, it doesn't give my relation with Pat a chance."

Garsten shrugged his shoulders slightly and ran a hand through the surprising silver hair.

" What *can* I say—except a lot of things that you know quite well already."

" Such as what ? "

" Well, for one thing, you're obviously a good deal less in love with Pat and a good deal more in love with this other girl than you're prepared to admit at the moment."

" Maybe. It doesn't feel like that. They're two entirely different things."

" Oh, quite. But they're both a part of being in love."

" Yes. But I don't think Pat and I are really a dud marriage. In most ways we're a good combination."

" I know you are."

Milne said, " Why, I've spilt all this over you is that I think there's a straightforward bit of delayed development in me that causes all this nonsense. And if so, I must try to get it right."

Garsten shook his head. " My dear old Felix—try to think of this as somebody else's story. Aren't you saying just what we've both had said to us by patients scores of times? 'My marriage isn't going very well. On the other hand there can't be anything fundamentally wrong with it. Therefore there must be something slightly abnormal about my wife. Please cure her. Or there must be something slightly abnormal about me. Please cure me.' It's the old cry. We've talked about it often enough, haven't we?"

"Oh, yes," said Milne slowly. "I know all about that. But the fact remains that however carefully I look at it, I still feel that it *ought* to work, and that it could be made to."

"Very likely it can. The question is, how well? What are you prepared to accept as a workable situation? The fact that you'd like to go to bed with somebody else doesn't mean that your marriage is valueless. It just means that it isn't as perfect as you'd like it to be. And that doesn't necessarily mean that there's anything wrong—*curably* wrong—with either of you." He shook his head. "Sorry, Felix. It's cheek to talk this elementary stuff to a person like you. But you know as well as I do that it's all wrong to go looking for complicated explanations when there are perfectly simple ones lying about."

"Oh, yes," said Milne. "But I've got a certain amount of reason for thinking there is something funny. Loewe dug up quite a lot of it when I was in Vienna."

"I don't doubt there's a lot that's funny. And you probably know what it is and even know how it got like that. It's exactly the same with me. I know perfectly well that some of the less satisfactory things about me go back to when I was four, when my father died. But I also know damned well nothing can be done about them now."

Milne said, "That's the devil of this whole business. Ability to diagnose is so far ahead of ability to cure."

"How many times have we said that? It's true even for ordinary patients. And for a chap like you who's in the racket, it's a hundred times truer."

"The essence of analysis is surprise," quoted Milne, with a rather bitter smile.

"Exactly. I don't say an analyst dealing with you or me wouldn't dig up a lot of stuff we didn't know about. I've seen some very queer stuff come out in practice analysis, even with the most experienced people. But though we may not know all about ourselves, we know the *sort* of thing. There's no real shock—no surprise. It may explain a lot, but it doesn't cure."

" I've never seen quite why it shouldn't," said Milne thoughtfully. " Except that knowing the game makes your mental defences so good."

" How about the personal relationship ? With a patient you build up a relationship, using all the tricks of the trade to do it. The patient doesn't see you doing it, and doesn't know how it's done. But you imagine yourself watching somebody try to induce a transference situation with you."

" It oughtn't to be impossible."

" It might not be for you, but it would for him."

There was a moment's silence.

Milne said, " This is all very depressing."

" I know. I'm sorry." Garsten threw himself into a chair. " But anyhow, Felix, even if it were possible, you don't really want to be cured of anything. Cure means change. And you can't afford to be changed."

" I'd certainly be only too glad to be changed in this respect."

" But my dear old horse," said Garsten irritably. " Let's talk sense. You know quite well that you can't change little bits of your character without touching the rest. Your ability to do your job and handle people depends on being the man you are." He sat up challengingly. " You say you have shop-girl tastes in sex. How often has that helped you in dealing with patients ? Thousands of times. I tell you, you don't want to be changed. What you want is a straightforward miracle that will make you the ideal husband for Pat without affecting you in any other way."

" Of course," said Milne. " That's the sort of thing everybody always wants."

" And do they ever get it ? "

" Maybe not. But the fact remains that there is an abnormality here. And quite apart from mucking up my relation with Pat, it strikes me as a bad one for a person in my job to have."

" But in God's name why ? Surely we've always agreed that if there were such a thing as a perfectly normal man he'd be about the worst analyst possible? Have you ever known an analyst who was any good, who wasn't more or less a queer in some direction?" He passed a hand impatiently through his hair. "Damn it, nobody but a queer would be conceited enough or fool enough to take the job on."

"What you're saying," said Milne after a moment's silence, "is that this isn't a thing anybody can deal with."

"If what you've told me is all there is in it, they neither could, nor should they try. The only person who can do anything about it is you. After all, you've been married how long? Ten years?"

"Twelve."

"Twelve years. You've had twelve years to look at your relations with Pat with an expert eye. If anybody knows the answers it'll be you. As long as you play straight with yourself, that is, and don't rationalise. The most that anybody like me can do for you is to remind you to tell yourself the truth and not cheat. You know the rest, and anything that can be done you can do for yourself."

"I don't seem to be able to."

"That's because you haven't been facing the facts. From what you've told me, the facts are that you're tired of Pat sexually and want somebody else; because of that you're very critical of all her faults; but in spite of it you want to go on living with her because you're fond of her and are used to it and she's a big part of your life. Well, that's a perfectly possible situation if you face it and don't flap. You may not have all you'd like, but you've got a lot more than many people. Me, for example."

Garsten got up. "So there it is. About all anybody can do for you is to tell you to go away and count your blessings. And only you can say if they add up to enough."

"It's a slightly lonely feeling," said Milne. "Lonely? Of course it is. But you can't have everything. If your job is to be an artifical daddy to anyone who comes along, you're bound to be out of luck if you ever happen to want an artifical daddy yourself. You know too much about them."

"Mind you," said Milne. "I think that's a thing which

puzzles people quite a lot. They can't see why a chap who knows all the answers for other people shouldn't know them for himself."

Garsten laughed shortly. " It always has puzzled people." He flung out his arms in the position of crucifixion. " He saved others, Himself He cannot save. He's only got to come down and they'll believe anything. But He goes on hanging there." His hands dropped to his sides. " Sorry, Felix. No miracles."

" No," said Milne, taking a deep breath. " No miracles."

Garsten said, " Do you remember the old advertisements for Monkey Brand soap ? They didn't tell you all the things it *would* do. They just said, ' It won't wash clothes ' and left it at that. It's time somebody did the same for this job. ' Admirable with tics and hysterical paralysis. Sovereign for claustrophobia and enuresis. Invaluable in depression, anxiety states and all neurotic conditions. But it won't just wash your personal dirty linen.' If we could put that on the label it'd save a lot of time and disappointment."

XII

A YEAR AGO Milne had said to Whiteley, " Well—there you are. There's no more I can do. The rest is up to you. I think you'll find it's all right now."

Whiteley had said anxiously, with a trace of the old stutter, " But I can c-come and see you sometimes ? "

" Of course you can. Any time you like. I hope you will."

He had watched Whiteley go down the path and out of sight, and had wondered as he always did at the end of that last interview whether more could have been done ; or if it could have been done differently ; or if anything *had* been done ; or if something had been done whether it would last. But Whiteley had gone down the path and out of sight, and Milne had heard no more of him until now.

Almost before they had shaken hands Milne knew that, superficially at least, Whiteley was one of his successes. There was still the faintest trace of a stammer. But the painful diffidence and the downcast eyes had never returned. Whiteley was fatter. His voice was louder. His manner was almost hearty. The new skin had grown over that raw over-sensitiveness ; and if the new skin seemed, if anything, just a trifle too thick, at least Whiteley would now pass as a normal man.

Milne said, " Well, how are you ? You look well."

" Oh, I'm fine," said Whiteley. " Never been better." He produced a pipe and pouch. " You don't mind this ? "

" Of course not." Milne watched, fascinated to see how the jutting pipe, clenched between the teeth, gave strength and squareness to the pointed face that he had known so well. " No more trouble over sleeping ? "

" Sleeping ? " said Whiteley between puffs. " The only trouble I have is with waking." He flicked out the match. " H-how are things with you ? "

" Oh, quite well. Lot of work."

" It must be a queer job," said Whiteley, looking at him appraisingly. " I've often thought of you, y'know—still sitting here, trying to sort things out for people."

" Or showing them how to sort them out for themselves."

" Well, yes, of course, that's it," said Whiteley, with a trace of relief. " I know you always used to say it was up to people to cure themselves really. I've found out how true that was."

" Yes ? " said Milne with an inward smile.

" Sure. You did a lot for me, of course. I'd be the first to admit it. But the finest thing you ever did for me was to stop the treatment and force me to take myself in hand. From the d-day I did that I've never looked back." He gave the curious characteristic blink and smiled at Milne with satisfaction.

" Well, it's something to be in a state to be able to take yourself in hand," said Milne drily. " Have a drink ? "

" Just a little one," said Whiteley with a wave of his pipe. " Just enough to drink your health. I don't drink much."

" You're practising again now ? "

" Oh, yes. Snatching a living at six-and-eight a time, you know." Whiteley wrinkled his brow. " Let's see—was I married when I saw you last ? "

Milne's thoughts flew back to the thin, stooping, young man going down the path. "No," he said gravely. "No, you weren't married then."

"Funny—I didn't realise we hadn't met for so long."

"It's well over a year, you know."

"Yes." Whiteley shook his head. "Of course in *some* ways it seems longer." In some ways, it was clear, it had been in another life.

"It was a phase," Whiteley was saying. "Just a phase." The word seemed to give him comfort. He had used it a dozen times in the last half-hour. "It frightened me, of course, and that's why I came to you. As soon as you kicked me out and forced me to tackle it, I found that I could beat it. I imagine that if I hadn't come I should have found that out for myself eventually. It was just a phase."

"There were a certain number of things that wanted clearing up, of course," said Milne gently.

"Oh, yes. Of course. I'd be the l-last to deny that you helped me a lot in the early stages." He shook his head with a reminiscent smile. "I was in a queer state. It seems funny to look back on it now. I remember crying once! D'you remember that?"

"Vaguely," said Milne. Day after day, week after week, it had gone on. "I can't, I can't," and then the floods of tears.

"But once you'd helped me put myself on the right lines it cleared up quite naturally." Whiteley blinked. "You know, I should have thought there'd be room for a lot more treatment of that sort. Just a chat and a bit of advice from someone like yourself without—all the other b-business."

Milne said, "Yes. But there's a certain amount of method in the other business."

"Oh, yes, yes. Of course." Whiteley waved his pipe. "But after all it's really a matter of faith, isn't it? You'll admit that I could beat it as soon as I thought I could?" He blinked violently. "I mean—all that stuff you told me about my parents and when I was four and so on—it's no more than the *setting* is it, for g-giving a man c-c——" he stumbled badly. "For giving a man confidence in himself. I mean, there's no harm in admitting that now. You had to do it, otherwise I shouldn't have believed I was better. I quite see that. But you don't suggest there was any more to it than that?"

Milne hesitated and noted the quick blink. "I don't think any one really understands exactly what happens," he said with a smile. "And anyhow, it doesn't matter much, does it? The only thing that matters is the result."

"Of course," said Whiteley. "The main thing is that after we finished I felt able to tackle things. I'd never deny that. That's what I always tell people when they ask me whether analysis is any good. I say, 'Well—I don't profess to know. Very likely I was going to get through this phase anyhow. But all I can tell you is that the man I went to was very nice to me, and worked very hard, and that very soon after I began to improve. You must make what you can out of that.' That's what I tell them."

"Fair enough," said Milne.

"After all, even you admit that nobody knows quite what does these things. I try to be objective about it. All the same," he added kindly, "I've mentioned your name to quite a few people. I've got a lot of contacts—clients and so on, you know. And if anything of the sort comes up I mention your name."

"That's very nice of you," said Milne gently.

"Not at all," said Whiteley, waving his pipe. "The least I can do. After all, there's no doubt you helped me a lot. I'd n-never deny that."

While Milne was waiting for Lucian he got out his file on Whiteley and made a few notes. The case had not ended a year ago. But with a bit of luck it was ended now. The ex-God Almighty had been successfully seen as a half-charlatan tradesman. The analysis was now seen as a slightly comic episode of the distant past. Another year and Whiteley would be quite sure; and then he would no longer have to protest so much, and a line could be ruled underneath, and it would all be over. Milne noticed with a grin that Whiteley had never paid the final month's bill. What a firm solicitors' letter any reminder of it would produce now!

Milne put the file away and went in search of aspirin. He had a headache.

Lucian was not only on time, but slightly early. He came limping up the path at a great rate, he had no stick, and he said, " Hullo, Felix ! " as he came in ; all of which Milne noted carefully and automatically and put mentally aside for future reference.

He said, " Hullo. You're on time. This is a record."

Lucian laughed. " It didn't take me as long as usual. My leg's getting run in."

Milne looked at the alert, smiling face and cursed his headache.

" I see you haven't got my stick," he said.

" Hell ! " said Lucian. " I meant to bring it back to-day. I forgot."

" Thought you might want it again," said Milne with a quiet smile.

Lucian shot a quick, almost suspicious glance at him, but continued to smile.

" You're going to make that mean something subtle ? "

" Subtle ? " said Milne. " I've got enough work to do with the obvious without worrying about the subtle. How are you ? "

" Well, what do *you* think ? " said Lucian, leaning back in his chair with a broad grin.

Milne looked at him thoughtfully and in silence for a moment. " You're feeling better ? "

" Better ? I'm feeling completely different."

Milne nodded. " Good."

" Ever since our last party. It's the damn silliest thing I ever heard of. But there's no denying it—that knock-out drop of yours did the trick. I can't tell you why. Nothing's really any different. But I just don't feel the same."

" Well, that's natural enough," said Milne, speaking slowly and thinking fast.

" But *why* is it ? I'm just completely puzzled by the whole thing. Why should—— ? "

Milne said, " You got a lot of stuff off your chest and it feels better without it. Haven't you ever had a boil lanced?"

"It was just getting it out of my system, eh?"

"Yes."

Lucian shook his head. "Well, if you say so I suppose it's right. But it seems a most remarkable thing to me. Still—the main thing is that it's happened."

There was a moment's silence. Milne caught again the quick, uneasy glance.

"Aren't you pleased with me?" said Lucian gaily. "I'm as pleased as hell with myself."

"Of course I am," said Milne with a slight smile. "But not quite as surprised as you are perhaps."

"You really knew that I should feel as much better as this?"

"I didn't know. But I thought you might."

"Do people always, after that stuff?"

"Oh, no. The stuff doesn't do anything. It's what comes out when you use it." Dully Milne cursed the headache again. To gain time he said, "Has your wife noticed the difference?"

"Moll? She certainly has. She damn' nearly wanted to ring up the police and give you in charge for witchcraft."

Milne hesitated for a moment and passed a hand over his hot eyes. "Well, this is fine," he said briskly. "Now we can get on."

The smile faded from Lucian's face. "Get on?" he said rather blankly.

"Yes. We had to get rid of that stuff before we could get any further. Now it's out of the way we can get down to it."

"But—but what are we to get down to?" said Lucian with a puzzled smile. "I feel perfectly normal now."

"What you mean is that you feel better."

"No. I mean I feel normal. As normal as I can be anyhow."

"That's what we've got to find out," said Milne shortly.

"Look, let me get this straight," said Lucian, leaning forward. "Do you mean you think I'm not cured?" Milne met the blue eyes. They flickered away for a fraction of a second and then resumed their puzzled look of inquiry.

"I don't know," said Milne quietly. "You're better. How much better I don't know. You may be completely well. I can't say for the moment. The next thing is to find out."

"Well, I've got no doubt about it," said Lucian positively.

Milne nodded in silence. Lucian's lips tightened. He was about to speak and then stopped and dropped his eyes. He smiled with something of an effort.

"Well, of course, Felix, you're the expert. But honestly I think you've done the trick already."

"You may be right," said Milne. "I hope you are." He was quite certain now.

"How *can* you find out?" said Lucian almost irritably. "What else is there to do?"

Milne said, "If you lance a boil and the boil clears up—that's fine, as far it goes. But what you're really interested in is what caused the boil, and whether it will cause other boils."

"You mean I might have more trouble later on?"

"Possibly."

Lucian shook his head. "I don't think it's at all likely. Apparently this stuff I told you has been worrying me more than I realised and that's what caused it. Now I've got it off my chest I'm quite all right. It seems obvious to me."

"Quite," said Milne. "But why did it worry you so much?"

"You don't think it was anything to worry about?" said Lucian bitterly.

"Not to that extent. Nothing is."

Lucian threw himself back in his chair. "Well," he said almost angrily. "What d'you want to do now? Give me more dope?"

"No, I don't think so," said Milne calmly. "What I want to do now is to find out a bit more about you. I hardly know anything yet. All we've done so far is to clear the ground of all the stuff that's accumulated in the last few years. It's important as far as it goes. But if there's a real problem, we shall probably have to go a fair way back in your history to get it."

"And how long will that take?" asked Lucian sarcastically.

"I don't know. It depends what we find."

Lucian's face flushed. "Oh, well," he said bitterly, "I suppose even psycho-analysts must live."

Milne looked at him with a broad grin and did not reply. Lucian stirred angrily in his chair.

"Well, I think I should warn you," he said coldly, "that I've no money and I simply can't afford to go on and on. It's going to be difficult enough to pay for the treatment I've had already. I'm not in a position to go making unnecessary experiments in case there might be something else wrong when I feel quite well. On that basis everybody ought to be being treated all the time."

"Now look," said Milne quietly. "Let's stop talking nonsense about fees and making a living and so on and use our brains. You say you're now quite all right?"

"Entirely. But that's only what *I* think, of course. You're the expert and you know better," said Lucian.

"Not at all. I'm the expert and I don't know. Therefore I must find out. Now, if you're quite all right, there's no harm done by making sure, is there? And if there still is a bit to clear up we may have saved a lot of time and trouble in the future."

Lucian stared at the table lamp in silence.

"You came here to-day," said Milne gently, "intent on getting me to agree that you were cured. When I said I wasn't sure you promptly started to try to make me lose my temper and quarrel with you so that you could walk out. Now that may be just disappointment—of course you want to feel that you're quite well and that it's all finished. But it *may* be that that bit of you inside that's been giving all the trouble is getting scared of how well you're getting on, and wants to put a stop to it before you can get rid of it entirely."

There was a long silence.

"Are you suggesting that I get fun out of being depressed?" said Lucian sullenly. "That I don't want to be well?"

"Not consciously. But there's always a bit inside everybody that doesn't want to be cured of these things. It's true of every patient I've ever dealt with. Curing people of these things means robbing an honest, hard-working neurosis of its living. So of course it kicks like hell and tells its owner to get the treatment stopped."

There was another long pause. Then Lucian turned suddenly.

"All right, Felix," he said, smiling. "You win. You're the boss. I expect you're right as usual." Milne, watching tensely, saw that tiny revealing flicker of the eyes, groaned inwardly, and smiled back.

"After all," said Lucian lightly, "it's damned nonsense to spoil the ship for a ha'porth of tar. The only thing is I don't see how the hell I'm going ever to pay you."

"We'll talk about that when you've got something to pay for."

"Well, God, I've got that now all right. Whatever happens, I can never thank you enough for what you've done."

"If you feel like that," said Milne, "the best thanks you can give me is to make this next bit as easy as you can."

"My dear man, anybody'd think the whole thing was for your benefit. Of course I'll do anything you say. You mustn't take any notice of what I said just now. It's just that I feel so much better and want to feel it's all fixed. You know how it is."

"Of course."

"One thing though," said Lucian. "And this is serious, Felix. I must pay for the treatment I've had up to date. That I do insist on."

"Why must you?" said Milne calmly.

"Well, after that particularly caddish thing I said, I shan't feel happy unless I do."

"Bunkum," said Milne shortly.

"No—seriously, Felix. I definitely shan't go on unless I pay up to date. This never-mind-about-money stuff isn't good enough."

Milne said, "You'll get a bill at the end of the month in the normal way." The cracked note of the conversation was ringing through his aching head intolerably.

Lucian looked doubtful. "You'll promise that?"

"Yes."

"All right," said Lucian, jumping briskly to his feet. "I shall hold you to that. Now then—when do you want me to come again?"

Milne hesitated. "You don't want to go on now?" he said bluntly. This time Lucian's eyes met his without a flicker.

"No," he said simply. "Go on next time, Felix. Not to-day."

Milne passed his hand across his forehead. It was hot and slightly damp. "All right," he said wearily. "Monday then? Same time?"

"Right," said Lucian. "And I'll remember to bring your stick back." He held out his hand. "Good-bye, Felix." It was the first time they had ever shaken hands.

As Lucian limped rapidly to the gate Milne saw clearly for a moment through a gap in his headache and went quickly towards the door. But the throbbing veil closed again and he stood at the window with his hands to his head, and through his fingers watched Lucian go.

They sat by the drawing-room fire and had tea, after the day's work, just the two of them, with the curtains drawn and the fire burning, and toast, and Patricia looking young and pretty. If there had been honey it would have been like Rupert Brooke. Ever since he had talked to Garsten he had carefully seen it all as being like Rupert Brooke. Only Rupert Brooke would have been deliciously improperly interested in Patricia's legs and he was not. He told her items from the day's work.

He said, "Do you remember Whiteley?"

"Whiteley?" said Patricia, wrinkling up her face. "I remember the name."

"Little solicitor cove. About eighteen months ago. I had him in to-day."

"All right?"

"Oh, yes. He slapped me on the back and smoked a pipe and said that I hadn't done him much harm and he'd taken the risk of mentioning my name to his friends."

"He didn't *really* say that?"

"More or less word for word."

"What did you say?"

"I thanked him nicely."

"But wasn't he the one you had an awful time with and were rather proud about?"

"Yes."

"And he says you didn't do him much harm?"

"He even says I helped in the early stages."

Patricia went very pink. "I never see quite how you stand it when they do that."

"Stand it?" said Milne roughly. "It's the best possible thing that could happen. He's got to get free of me somehow. How the hell is the poor devil to do it if he doesn't come and patronise me?"

"Oh, I know all about that. But it's irritating all the same."

"If it doesn't irritate me I don't see why it should irritate you," said Milne curtly.

"Don't you, pet?" said Patricia with a smile.

"No. That's the difficulty over telling you anything about this stuff. You go up in the air as though what mattered was me instead of the patient."

"Sorry," said Patricia wearily. "Then that was fine?"

"I was very pleased with him," said Milne shortly. He took a deep breath and smiled. "This is nice, Rhino."

Patricia said nothing but came and leant against his knees. Mechanically Milne began to stroke her hair. There was a long silence. Milne shut his eyes and sought hard for something to say. If somebody didn't say something quickly, they would begin to talk; and that was to be avoided at all costs.

"Your hands are very hot," said Patricia suddenly. She turned and looked up at him. "Are you all right, honey?"

"Headache," said Milne.

"Bad one?"

"Moderate to bloody."

She got to her knees and put a hand on his forehead. "You've got a temperature, my boy. Bed."

"Nonsense," said Milne without conviction.

"Bed," said Patricia firmly. She rose and held out a hand. "Come on. Bed's a nice place. You try it. You'll be surprised. I thought there was something."

His temperature was just under 101°. Patricia had switched on the electric fire, but he shivered as he took his clothes off. Patricia was going around with that extraordinary deftness and quickness which always came with clinical thermometers. At 98.4°, Patricia dropped everything that she remembered to get and forgot everything else. After that, for every 0.1° upwards she became more sure-handed, more thoughtful and more competent.

Milne said, "Picture of gent swinging the lead in order to be fussed over. What you ought to be is matron in a flash nursing home. You'd make a fortune."

"Get in," said Patricia. She looked at him thoughtfully. "I wonder if I'd better get Sands to you?"

"Good God, no. He'd say I was suffering from pyrexia of uncertain origin. That's not worth half a guinea."

"Maybe," said Patricia unheedingly. She looked at him again. "I'll give you a few hours and see how it goes," she said at last. "The veganin may do it. Think you can go to sleep?"

"Feels like it," said Milne. He shut his eyes. It was an exquisite relief to be lying down. "I let that man Lucian go," he said vaguely. "I shouldn't have done that."

"Well now, let yourself go," said Patricia. "Good-night, pet."

She bent down and kissed his forehead.

"Good-night," said Milne. "Gentle Rhino. Nice Rhino. God, I am spoilt."

When she had gone he lay with his eyes shut for a while, but after that he opened them and stared at the ceiling. Lying in bed alone it was easier to think about it calmly. He had been trying it now for ten days and it wouldn't do. He was the luckiest man in the world and he could see it, but he did not feel it. There must be somebody in the world—thousands of people—who would give anything for Pat—and give anything to her. But he was not one of them. That much was clear now. He shut his eyes and deliberately let the rigid muscles of his loyalty relax. She was a darling. There was no doubt about that, even speaking within these four personal walls. And she left him cold. And there was no doubt about that either. He could go on, because there might not be more than they had together. Or he could stop, and chance it that somehow he could find more. A week. That's all it would mean. A week of complications and arrangements over money and where to stay and so on. And after that it would be past, and he would have all life in front of him, free and unmortgaged, to make whatever bloody mess of it he pleased. The phrase " gratitude and loyalty " came into his head from somewhere. He grinned sardonically. " Gratitude and loyalty " to the Rhinoceros. Then he realised that for purposes of this kind Patricia could not be the Rhinoceros. The Rhinoceros was his person—a part of him. And it was decided now that Patricia was not him, but a woman to whom he was married and therefore not the Rhinoceros any more. His headache had almost gone. But when he realised that Patricia could not be the Rhinoceros any more the tears came into his eyes. It was the thought of finality which always affected him strongly.

XIII

Norris Pile was standing in the hall, apparently reading a torn two year old notice on the board. He was even more astounded and delighted to see Milne than usual. He said, " You're looking well, Felix." He always told everybody they were looking well, on principle.

" Looking well ? " said Milne indignantly. " I'm at death's door. At least, I was last night. I had a temperature of 101°. Like a fool I went and took it again this morning and it was normal. Otherwise I could have stayed in bed and been fussed over for a week."

The hearty smile had faded from Pile's face and had been replaced by a keen diagnostic glance. " Yes," he said solemnly. " You don't look too good. Been overdoing it, I expect." The patient was always right. Pile shook his head. "I hope you haven't got too much to-day?"

"Oh, I'm all right," said Milne. "I was only fooling."

They walked towards the stairs. "By the way," said Pile suddenly, thinking of it for positively the first time. "What time's your first patient?"

"Half-past three."

"Half-past? Then that would give us a few minutes for a chat? I've got a thing I want to tell you about."

"Sure," said Milne.

When Pile sat down in his swivel chair he squashed out sideways so as to fill it completely. Milne always expected it to come up with him when he got up, but it never did.

Pile said, "Well, Felix—we're not going to get the money out of Freethorne."

"Not?"

"No." Pile took off his glasses and began to polish them vigorously. His face wore a look of mingled sadness, firmness and nobility.

Milne said, "I thought he'd promised it to you. I suppose the sight of all of us was too much for him. We did pull his leg rather."

"Well, there it is," said Pile. "We aren't getting it."

There was a moment's pause.

"Well, I'm very sorry, Norris," said Milne, not quite understanding. "Frankly, I don't think money's the chief need here. But it would have been nice to have it. Apart from anything else, it would have been a sort of—of formal recognition."

"It meant a great deal," said Pile with quiet heroism. "My plans—my visions for the future—were all built round it. But there——" He waved aside his visions and sighed.

There was another silence. Milne strained his ears vainly for the prompter's voice.

"What made Freethorne change his mind? Did we let you down?"

"My *dear* Felix——!" said Pile with a violent flourish of his glasses. "My dear man! Let me down! As though you people here *could* let me down. With all the brilliant and unselfish work that's being done——"

"Who didn't he like?" said Milne, beginning to see the light, though still faintly. "Garsten did crack him rather hard. Or was it me?"

"No, no. Nothing of the kind. Between ourselves I don't think he even noticed Garsten's irony. He isn't used to people being ironical, you know. It wouldn't occur to him that anybody would laugh at him."

"Well then, what was it? It must have been pretty serious for him to turn the whole thing down."

Pile rubbed slowly at his glasses. "He didn't turn it down, Felix. He was quite willing to place the money at my disposal." He turned quickly. "But on terms which I could not possibly consider. I told him bluntly, 'Sir George, I want that money. I need it badly for this work. But I don't take money on those terms. You can keep it.'" He brought his huge paw down on his desk with a bang.

"What did he want then?"

Pile held his glasses up to the light and peered through them.

"He wanted me," he said slowly, "to get rid of Paston."

"Oh, it was Paston? I thought they didn't seem to be much of a hit together. And you refused?"

"Of course." Pile threw out a hand. "The staff here have been loyal to me and to the work. They have a right to expect me to be loyal to them."

Milne nodded. "Yes. Of course poor old Paston does tend to say the wrong thing for people like that. We ought really to have kept him out of sight."

"Oh, he had no *personal* objection to Paston," said Pile heavily. "I wouldn't have minded so much if he had. Between ourselves, Paston's a doubtful asset, Felix. But Freethorne was after a—a matter of principle."

The lights went full up at last. "You mean," said Milne quietly, "that he objected to your employing unqualified people?"

"That's what it came down to," said Pile. He began to speak very quickly. "So of course I said but this is absurd. My best man is a lay analyst. A condition like that shows that you're completely out of touch. Rather than accept a condition like that I'd close the place down to-morrow. You can keep your money. When I think of all the brilliant and unselfish work that's being done——"

Milne made up his mind bitterly but without hesitation. "Oh, come, Norris," he said gently. "After all, Paston and I are the only unqualified people you've got. We shouldn't be much loss."

"My dear Felix, don't be absurd."

"Two thousand pounds is two thousand pounds. You can't turn it down on a point like that."

"Can't turn it down?" said Pile emphatically. "I can, and I *have*."

"Then you must obviously see Freethorne and say you've changed your mind."

"My boy, you're worth far more than two thousand pounds or twenty thousand. This is a clinic not a bank. Besides, we can't possibly let this absurd Trades Unionism interfere with our work. It's one of the things I'm most keen about."

Milne's throat was very dry. He swallowed quickly and said, "Oh, I don't know. It's quite reasonable from Freethorne's point of view."

"*Reasonable*——!"

"Of course," said Milne dully. "This is a Trust Fund. Anything that it supports must be Caesar's wife. We both know that there are some damn good unqualified people in this job. But there are a lot of shockers too. Keeping to qualified people doesn't mean you get rid of all the duds. But it gives you a better chance."

"Possibly," said Pile. "But still——"

"Paston's a shocker. You've no right to ask Freethorne to give you money to support anything he does, and you know it. If Freethorne knew his business he'd pay you the money to keep Paston away from patients. Well—that's what he is doing. You can have the money or Paston."

"I don't give a damn about Paston. But how about you?"

"I'm the limiting case. At least I like to think so. But you can't work on limiting cases."

"*No!*" said Pile. He wriggled his shoulders and settled down even more massively in his chair. He looked much happier now. " No, Felix. Your attitude about it's grand. If I were in your place I should be furious. I might have known you'd think only of the job. But I won't have it and that's flat. I've told him so, and there's no more argument about it. I'd rather close the place than agree to your going."

Milne swallowed again. " All right, Norris," he said rather huskily. " Then that leaves it up to me."

" How d'you mean, old boy ? "

" I shall resign. Then you can kick Paston out and everything will be fixed."

" But I tell you, Felix, I don't *wish* it," said Pile feebly.

" You can't have everything you wish," said Milne drily.

" And anyhow—what'll happen to your patients here ? "

" They can come to my place—the ones I'm dealing with now."

" You mean you'll go on giving them treatment ? "

" Of course."

Pile shook his head mournfully. " I don't like you to do this. Even for the sake of the place, Felix. It's too much. I——"

" Oh, for Christ's sake——! " said Milne suddenly. He got up and went to the door. Half turning, he said, " That's fixed then, Norris. I'll tell my patients to-day and this'll be my last appearance. Cheerio."

It was ironical that his first patient should have been Harrison. Harrison had been under treatment for nine months, and had reached the peak of the God Almighty stage. Milne was omniscient, omnipresent, all-powerful. What he said was wisdom and truth. He was the only person in the world who understood life, and particularly Harrison's life. The whole point—indeed the only point—of Harrison's existence was the two hours a week that he spent in the presence of God. He was a brisk, business-like young schoolmaster, and he worshipped in a brisk, business-like, schoolmasterly way, which was much more disconcerting than a dozen romantic and tearful Lady M.s.

Milne sat rather wearily on his pedestal and let Harrison pour over him, in blunt, manly and unsentimental phrases, all the flood of sentimentality that had been dammed up, and misdirected and distorted in a complicated life of twenty-eight years. He had meant to begin, that afternoon, the cautious process of prying the transference loose—the process that would end with Harrison as a Whiteley, his emotions flowing quietly down the desirable channels, and Milne himself as a queer, shadowy, slightly comic figure in the past, remembered, like an early mistress, either with dislike or faintly amused patronage. But this was no afternoon to begin a major operation.

Milne said, "By the way, after to-day we shan't be meeting here."

"Shan't be meeting?" said Harrison sharply, with a quick, scared glance.

"Not here. We shall carry on, of course. But I shall want you to come out to my place."

Harrison's blunt, snubby face broke into a smile of relief. "D'you know, I thought for a moment you meant you were throwing me over. I was going to say——"

"No, no. Of course not. I just want you to come to my consulting room instead of here."

"I shall like that," said Harrison thoughtfully. "I've often wanted to see your house. I can imagine the room you work in."

"Can you? All right then, tell me what it's like."

"Well, of course this is complete nonsense," said Harrison, the common sense schoolmaster coming to the top for a moment. "But I've always seen it as a sort of library, with bookcases going up to the ceiling, and leather armchairs and a french window opening on to a lawn."

"Is there a clock in it?"

"Yes. Over on the far side away from the door."

"Who's sitting at the desk?"

Harrison hesitated. "Well, you, of course."

"You think again," said Milne with a smile.

Harrison thought for a moment. Then his face gradually relaxed into a delighted smile.

"You know you're a complete wizard. You are really. There was a time when you would have been burnt for half the things you do with me."

" It's your father sitting at the desk, isn't it ? "

" Yes, of course it is. But how in God's name did you know ? "

" Because you've just given me a perfectly good description of your father's study. Don't you remember ? It was one of the first things you ever told me about."

" But why should I think your room would be like that ? "

" Try thinking that out for yourself."

" You mean I wish you'd been my father ? " said Harrison promptly. " Well, my God, that's true enough."

Milne said, " Let's say that you're mixing us up a bit at the moment. Anyhow, the main thing is that I want you to come out there next week. That all right ? I'll give you the address."

" Write me a letter giving it," said Harrison hopefully. " I haven't got any letters from you."

" No," said Milne firmly. " You can just shove it down."

" All right," said Harrison, rather disappointed. He fumbled for a pencil. " Aren't you coming here any more, then ? "

" No," said Milne curtly.

Miss Lucas was late. While he was waiting for her, Garsten wandered in. He said, " Look, Felix. Hans is still yammering about getting some group therapy going. What d'you think ? "

" I think you might try it."

" So do I. Shall we tell Norris we're going to ? "

Milne hesitated and then said, " Well, I'm not much concerned. This is my last appearance."

Garsten turned quickly and said, " *What ?* "

" I'm packing up to-day."

" But—in God's name, why ? "

" Oh, I don't know. I haven't really got the time and so on."

" Well, Christ ! " said Garsten, rather hurt. " You might have told me. When did you decide ? "

" Only to-day. I've told Norris."

" What's he say ? "

" Oh, the usual sort of thing."

"He'll be shaken to the wick," said Garsten. "So will everybody else for that matter. Including me." He shook his head. "I don't blame you, of course. I've nearly packed up myself half a dozen times lately. But——"

There was a slightly questioning silence.

Garsten said, "You're just fed up with the place?"

"Oh, yes," said Milne carelessly. "And I've got a lot to do with my own stuff. I shall carry on with the people I'm treating now at home and then stop."

Garsten nodded and sat down astride the arm of a chair. "This is a blow," he said moodily.

"I'm sorry myself in some ways," said Milne.

"If you go," said Garsten slowly. I think I shall pack up too."

"No," said Milne sharply. "You can't do that."

"Why can't I?"

"Well, damn it, we can't all leave Norris flat."

"Nothing could leave Norris flat. He's not a flattenable man. Anyhow I've got a practice too, you know, Felix."

"Yes, but you mean a lot more to the place than I do. You're the only person of any standing that Norris has got behind him."

"Bunkum. If it comes to that, you're the best clinician he's got by a mile."

"I don't think many people would agree with you," said Milne rather bitterly.

"Well, anyhow, it's a blow," said Garsten. "Particularly sprung on us like this. Oh, well——" He shrugged his shoulders. "I suppose I must go and see if the next victim has turned up."

He was afraid it wouldn't work. As he came down the stairs to the common-room, he heard Garsten's angry voice in the office. He went straight in. Garsten was standing in front of Pile's desk with his face pale with fury. It looked ghastly with the dark eyes and the silver hair. Pile had pushed his chair back from the desk and seemed to be almost cowering against the wall. As Milne came in Garsten was saying, "I've never heard such bloody gutlessness in my life. Why——"

Milne said, " Hallo—what's happening ? "

" Ah, hallo, Felix ? " said Pile with much relief. " We were just discussing——"

Garsten half turned. " Look," he said in a strained voice. " He's told me about this, and I've just been telling him what he is."

" I've been trying to explain, Felix," said Pile helplessly. " You'll bear me out that my attitude——"

" I don't need to be told about your attitude," said Garsten furiously. " Your attitude is to sell Felix down the river for twopence ha'penny from that bastard Freethorne. Well, you can bloody well have it, and I hope it chokes you."

Milne said, " Steady the Buffs. It isn't anything to do with Norris."

" That's what I've been trying to tell him," said Pile pathetically. " The line I took——"

" Norris was all in favour of telling Freethorne to go to hell," said Milne quietly. " But it so happened that I wanted to get out anyhow, so it all fitted together rather well."

Garsten gave a snort of derision. " Sure—it fitted like a glove. Norris tells you with tears in his eyes that he can't have his bloody money if you stay, and you discover that you want to go. What a bit of luck."

" I left Felix in no doubt about my feelings," said Pile with dignity.

" I'll bet you didn't. That's why he's going."

" Look," said Milne wearily. " This isn't getting us anywhere. What else could Norris have done ? He told Freethorne to go to hell."

" Then why couldn't he have kept his mouth shut, instead of coming and weeping on you about it ? "

" But what does it matter ? I don't care."

" Maybe you don't, but I do." He turned to Pile with suddenly renewed anger. " Quite apart from losing Felix, don't you see that this is throwing your hand in about the use of lay analysts ? It means that for a couple of thousand miserable pounds you're going to toe the line and say that any medically qualified nitwit is better than a chap who's given his life to the job."

"Well, Felix himself thought that it was reasonable only to have qualified people," said Pile sullenly. "I didn't agree," he added hastily. "But it's a possible point of view."

"Of course Felix thinks it reasonable" said Garsten angrily. "I've talked to him about it often enough. He thinks it as reasonable as hell. God, Norris, you're just about the champion self-kidder of all time."

"It doesn't help to be insulting," said Pile with dignity.

"It helps a hell of a lot, my boy," said Garsten. "Because maybe if I'm insulting enough I shan't hit anybody on the nose, which I feel very inclined to do."

"Oh, come on," said Milne impatiently. "Snap out of it, Jim."

"I am snapping out of it," said Garsten. "And that pretty damn quick. I'm through."

Pile gave a low wail of dismay. "You can't possibly do this. It's completely unfair. I've tried to act for the best in very difficult circumstances, and all I get is abuse and resignations. You must see that you're putting me in an impossible position."

"You'll get a hell of a lot more resignations when people know about this," said Garsten with satisfaction.

Milne said, "Look, I'd like to have a word with you about this alone. Come on."

"Yes," said Pile eagerly. "Talk it over with Felix. Don't decide anything for the moment. Think it over. We're all rather upset." He surged on to his feet and waved eagerly towards the door. "Go and talk it over with Felix."

They walked up to Milne's room in silence. Garsten sat down and passed a hand over his eyes.

Milne said, "You can't go, of course."

Garsten did not reply for a moment. "I know," he said at last. "But equally I can't stay after this. So what?"

"Why can't you stay?"

"What, and work with that slack-gutted ton of uselessness?"

Milne said, "What the hell's he got to do with it? He doesn't make any difference to you. You come here to work, not to play with Norris."

" I can work quite well in my own practice."

" Then why did you come here in the first place ? "

Garsten did not reply.

Milne said, " You came here because it gave you a chance to treat people who needed it and couldn't afford, or thought they couldn't afford, to come to you privately. That's why I came. That's why we all came. It seems to me that was a pretty sound reason. And it isn't altered because I happen to be going."

Garsten looked up and said, " What say we all clear out and start a proper show of our own ? "

" Where does that get us ? "

" We could kiss Norris good-bye and leave him to play penny nap with Freethorne. We could get rid of Paston. And we could do some decent work."

" You'll get rid of Paston anyhow on this. And you know Norris is all right really. If his cheeks didn't wobble you wouldn't have much against him. Maybe he does go to committees a bit, but he's done a lot for this work in his way."

" So you think we just ought to let you go and say, ' Well, well—too bad. But the great God Freethorne has spoken '?"

" I think you ought just to carry on with your job and let me work out my own salvation," said Milne slowly.

" Oh, it's not your sweet eyes that I'm worrying about," said Garsten bitterly. " It's the poor bloody patients. Somebody has to think about them at times."

" Well, it won't help them much if you walk out in a huff," said Milne bluntly.

There was a long silence.

" I'd like to talk to the other people about it," said Garsten doubtfully.

Milne said, " No—that's out. Otherwise we shall have to tell them the whole thing and they may kick up a fuss." He stopped suddenly and then added, " Look—I've been being reasonable about this all the afternoon and I'm tired of it. Suppose you take over now ? "

Garsten looked at him thoughtfully for a moment.

" That seems fair enough," he said gently. " You'd really rather just go ? "

"Yes. Far rather."

Garsten nodded. "I suppose so. I'm not sure you're right, but there it is. Now let's go and have a drink."

"Too early," said Milne. "Anyhow we've got to go down and have tea. I shall tell them I'm packing up and if you'll kindly prod Norris in the belly if he starts to jabber and spill the beans, I'll be obliged."

So they went downstairs. Garsten said, "I wonder what Norris will buy with his two thousand pounds?"

Milne said, "It wouldn't be a bad idea if he used it to pay himself back a bit of what he's spent on the place. It owes him personally about ten thousand, apart from the overdraft."

It was well after six when they left the Clinic. Garsten asked him to come home and have a drink, but Milne refused, and Garsten saw and didn't press it

They parted in Belgrave Square, and as Milne walked up to Hyde Park Corner he found himself suddenly fantastically angry. From the moment that he had seen what Pile was getting at he had felt peculiarly calm and reasonable and controlled. It had been no effort to defend Pile, to pacify Garsten, and to bluff Hans and the rest. But now there was nobody to deal with, and that was different.

He hesitated at the Tube entrance, but he knew that the thing had to be dealt with before he saw anybody else, and he went and sat on a seat in the Green Park. It was nearly dark and slightly foggy. The first thing to do was to be angry, so he was angry. He swore, using the words that meant real anger to him, about Pile and Freethorne and doctors. He sat there and let it go inside him, and it made him shake.

He got up and walked blindly down the path to the Palace, and back up again to Piccadilly, and on the way he told himself that seldom had a man made such a fuss about ceasing to do a great deal of hard work for nothing. But that dog wouldn't bark, and he knew too much to force it.

He knew more than that. He knew that what was really required was somebody to sit back quietly and be told the whole story, with all the bitterness and all the unfairness of it. Not taking sides, or supporting or opposing, but just listening. And then, as it came out it would change, and the listener would barely have to say anything, because it would all have become clear enough, and small enough, not to matter. But there was nobody to sit and listen. The only man who could have done the job was walking blindly round the Green Park feeling sick and rather shaky.

He thought of going round the Park again, but it was pretty clear that the whole thing would come round with him, so he crossed Piccadilly and went into the Berkeley, and ordered a whisky and soda and drank it quickly. He ordered another, and realised that the immediate difficulty was that he couldn't possibly go home and tell Pat all about it. Not because of his pride—that didn't arise ; but because Pat would be furiously and irrationally and childishly angry for his sake. And that, at the moment, was unfaceable. Pat, pink with anger and attacking everybody with the wrong end of the stick on his behalf, was no answer to anything. Like Garsten, but worse and much more irritating because less reasonable. He drank his second drink and decided, without surprise, that he knew exactly what he wanted, and went to get it.

Barbara answered the telephone herself.

Milne said, " This is Felix. Get your fighting irons on. We're going out."

" Are we ? When ? "

" Now. To-night."

" Darling, I'm terribly sorry, but I can't."

Milne said, " No—it isn't like that. We've got to go out to-night. See ? Not just ordinary. It's important."

" But, Felix, dear—I've got a thing. Booked and so forth."

Milne said, " Look, Bab—do you like me ? "

" Felix, I like you very much. But the fact remains——"

" All right. Then come. And for Pete's sake come quickly."

Barbara giggled and said, " Scarcely for *Pete's* sake, darling, surely ? "

" I don't mean your Pete. I mean the other Pete. Anyhow, you'll come ? "

" No, Felix—seriously. No can do. If I'd known earlier——"

" What is your thing ? "

" Well——" said Barbara hesitantly.

" You haven't got one. Don't lie to me, trollop."

" I've got people coming."

" What people ? "

" The Duke of Plaza Toro and his mistress," said Barbara helplessly. " She has dyed hair and false teeth."

" That may be. But you're coming out with me. They'll like it better if you're not there anyway."

" No," said Barbara. " Fooling apart, the fact is that Pete's in the frozen north——"

" Oh, marvellous ! "

" —and he's going to ring me up during the evening and I've promised I'll be here."

" Well, that settles it," said Milne calmly. " What a fuss ! Go put your clothes on. Not too lush because I'm in a decayed lounge suit."

There was a fat man in a dinner jacket waiting impatiently outside the telephone box. Milne rang up Patricia and just said, " Look, I may be late. Dining out. Don't wait up for me."

Patricia said, " All right, honey. Got your key ? " in her most unsurprised voice.

" Yes, thanks," said Milne. " Dining with Garsten," he added. To say that was childish, unnecessary, and somehow final.

" Right," said Patricia. " See you when I see you. Don't get too tight."

The fat man was in such a hurry to get into the box that he and Milne stood for a moment dodging in the doorway. Milne wondered idly whom he was ringing up, and why.

As they were dancing, Barbara disengaged her left arm and glanced at her watch.

" Look," she said. " Far be it from me to interfere with a

good party, but the man Pete will ring up at about ten, and it is essential that I should then be sitting by the fire making a noise like a woman darning."

"Why?" said Milne.

"Well, between ourselves, I think that's partly why he's ringing up—to see I'm not on the tiles."

"Is Pete coming all over jealous?"

"Not exactly. But he's always felt that there might easily be a catch in it with me, you know."

"Over-sexed," said Milne calmly. "But you can't really expect me to worry about Pete's troubles, can you?"

Barbara said, "You're very *tough* to-night, Felix. Tough and joyful. Why are you joyful?"

"Anybody would be joyful dancing with you, darling. Even if he were sober."

"Nicely put," said Barbara. "That'll larn her. But seriously, I shall have to go soon. Very soon."

Milne shook his head. "You should never use the same tactics twice," he said. "Shows a lack of imagination. I've left parties early with you before."

"Well, nobody's asked you to come this time."

"Have you ever been rung up in the nude, Bab?"

Barbara hesitated. "Taking that question purely at its face value—I have, and it always makes me shy. If the telephone's in the room I always clutch coyly for a garment." As Milne did not answer she said, "Why?"

"I was just wondering."

As they sat down at their table Milne said, "Say when you want to go and we'll get a cab."

Barbara looked at him for a moment and said, "Look—we don't want another mess like last time."

"We do not. And we're not going to have one."

"That's all right then," said Barbara with relief.

"It is," said Milne calmly. "Come on. We'll go now."

The house was still almost irritatingly comfortable, inside. Milne said, "Come and sit over here, Bab."

Barbara hesitated and then, with sudden decision, sat down on the sofa beside him.

" All right," she said rather wearily. " I'm a bitch. So what ? "

Milne put an arm round her and kissed her hard.

" Yes," she said. " Yes. But I'd like to know, Felix."

" What would you like to know ? "

" What's wrong. How come ? Why ? All those things."

Milne said, " Darling, do you want a hard-luck seduction story ? " He felt very tired and rather drunk.

" But there is *something* wrong," she said, looking at him with the slanting blue eyes.

" What makes you think so ? "

" I'm pretty obviously being used as something. Oh, don't worry—I'm not proud. That's my trouble. I only wondered what it was."

Milne said, " This is no time for philosophic introspection." It took him quite a while to say it.

The telephone rang. Barbara jumped and said, " God—I'd forgotten about Pete."

Milne said, " You may sound as though you're knitting, but you don't *look* a bit like it." He lay on the sofa with a fatuous smile as she picked up the receiver.

Barbara said, " Hallo. Yes——? " Her head came round quickly towards Milne. He sat up as he saw her face.

" *Hallo*, darling ! What ? " she looked wildly at Milne. Then she said quickly, " Look, darling, I can't hear. There's a hell of a row going on. Wait a mo' while I switch it off." She put down the telephone, covered the mouthpiece with her hand and said quietly and rather precisely, " That is Pat. She's asking for you. Now what ?—and fast."

Milne said. " Pat ? " He jumped up and put out a hand for the telephone.

Barbara said quickly, " It's O.K. for her to know you're here ? "

Milne said, " Yes. She wouldn't ring unless——"

Barbara said, " All right. Wait a minute." She picked up the telephone and said, " Hallo, Pat ? That's better. What did you say ? Felix ? Yes. He's here. Hold on a mo'."

She handed Milne the receiver in silence. He said, " Hallo, darling."

Pat's voice said, " Look, honey—I've been phoning all over London after you. The police rang up for you about half an hour ago from that man Lucian's house."

" The police ? "

" Yes. They wouldn't tell me what it was all about. But they wanted you urgently. I thought I'd better get you."

" I expect he's pinched another watch," said Milne curtly. " I'll go down and see. Thanks, honey. Cheerio." He put down the receiver and looked at Barbara for a moment. But he did not notice her. His hat and coat were flung across the side-table. He grabbed them and said, " Where's the nearest cab rank ? "

XIV

HE WASTED five desperate minutes hunting for a cab. But there were no cabs, and in the end he half-ran, half-walked to the Underground. He told himself again and again that the police ringing up might mean anything. But this was reason, and there was a coldness inside him that was something a good deal more certain than reason.

In the racket of the train he formulated curt answers to the unspoken questions. Yes, I knew. Yes, I warned her. No, I did not insist. Yes, I saw something was wrong last time. Yes, I let him go. Yes. Yes. And finally, always, grotesquely feeble, " I had a headache."

A fat elderly woman in a fur coat leaned towards him and said, " Would you mind telling me when we get to Victoria ? " He smiled agreeably and nodded and went on smiling mechanically into vacancy. If it had happened, his part in it would look like either criminal negligence or pure lunacy. He tried to decide if it felt like either, but could not. One worked on a guess. There was no other way to work. And if the guess happened to be wrong, there was no way of going back and deciding whether the guess had been justifiable or not.

He realised that he was still smiling and stopped deliberately. The train slowed down. Every few yards there was a sign saying, " Victoria " in large letters. Porters bawled " Victoria." The elderly woman went to the door and said to another passenger, " Is this Victoria ? " She got out, casting an angry backward glance at Milne. He smiled and bowed to her. Technically, the only inexcusable mistake had been to let Lucian go that last time. He had started something and then left it. One should never do that.

In the train he had lost the sense of urgency, but when he got into the street it came back. He half-ran to the block. There was no one in the hall and he went up to the third floor and rang.

A policeman in uniform came to the door.

Milne said, " My name's Milne. I believe you've been trying to get hold of me."

The policeman said, " Oh, yes. Dr. Milne." He had an almost comically refined accent. " The superintendent's round at the hospital. Perhaps it would be best if you were to go round there, Dr. Milne. I know he wanted to see you."

Milne said, What's happened ? Is it Mrs. Lucian ? "

The young man looked at him oddly and hesitated. " Yes," he said, after a moment.

" Is she—all right ? "

The policeman said, " I think probably it would be better if you'd see the inspector, Dr. Milne. The hospital's just round the corner. Sorry, but you understand my position, don't you ? D'you know where it is ? Only a few yards."

The inspector was a grey-haired man in a well-cut blue lounge suit. He looked like a bank manager.

He said, " It's good of you to come along, Dr. Milne."

Milne said, " I'm not a doctor. Is she all right ? "

" Well, no, she's very far from all right. But she's alive. You say you're *not* a doctor ? "

" No. I'm a lay analyst."

" Oh, yes. But you'd been treating him ? Knew his mental state and so on ? "

"Yes. Will she live?"

The inspector shrugged his shoulders. "She's got four nine millimetre Luger bullets through her, poor kid."

Milne said, "He *shot* her?"

The inspector looked up sharply. "Yes. Why?"

"I'm surprised it happened that way."

"But not surprised that he did *something*?" said the inspector.

Milne met his eyes and realised with a sudden shock that he mustn't talk—mustn't say things. He shook his head doubtfully and did not reply.

"We'll have to talk about that later," said the inspector. "*She* told us to get hold of you."

"Where's Lucian himself?"

"We haven't got hold of him yet. He's bolted."

"Bolted? I didn't realise that."

"Yes. Can't have got far. It only happened about nine o'clock." The inspector hesitated. "I'm not quite sure what to do. Earlier on she was very keen to see you and say something. But I'm afraid she may be past it. Hold on a moment while I go and see how it is."

He went out. Milne took off his coat and hat and threw them on the table. He could smell the characteristic hospital smell. She had four nine millimetre Luger bullets through her. He thought of her sitting curled up in the chair. "It's just not on, Mr. Milne." She was going to die, but that wasn't what he was thinking about. Dr. Milne. You were treating him, weren't you? Not surprised that he did *something*? Yes, I let him go. I had a headache and I looked through my fingers and let him go. Let him slip through my fingers.

The inspector came back and said, "I don't think it's much good—not at the moment anyhow. But they say she may have patches when she'd know you. You'd better come in, just in case."

He had thought she would be lying in bed looking beautiful and pathetically small and being brave, but it wasn't like that. She was lying in bed looking ugly and shrunken, and she no longer looked like a child but like a dwarf woman. They had the transfusion apparatus beside her but they weren't working on her for the moment. Her eyes were open and she was conscious. But she was not being sweetly brave. She was groaning, and very frightened.

She said, "Well, I didn't know he'd do it. I didn't know he'd got it. Oh, Christ, do something for me. Quick! Do something." Her head rolled to and fro and she began to groan regularly with her slow breathing. A rather young, very clean-looking doctor walked over to them.

The inspector said in a low voice, "This is Dr. Milne. Mr. Milne. Dr. Hayling. She was asking for him a while back. Think she'll recognise him?"

Hayling said, "Don't know. Can try." He went over to the bed and said quietly, "Look, old dear—here's Mr. Milne. You wanted him to come."

The black head with the dirty yellowish-white face rolled towards him. Milne stepped forward and said, "Hallo, Mollie." There was phlegm in his throat and he gave a little grunt to clear it.

For a moment the regular groaning stopped and she looked at him. But there was nothing in the dark eyes except terror, and after a moment the head rolled and the groaning began again. Hayling looked at her for a moment and then with a jerk of his head took Milne by the arm and led him a few yards away.

"No good at the moment," he said in his clipped undertone. "Not here much. May come out though. Can't guarantee it, but she may. See?"

Milne said, "Is there any chance for her?"

"No," said Hayling promptly. "One was all right. Other three all bastards. All through-and-throughs except one that hit her pelvis. Nine millimetre high velocities."

Milne looked at the rolling yellow face. "Won't be long now?"

"Couple of hours. It won't go on like this long."

She spoke again in a sort of sobbing groan. "I never had a chance. Gee, I didn't know. I never even moved. He didn't look that way. Do something quick. I'm hurt bad. Bad."

Hayling touched Milne's arm. "Try again. Only way. Keep on trying."

He went forward to the bed and bent over her.

"Mollie!" he said sharply. "It's Felix Milne. Milne."

Her eyes came slowly round to him but they wandered away at once. Then they closed tightly and she began to utter queer shrieking regular sobs.

Milne turned quickly away. Hayling said quietly, "Sorry. But that's the only way. Keep trying."

The inspector came over to them. Milne noticed that his face was a curious grey colour. He said to Hayling, "If we talk outside can you call us if——?"

Hayling said, "Sure. If she comes back. May not, of course."

Milne and the inspector went back to the waiting room outside. The inspector took out a cigarette case and they lit cigarettes in silence.

The inspector said, "Bloody business. She's a friend of yours?"

"No—except through her husband being a patient," said Milne. He sat down rather heavily. He was feeling sick.

"Can you help with this at all?" said the grey-haired man. "I take it he's gone crazy?"

Milne said, "Yes. Schizophrenic."

"You were treating him for that?"

"Not exactly. I'm not an alienist."

"But he had some mental trouble? Wasn't normal? That's why he came to you?"

"Yes. He had a bad time in the war. Prisoner with the Japs, and was tortured and so on. It had left him in a mess mentally, and I was trying to clear it up."

"And it'll just have gone wrong suddenly?"

"Yes."

The inspector nodded in silence.

"Had he ever been violent before?" he said after a pause.

Milne hesitated. The grey-haired man said quietly,

"I'm not trying to pump you. I'm only trying to sort it out. But you weren't altogether surprised?"

"It was always on the cards," said Milne dully. "I warned her."

"Oh, you did?"

"Yes."

"That he might attack her?"

"Yes. She wouldn't listen, of course."

"They never will," said the inspector, shaking his head. "I had another case six months ago. Same thing. Woman with her son. Ought to have had him put away of course, and she wouldn't. End of it was he put her in hospital for months. Marvel she's alive."

"Your people'll pick Lucian up easily enough, I suppose?"

"Oh, yes. He can't have got far." He cocked an eye at Milne. "He's still got the gun. At least we haven't found it. He'll use it now, eh? If he gets a chance?"

"I don't know," said Milne slowly. "You can never tell with schizophrenics. But I should doubt it."

"Why? If he's crazy?"

"He probably won't realise that he's done anything wrong. They don't as a rule. You don't want to take any chances though."

"No," said the inspector grimly. "They know that."

Milne said, "He may have killed himself. Quite probable."

"All the better if he has, poor devil," said the inspector curtly. "About the best thing that could happen really." He jerked his head towards the door. "What was he like with her when he was normal? Did they hit it?"

Milne said rather hoarsely, "Oh, yes. She—— He loved her all right."

"It often seems to be like that," said the inspector. "This boy worshipped his mother."

Milne got to his feet and said, "Is there a lavatory anywhere near here, d'you know?"

"Just round to the right," said the inspector. "Second door."

The lavatory smelt strongly of disinfectant but it was cool. He felt sick, but not sick enough to be any use. His mouth was dry and he made a cup of his hands and drank some water. He stood for some minutes leaning against the wall with his eyes shut. But he was afraid Hayling might come for them, so he went back. The inspector was just lighting another cigarette.

" The extraordinary thing about this," he said, as though Milne had never gone out, " was that she got out of the flat and called the porter after he'd shot her."

" With four bullets in her ? "

" Yes, sir. With four bullets in her. The porter found her lying outside her door."

" And he didn't see Lucian ? "

" No. He can't have been gone long. But she'd been shot in the bedroom and I think she'd been unconscious for a bit."

There was a long silence.

The inspector said, " I suppose he must have known there was something wrong with himself, or he wouldn't have come to you ? "

" She made him," said Milne briefly.

" Ah. So she knew ? Even before you warned her ? Of course—you told me he'd threatened her."

Milne said bitterly. " No," he said gently. " I didn't tell you so, and as far as I know he hadn't."

" Ah," said the inspector with a keen glance. " I misunderstood you." He shook his head with a frown. " Then I don't quite see how she knew there was anything wrong."

Milne suddenly felt very tired of it.

" It's not really very deep," he said wearily. " He hadn't threatened her but he'd had at least one previous shot at murdering her and possibly two. That's why she made him come to me."

" Oh," said the inspector. " This wasn't his first go, then ? "

" No."

They looked at one another for a long moment in silence. Then the inspector dropped his eyes and gazed thoughtfully at his cigarette.

" Being wise after the event," he said slowly, " which is always the easy time to be wise—it might have been better if he'd been put away before, mightn't it ? "

" How ? " said Milne shortly. " He wasn't certifiable."

" Not after trying to murder her ? "

" No. It was an isolated thing. He was normal enough most of the time."

" All the same," said the grey-haired man, " if she'd come to us on it, I reckon something could have been fixed. But there you are—they never will."

" She didn't want him locked up. She wanted him cured."

" Oh, sure. That's always the way. They think they're doing a kindness, and then——" He shrugged his shoulders. " Still—you say you warned her ? Told her he was dangerous ? "

" Oh, yes."

" Of course it makes it a bit awkward, your not being a registered doctor," said the inspector bluntly. " It's amazing what you can get away with if you're a doctor. I suppose it's because you've got the whole profession behind you. I never see it myself. I've had too much to do with doctors. But you know what it is."

Milne nodded, but said nothing.

" I'm not suggesting any blame attaches to you," said the inspector hastily. " These things happen, and nobody can really tell, doctor or not. But it's a good thing you warned her."

Hayling came in quickly. He said, " Look—I've got her doped up so that she's not in so much pain now, and I think she's a bit more with us. If you want to try, now's the time." As they hurried along the corridor he said, " I think this is your last chance."

Milne said, " She's going out ? "

" She may last quite a while, but she'll get more dopey now. Mind you, I wouldn't put too much reliance on anything she says. She's only half here."

They went in. She was lying quite still. Hayling said, " Look, old dear—here's Mr. Milne that you wanted to see."

The dark eyes came round and this time they saw him.

Milne said, " Hallo, Mollie. What have they been doing to you? "

She said, " Hallo, Mr. Milne," very slowly and drowsily. Her face creased into a ghost of the old grin, showing her teeth. " How right you were, eh ? "

Milne heard a tiny movement from the inspector at his elbow. The eyes shifted from him to the inspector, and stayed on him for a moment thoughtfully. Her eyebrows flickered and she said slowly, " Mr. Milne here told me this might happen and I didn't believe it."

" Well, you couldn't know, could you ? " said the grey-haired man gently.

" I stuck around," she said drowsily. " But he told me. He's a good guy. He knows it all."

She lay for a moment in silence. Then she frowned. Her eyes roved round until they found Milne again.

" Say, Mr. Milne," she half whispered. " What's going to happen to that boy Adam ? I reckon I'm going to roll up. And then what ? He can't get along much, see ? "

Milne said, " He'll be all right. I'll look after him."

Her face lightened. " That'd be grand if you would," she said more distinctly. " Only he's used to you now." The painful frown reappeared. " You'll have to explain," she said. " Otherwise they won't see. You'll have to tell them he's all right most times, and that you're going to get him right." She closed her eyes. " You sure have done a lot for that boy Adam, Mr. Milne." Her voice was becoming very thick and drowsy. " You want to watch your step," she muttered, " there's nothing to it if you watch your step. Just laugh it off, and keep watching. I was a sap. I wasn't looking. I didn't know he'd got it." The ghost of a smile appeared again. " Don't know what we'll use for money, Mr. Milne. We never got any."

Her eyes opened again and fixed themselves on Milne. " That's O.K., then ? " she said.

" Yes," said Milne. " I'll look after Adam. You go to sleep."

" Fine," she said. Once more she painfully sought and found the inspector. " Mr. Milne here told me," she said very carefully. " He told me I ought to go. But I wouldn't.

I hung around. I would hang around in spite of what he told me."

"Yes, my dear."

"O.K.," said Mrs. Lucian. Her eyes closed and her head rolled slowly away from them. There was a long silence. Hayling stepped forward and looked at her closely.

"I think that's all you'll get," he said quietly.

"Is she gone?" said the inspector in a low voice.

"Oh, no. She may last for quite a bit yet. But I don't think she'll talk any more."

As they turned to the door he said in a low voice to Hayling, "You'll keep her under now? There's no point in——"

Hayling gave his arm a quick pat, opened the door and said "Cheerio."

The inspector lit a cigarette and said, "The car's coming round now. Sit down and have a smoke."

Milne said, "It's very good of you to send me back. I wouldn't bother you but everything will have stopped by now and it's rather a way to walk."

"Oh, that's all right," said the inspector politely. "Good of you to come down."

"They haven't picked him up yet?"

"Not a word. It won't be long though. Takes a bit of time to get everything started." He looked at Milne thoughtfully for a moment. "Nasty business," he said moodily. "Only a kid too, wasn't she? American?"

"She's older than she looks. It's being so small makes her look young."

"War marriage?"

"Yes."

"Got a lot of pluck. Must have, to have stayed with him like that. Turned out wrong, but still——"

Milne said, "She had all the guts there are."

"That's right," said the inspector, turning quickly away. "I think they'll have got the car round by now."

Milne got up and said, "Look—when they find Lucian, you might let me know."

"I will, sir."

"Only if you have any trouble I might be able to help."

The inspector paused. "Yes," he said thoughtfully. "That's true. You mean you can handle him?"

"I don't know. But I'd like to be there if there's any handling to be done."

"Yes. All right. If it comes to that I'll give you a ring. I'll let you know, anyhow."

The car slowed down quickly at a crossroad, jerking him upright. Milne realised that he had been nearly asleep. His head felt thick and heavy, and he remembered that earlier in the evening he had been fairly drunk. He glanced at his watch. That was only just over two hours ago.

He realised that there were other parts of life and deliberately tried to think about them. But they gave him nothing to bite on. He looked at the back of the uniformed driver, and decided that Lucian would undoubtedly be dead by now. If he had been a paranoid it would have been different. But a schizo of Lucian's type would be dead or wandering in a memoryless fugue. Mollie had been his only attachment to life. Killing her would be just a part of getting out. He suddenly realised that he would never know now what had been underneath with Lucian—the real thing that was wrong, apart from the Jap business and so on. That brought him back to the last time, and he went over it again. For the life of him he couldn't see anything wrong with it, up to the point where he had stood and looked through his fingers and let Lucian go. It was just the one, simple, elementary mistake. He had a headache and that killed Mollie.

He became interested in cause and effect, and tried to work back to why he had had a headache, but the car pulled up at the gate. He gave the driver half a crown and the driver said it wasn't necessary and took it and thanked him and the car whined away as he went up the path.

There was a light on in the consulting room. He took off his hat and coat and went in.

Lucian and Patricia were sitting opposite one another by

the fire. They both got up. Patricia smiled at him and said brightly, " Oh, hallo, darling ! We've been waiting for you for ages."

Milne stopped and said, " Hallo, Lucian."

Lucian smiled but did not say anything. He was wearing a black evening overcoat and a dinner jacket. He looked very big and handsome. Pat said, " Mr. Lucian came in to return your stick."

" Oh, you've brought it back at last, you scrounger," said Milne.

" Yes," said Lucian. " It's in the hall. Back where it belongs."

Milne came a few yards nearer. Keeping his eyes on Lucian he turned his head towards Patricia and said reprovingly, " You should have phoned me, darling, and I'd have got back sooner."

Patricia smiled at Lucian. " Well——" she said.

" I was against it," said Lucian gently. " I knew you'd come anyhow."

" He's told me all about it," said Patricia. " I told him you'd gone down to see."

" Oh, yes," said Milne. He noticed that Lucian had moved slightly so that the arm of his chair was now between them.

" I'm sorry to have bothered Mrs. Milne," said Lucian easily. " But she's been most kind and understanding." He flashed an intimate glance at Patricia and said, " I think you see now, even if nobody else does."

" Of course I do," said Patricia, smiling back at him. " Give me a cigarette, darling."

" Sure," said Milne. He offered his case. Lucian shook his head with a smile. Patricia took a cigarette and Milne lit it for her. The flame flickered slightly but the cigarette was as steady as a rock.

Lucian said rather pompously, " I had to come and inflict this tedious tale on Mrs. Milne in case I had to go before you arrived. You know of course that I've killed women, and though other people can think other things, I thought you ought to know because you always wish to know. So I trespassed on Mrs. Milne's great kindness——"

" Of course," said Milne, " I want to hear all about it. By the way, have you still got that gun ? "

" Yes," said Lucian briefly.

" What is it ? A Luger ? "

" Yes," said Lucian, putting his hand in the right-hand pocket of his overcoat.

" Well, you'd better give it to me, hadn't you ? "

Lucian said, " It's back in its proper place in the hall."

" No, it isn't. It's in your pocket.

" We're talking about different things," said Lucian. " Anyhow it's not important."

Milne shrugged his shoulders. " All right," he said indifferently. " By the way, if you've heard the story before, Pat, you'd better get off to bed. It's late." He turned to Lucian. " You don't mind if Pat goes and leaves us to talk ? "

Lucian frowned. " But she'll ring up the police," he said peevishly.

" What if she does ? You'll have to explain it all to them sooner or later. I should have thought it would be a good idea to get them along now."

" No," said Lucian with a cunning smile. " She'll go out of here, pretending to go to bed, and she'll ring up the police." He shook his head knowingly at Pat. " You see, I know about women. Not that you haven't been very kind, Mrs. Milne." He leant back in his chair with his hands in his overcoat pockets. " This is all quite clear now," he said. " In some ways it's a pity it wasn't clear before. My father gave her a terrible time, but I loved her very much. I was only a child, of course. Nevertheless she was unfaithful to me with him, so I killed him first and then I shot her. You'll agree that that was reasonable ? In France I believe they recognise it. Crime passionel and so on."

Milne said, " How long ago was it that you shot her ? "

" Oh, it's years ago now." He smiled rather crookedly. " The interesting thing is that if she hadn't been unfaithful to me with him I should never have been born." He looked at Patricia. " Mrs. Milne pointed that out to me."

" What I didn't quite see, Mr. Lucian," said Pat calmly,

"was how Mollie came into it. I quite understand about your mother. But——"

Lucian's face seemed to crumple. "I don't wish to talk about Mollie," he said painfully. "She was a grand kid and anybody who says anything different is a damn liar." He turned to Milne. "You know what I thought about her, Felix. He worshipped that girl." He chuckled suddenly. "Of course what was funny was your taking all that trouble over the Japanese business, which wasn't of the slightest importance."

"I thought it probably wasn't the whole story," said Milne. "I suppose you didn't feel like telling me all this before?"

"No," said Lucian, frowning. "Not until it was cleared up." He looked at Patricia again with the queer intimate smile. "I'm really not telling you the story as well as I told it to Mrs. Milne. She understood, being a woman." He paused and added, "Look, I don't want to bore you, Mrs. Milne. Please go to bed if you're tired."

Patricia hesitated, still smiling mechanically. "Wouldn't you mind?" she said. "I am a bit sleepy."

"Of course not," said Lucian promptly, rising. His hands were still in his overcoat pockets. Milne got up too, edging a little closer.

"All right then. I'll say good-night," said Patricia. Lucian bowed. "Good-night, darling," she said, turning to Milne.

"Good-night," he said. He caught her hand for a moment and pressed it. His eyes never left Lucian. As she went he moved between them. Lucian stood quite still until the door had closed behind her. Then he turned away with a chuckle.

"I'll bet you five bob she goes straight away and rings up the police," he said, looking at Milne with a boyish grin. "They're all the same. But she was very nice to me. Very nice. I was a bit taken aback when I found you weren't here. I didn't know quite what to do. We'd never met, you see. But she put me at ease at once." He paused and shook his head. "But she'll try to ring up now. They're all the same. No principles. I knew of course, but she watched me like a cat watching a mouse, so what could I do?" He sighed and took the Luger out of his pocket.

Milne said, " Give me that, Lucian."

" This?" said Lucian. " Sure." He changed the big automatic into his left hand and held it out. At the same time he swung a blow at Milne's head with his right fist. Milne saw it coming rather late, but dropped his head in time to take it on his skull instead of on his jaw. Even so, it sent him staggering backwards. He tripped against a chair and went down heavily.

Lucian shouted, " Sorry, doc. Sorry, doc!" and rushed to the french window. He still had the automatic in his left hand and he fumbled for a moment with the bolts. As Milne staggered to his feet he got the window open and dashed out. Patricia was standing in the doorway, very white.

Milne yelled, " Lights out, ass!" She hesitated for a moment and then it was dark. Her voice said breathlessly, " Felix—are you all right?"

" Yes," said Milne. " Keep to the side." He felt very dizzy. He said, " Damn it!" and staggered over to the open window. Patricia grabbed his arm and said, " No. Not in the dark." He stood and listened but there was complete silence outside. He said heavily, " To hell with it. I was slow. But I couldn't be sure which way it was going to break."

The inspector said, " How the hell did he get up there anyhow?" He tilted his black Homburg on to the back of his head and gazed at the huge office block discontentedly. The young sergeant said, " There's a fire escape down that side. He must have gone up that and then walked along the ledge."

" Then he's crazy all right," said the inspector drily. " No doubt about that anyhow."

" I haven't tried to get out to him," said the sergeant rather apologetically. " I thought I'd wait till you came. But I reckon if I could get out of one of the windows just above, I could drop down and work my way along and round to him."

" Well, you're not going to, son. He's crazy, and he's

got a gun. We don't want to go getting anybody killed. Let him sweat for a bit until it's lighter and we can see what we're doing."

"I don't think he'll *fall*," said the sergeant. "He's safe enough now he's got there."

Milne said, "I think he may quite well jump."

The inspector shrugged. "Well, if he does that'll save us the job of going and getting him," he said calmly.

"Can you do anything about catching him? Net or something?"

"The fire people'll do that. They'll be here any time. They're bringing a floodlight too, so we'll be able to see what we're doing."

They stood in silence for a moment, gazing upwards. In the half-light Milne could just see the dark patch of Lucian's figure against the white stone of the big building.

Milne said, "Has he got his back to us? It looks like it."

"Yes, sir. There's a parapet running along, and then a sort of niche goes in. I suppose it was to put a statue in or something. It's the same right the way down to the second floor. He's sitting on the parapet with his back to us. I don't reckon he'll fall unless he overbalances."

"Does he know you're here?"

"I think so. I've shouted to him from here, and I went up inside and shouted to him out of the window. Of course I couldn't see him because he's round the corner. He didn't answer, but he must have heard."

"He didn't say anything?"

"Not a word. Never even moved since I've been here."

It was growing lighter rapidly. Milne could make out Lucian's back more clearly now. He seemed to be sitting quite still, with his head sunk forward. He looked very small up there, and incredibly lonely.

Milne said suddenly, "I think I must get up to him."

"You can't do it, sir," said the sergeant, shaking his head. "He's on the sheer wall, see."

"I could go up the fire escape and round, like you said."

The sergeant smiled. "I wouldn't try that, sir," he said gently. "It'd be a tricky climb even if you're used to scrambling about on places. I'll go if you reckon someone ought to," he added simply.

"*No*," said the inspector irritably. "Nobody's going to break his neck for the sake of quarter of an hour. I tell you he's got a gun, and he's as like as not to shoot you if you did get up there."

"I don't think he'll shoot me," said Milne. "And I might be able to get him to come down."

"Well, what if you do?" said the inspector bluntly. They looked at one another for a moment in silence. The inspector shook his head and turned away. "It's not worth risking a good chap's life for any good that it'd do us. Or any good that it'd do him, poor devil." He turned to the sergeant and snapped, "Go and see where the hell the fire people are."

Milne looked up at the small figure perched on the face of the white building, and as he did so it moved. The back straightened and the sunk head came up and back as though Lucian was looking upwards. Then the head slowly sank and the back bent into the same position as before. It was a movement of utter weariness.

He made up his mind. He turned to the inspector and said, "Look, I'm sorry, but I can't just let him stay up there. It's all right for you, but he's my patient. If I hadn't let him go this wouldn't have happened." He stopped and added shamefacedly, "You do see, don't you?"

The inspector shook his head and said irritably, "That's all very well, Mr. Milne, but——"

"And anyhow," said Milne quickly, "even when you've got everything and everybody here, he's still got a gun and somebody'll still have to go up and take a chance of being shot. Far better let me talk to him."

The inspector hesitated. "I don't mind your *talking* to him if you think it'll do any good. As long as you don't go trying to get out there. How about going up inside and calling to him? Maybe he'll take some notice of you."

"I doubt that'll do it," said Milne thoughtfully. "But it's worth trying."

They went into a big room that looked like a drawing

office. There were tables and drawing boards all over the place.

The sergeant said, " This is the top floor. He's just below this, round the corner there."

" How far round ? "

" About twenty yards, I should think. If you give him a shout out of the window I think he's bound to hear you."

Milne went to the end window and opened it. About seven feet below was a gutterway with a narrow parapet. The whole thing was only about a foot wide. Ten feet beyond the window to the left was the corner of the building. Milne glanced down. A hundred feet below, and directly beneath him, a policeman was standing in small but perfect plan view.

Milne said, " He can't have gone along that. He'd never have got round the corner."

" Must have," said the inspector. " There's no other way."

Milne leant out and shouted, " Lucian ! " His voice was hoarse and cracked. He saw a white flicker as the policeman below looked up. There was no reply. He cleared his throat and shouted, " Lucian ! This is Felix Milne. Can you hear me ? " There was still no reply. He waited for a long time, but all he heard was a distant clanging.

The sergeant said, " That's the fire people."

" Shut up ! " said Milne, still listening tensely.

After a long pause he drew his head in and said, " Not a sound. I think he must have heard, don't you ? "

" It was just the same when I tried it," said the sergeant.

Milne said, " I'll have one more go." He leant out again and was about to call when he heard a sound. It seemed almost uncannily near, and it was a queer, muffled, choking noise. For a moment he could not understand what it was. Then he recognised it. He gave a sudden gulp and began to shout, " It's all right, old boy ! It's all right ! Hang on a minute. I'm coming to you."

He turned back into the room and said, " Get me a rope down from the roof. I'm going round."

" Now, listen," said the inspector.

Milne said, " God damn and blast it. Get me a rope down or I'll go without it. Can't you hear ? "

A bell clanged below.

The sergeant said, " Here we are. They'll have ladders."

The sun was just rising and the top of the building was in sunshine. Lucian was just below the rim of shadow. He was still sitting in the same position. The top of the ladder was only a few feet from him but he had not looked round.

The officer looked at Milne curiously and said, " Have you been up one of these things before ? "

Milne shook his head.

" Well, the main thing is to go slow and steady. Remember it's a long way up. Stop and rest when you feel like it. Keep your head up and don't try to look at your feet. You'll be all right as long as you take it steady. Hook on your belt when you stop." He turned to the inspector. " Be better really if he had someone behind him, y'know."

" He says not," said the inspector briefly.

" He's more likely to come if it's only me," said Milne.

" As you like," said the fireman, shrugging.

" O.K., sir," said the inspector without enthusiasm. "It's all yours. But for goodness' sake don't get too close to him. Not where he can reach you. You keep out of reach and you'll be all right. We've got him taped from down here if he tries shooting."

Milne nodded, wiped the palms of his hands on his trousers and walked forward. At the foot of the ladder he turned his head and said, " I shall try to get him to come down. If he won't, I'll try and keep him talking while somebody else gets up. I still think you'd be better from the roof."

As he started, he heard the inspector mutter savagely to the fire officer, " Now, if he doesn't fall off and break his bloody neck, or get a bullet in him, we're just about as far as we were before."

" He may do the trick," said the fireman cheerfully. " He's got guts to try, anyhow."

" Oh, he's got guts," said the inspector moodily. " But the other bloke's got a gun."

He had always been afraid of heights and climbing, and

for a man of his moderate size and weight he was clumsy. Being afraid, he kept his body in too close to the ladder, so that there was no room for his knees to bend as he climbed. He had to bring his feet out and round with an awkward, splay-footed movement. The temptation to look down to see that his foot was firmly on the next rung was strong, but he remembered the warning and kept his head rigidly level.

But if it would have been frightening to look down, it was nearly as frightening to look straight ahead. Always before when he had climbed a ladder, the wall had been comfortingly close. This time it was far away. He was alone in space. He had not reckoned with the ladder being so far from the wall. It brought a sudden qualm of helplessness and sickness, and in desperation he threw his head back and looked upwards. The rungs of the ladder rushed away from him in frightening perspective. But looking upwards he could forget his awkwardly-groping feet, and at the top, just to the left, he could see the fore-shortened black square of Lucian's back, which steadied him slightly.

He was between the second and third floors now. Despite the fireman's warning he had climbed as quickly as he could, and he was beginning to pant. Once he did not raise his foot far enough, and his toe kicked against the rung, sending a jar through his whole body as he tightened up convulsively. His thigh muscles shook as he shifted the weight from one leg to another, and he stopped for a moment to rest.

This was a mistake. He was level with the top of the third floor windows, and instinctively his eye followed the line of them along the face of the building and down to the ground below. He gave a little grunt of terror and shut his eyes, leaning his body closely against the ladder. For a moment nothing seemed to work, except his hands clinging convulsively to the metal, and he seemed suspended by them. But his mind slowly came back from the space beneath him, and he could tell himself that there was no more danger of falling than there had been in the first half-dozen rungs, and that what he was doing was just walking up a particularly safe, strong ladder.

But even so it was difficult to start again, because he did

not want to open his eyes, or shift his hands from their cramped hold. He was safe enough if he did not move, but if he moved he would fall. He did not want to go down again. It never entered his head. He only wanted to stay still and safe with his eyes shut. His feet were all right, and he shifted one up to the next rung. His hands moved up automatically, and so did the next foot, and then he realised that he got on just as well with his eyes shut, and went on like that, counting the rungs as he climbed.

He had counted fifty since he stopped and he knew he must be near the top. The ladder was whipping a little now and his hands were aching dully but he was quite all right—far better than he had been before. The only trouble was that he could not stop and open his eyes or he would fall. He had a grotesque vision of climbing conscientiously to the top and off into space with his eyes shut.

He heard some sort of shout from the ground and knew he must be near, and threw back his head and opened his eyes, still climbing. He was close into the wall and there was a buttress with pigeon droppings all over it, and about ten feet above him was Lucian's back. His black overcoat looked green and shabby because the sun was full on it now. He was sitting quite still with his head in his hands.

Milne felt drunk but not at all frightened and rather happy. He said, " Lucian."

Lucian said, " Yes ? " without moving.

" This is Felix."

" Yes."

Milne said, " I've come to get you down. There's nothing to worry about. I'll look after you."

" Yes," said Lucian. He still hadn't moved.

" I'll stay here with you, and they'll send up and get both of us."

He suddenly realised that he didn't know quite how. He said foolishly, " You're all right, aren't you ? "

" Yes," said Lucian again. He took his head from his hands and sat up, but did not turn round.

He said, " It was the only thing to do. I quite realise that it will be misunderstood. But what does that matter ? Standing there naked he was magnificent."

"You've given me a hell of a climb," said Milne cheerfully. "How did you get here anyway?"

Lucian said, "I bashed his skull in and then shot her. His skull didn't crush. The stick bounced off it and stung my hands." He suddenly slumped forward and said, "The bitch went to bed with him," and started to cry.

"Never mind," said Milne quietly. "It's all over now." He heard a scuffle above him. They were up there, but he could see nothing but the sharp unbroken edge of the roof against the sky. He raised his voice so that they could hear, and said, "I should think you'll be glad to get down. You must be pretty cold."

Lucian stopped crying and said, "Yes."

"You can't reach this ladder or you could have come down with me. Do you mind ladders? I hate the damned things. Scare me stiff."

There was more scrambling above and a voice said, "To your right. Your *right*."

Lucian's head came up sharply. He said, "Felix?" in quite a different voice.

Milne said, "Yes, squire?"

"There's a thing I want to ask you before we go down. Privately."

"Yes?"

There was a long pause and then Lucian said, "You don't think it hurt her?"

Milne said, "Oh, Lord, no. She never felt anything."

Lucian turned his head sharply. "You're sure of that?" he said with a queer hesitant smile. His face was white but strangely smooth.

"Quite sure."

"That's fine," said Lucian. "Then we'll go down now." He stood up. Milne said, "Wait——" but Lucian brought the automatic up like a flash and seemed to fire as it was coming up. His body swayed backwards and then fell forward again awkwardly into the niche with the side of his face jammed against the wall.

Milne looked at him dully and then shut his eyes and leaned wearily against the ladder. He was quite all right as long as he stayed still, but he didn't see how he was going to get down. They were shouting on the roof. He kept his eyes shut and called, " All right. No hurry now."

The sergeant gave him the letter as he was getting into the car, but he hardly noticed, and forgot it until they were almost home. Then he put his hand in his pocket and found it. It was addressed to Dr. Felix Milne. He was hurt about that, but of course Lucian hadn't written it at the end. He tore it open, and inside were four pound notes and two ten shilling notes. He looked at them for a moment and then put them back in the envelope, put it in his pocket and shut his eyes. He had been up all night and was very sleepy.

XV

" YES," said Mr. Grandison. " Yes. I see. What a very sad business." He blew out his cheeks, held them distended for a moment and then gave one side of his face a sharp pat, like a man bursting a paper bag. " I often think that's one of the worst aspects of war," he said thoughtfully. " Not only the tragedies that it causes directly, but the tragedies it leaves behind it." He tilted his head back and with his sharp nose in the air looked at Milne calmly. He wore glasses which were not round, but semi-circular. The idea presumably was that he could look through them to read and over them when he was not reading. In practice he looked at people through them and read over them.

Milne said, " It's only fair to tell you that I didn't wish to be represented. But my wife was very keen on it. So——"

" Ah," said Mr. Grandison. He dropped his chin on his chest, peered over his glasses at his notes and shook his head. " Well, Mr. Milne, I must say I think it's a wise decision. A very wise decision. That's the trouble with a coroner's court. You never know. In a court of law you know where you are. At an inquest you don't."

" The facts are clear enough," said Milne wearily.

" Ah, yes. I don't doubt they are. It's the coroner's job to determine the cause of death. From what you've told me there's no doubt what his verdict will be. He murdered her and took his own life while the balance of his mind was disturbed and there you are. No more to be said. But in *arriving* at that verdict, Mr. Milne——" He shook his head again. " That's what we've got to watch."

Milne got up and walked over to the window. After a moment's pause he said slowly, " I'm definitely not prepared to do anything just to avoid criticism."

" Oh, quite," said Mr. Grandison drily. " As long as it's justifiable. But I take it you don't want to be criticised just for the fun of it ? "

" You think that's likely ? "

Mr. Grandison blew himself into a paper bag and exploded himself. " In a case like this," he said, " you may get criticism—or at least insinuation—from two sources. His or her relatives. Or the coroner."

Milne shrugged his shoulders. " Well ? " he said sullenly.

" Oh come, Mr. Milne," said Grandison rather irritably, cocking his head back at an extreme angle. " You're a professional man. I take it you did your best for this young man ? "

" Yes."

" Well then, you owe it to yourself to show that you did. You're not conscious of having made any mistake—in the light of what you knew at the time ? "

Milne hesitated. " No."

" Very well. That's all I'm saying. When anybody dies suddenly, Mr. Milne, you can take it for granted that the relatives will think somebody's to blame. And usually it's the unfortunate doctor. They may not attack you. I'm not saying they will. But they might—particularly the *wife's* relatives."

" I don't know whether she had any relatives over here. She was an American."

" I see. Well, anyhow that's one thing that must be watched. The other thing is the coroner. His job is to determine the cause of death. But if he thinks there's any blame attaching to any one, he can say so." He blew up and exploded again. " Lefage—the coroner in this instance—is a doctor," he added briefly.

Milne turned away from the window. " Oh, is he ? "

" Yes. He's a doctor. Very much so. He's also an extremely awkward person. You see what I mean, Mr. Milne ? "

" Oh, yes. I see what you mean all right."

" Right," said Mr. Grandison briskly, tucking his chin well in and peering at his notes. " Well now, my job is to *watch* the proceedings on your behalf. I don't ' appear ' for you. In fact I'm only there by the coroner's courtesy. And if everything goes smoothly I just sit quite quietly through it and never say a word. And afterwards——" he gave a little giggle, " I collect my fee and that's all. *But*——" He threw his head back and wagged a finger. " *But*—if anything that's said in evidence appears to be reflecting on my client—yourself—either professionally or personally, then I get up and I ask permission to put questions and—and generally deal with it."

" Yes," said Milne patiently.

" Now I take it your evidence will be that this couldn't have been foreseen—that there was nothing to suggest that he'd go mad—that it was one of those unfortunate things that no human skill can avoid ? "

" My evidence," said Milne wearily, " will be that I didn't foresee it, that the evidence that he'd go mad wasn't conclusive and that I hadn't enough skill to prevent it."

" Yes. Yes, I dare say," said Mr. Grandison shortly. " But you'll have to take a stronger line than that in court, won't you ? *I* see what you mean. But to the average man that just sounds as though you think you were to blame."

" I'm not at all sure that I don't."

" You'd said you'd made no mistake ? "

" Jesus Christ," said Milne without heat. " The man's dead and so's his wife. He was my patient. I'm not conscious of having made any particular positive mistake—not one I could know about anyhow. But I'm damned if I'm going to say that no human skill could have saved him. I leave that sort of thing to the doctors. If they leave a swab in a man and it kills him they'll always go into court and say it was only superhuman skill that kept it from being a case of instruments. But I'm not a doctor and so I don't have to be infallible. I did my best for Lucian and it wasn't enough. That's all there was to it, and if anybody wants to make more out of it than that, they're welcome."

There was a long pause. Mr. Grandison blew himself up and exploded thoughtfully.

"Yes," he said rather dispiritedly, "I think we're really saying the same thing. It's a matter of phraseology." He picked up his notes. "Now could we just run through this again and make sure that I've got the facts right?"

The court was in a back street, in what looked like a disused schoolroom. As they were going in Patricia said, "Hallo—there's Jim Garsten."

Garsten came over to them. He was wearing a black coat and striped trousers. With his silver hair he looked almost vulgarly distinguished.

He said, "Hallo, Pat. Hallo, Felix. I hear we've got old man Lefage for this business."

Milne said sarcastically, "You've come in the wrong clothes. This is an inquest, not a wedding."

Garsten took no notice. He said, "Are they calling you, Pat?"

"We're not sure yet. They don't think so, but I was warned to be here."

"Yes, of course. You had quite a bit of time with him alone, didn't you?" He glanced round with a slight frown. "Listen, Felix," he said in a low voice, "this old boy Lefage is rather a perisher. You know he's a doctor?"

"Yes."

"Well, he's the wrong sort of doctor, and he might go awkward. On the other hand I think he's honest. The main thing to do is to keep your temper and don't let him rattle you." He smiled slightly. "There's no real need to tell you that, because you don't get hot under the collar like I do. But he can be a bit of a bastard. Just don't let him draw you."

"No," said Milne. He was not listening much. His eyes were wandering round the dingy little room. He watched a man sharpening a pencil. It broke twice before he could get a point on it. He had a notebook and Milne decided that he was a reporter.

He realised that Grandison had appeared and was talking to Pat. He and Garsten were standing alone. He must say something to Garsten. He said shortly, " Why did you come? "

Garsten smiled slightly. " Just technical interest. Mixed with morbid curiosity."

There was a long silence.

Garsten said, " I think you and Pat have to sit over there. See you later."

The coroner looked very old. He wore a stand-up collar with a black tie threaded through a ring, and his neck was very thin and stringy and waxy in colour. The remaining hair round his temples was quite white, and he had bushy grey eyebrows that reminded Milne vaguely of Freethorne. He came in as though he was in a tremendous hurry.

When Milne noticed him again the coroner waved a hand towards where Grandison was sitting and said, " Now—if I could just know who's who." His voice was very hoarse. Milne waited for him to clear his throat but he didn't.

A rather handsome man with wavy hair who was sitting next to Grandison got up and said, " My name is May, sir. I am here, by your courtesy, on behalf of Mr. Ogden Lucian, next of kin."

" Father? " said the coroner curtly.

" Uncle, sir."

" You barrister? "

" Yes, sir."

" Yes? " said the coroner, writing.

Grandison rose. " William Grandison, sir," he said, tilting back his head.

" Yes," said the coroner. " You're solicitor, aren't you? Who you for, Mr. Grandison? "

" Mr. Felix Milne, sir."

" Ah, yes, Mr. Milne. Any one else? "

A tall man in dark glasses rose and said loudly, " Parkinson, Solicitor. I am here, by your courtesy, sir, on behalf of the City and Home Counties Syndicate."

" On behalf of *who*? " said the coroner, looking up with a frown.

" The City and Home Counties Syndicate."

" How they come into it ? "

" Some of the events took place on their premises, sir."

" Oh," said the coroner in a sort of derisive growl. " All right, Mr.—Mr.——"

" Parkinson."

" Yes. Anybody else ? Right." The coroner took his watch out of his pocket and laid it on the desk. " Right," he said again. He still didn't clear his throat.

In the slight pause that followed the sitting down of Mr. Ogden Lucian, Milne knew for the first time that there was something slightly wrong. It was not that his mind was wandering. In fact he was seeing and hearing as acutely as he had ever done in his life. But his attention was highly selective, and he realised uncomfortably that it was selecting the wrong things. He had noted every detail of Mr. Ogden Lucian's appearance and every inflection of his voice. He had decided that Mr. Ogden Lucian was one of those civilians who look and dress so like a caricature of retired army men that they cannot possibly have ever been soldiers. He had noted the black tie, the bowler hat, and the general solemn but restrained air of grief usually reserved for the funerals of fairly distant relatives. He had also observed the coroner and reached conclusions about his blood pressure, his home life and his parents. But he had no clear recollection of what the coroner had asked Mr. Lucian, or of what Mr. Lucian had told the coroner.

This alarmed him. He turned to Pat and whispered, " I'm not really taking this in." She did not catch it and said, " What, darling ? " But another man had appeared, and Milne did not reply. Pat squeezed his arm, and he pressed her hand against his side and leant forward with his chin in his hands and tried to listen whilst the police surgeon explained why a woman with four bullets in her body and a man with his brains blown out should have died.

The inspector still looked like a bank manager, and the coroner called him " Inspector " and seemed to know him. But it was not until he said, " She kept calling for Mr.

Milne" and the coroner said, "Milne?" that there was any coherent thread.

The coroner said, "Oh, yes. He was the psychologist—or psycho-analyst, wasn't he? Well—she asked for him?"

"Yes, sir. She gave me his telephone number and I rang him up. Mr. Milne was out, but Mrs. Milne said she would try to get a message to him. Meanwhile we took Mrs. Lucian to hospital. By the time we arrived she was unconscious again."

"Wait a minute. You're going too fast," said the coroner huskily. For the twentieth time Milne waited agonisedly for him to clear his throat, but he did not. Instead he wrote what appeared to be one word, looked up and said sharply, "Well? Go on."

"She rallied after the transfusion but made no further statement for some time. She was conscious but not rational. She kept repeating that she hadn't had a chance and hadn't known he'd got it."

"Got what?"

"I imagine the pistol, sir."

"Well, then, she did make a statement, didn't she?"

"If you like to call it that, sir."

"What else can you call it? She said again that she didn't know he'd got the pistol and hadn't a chance. That's a statement, isn't it? All right, go on."

"Then Mr. Milne arrived."

"Yes," said Mr. Lefage irritably. "Don't keep stopping, inspector. Just go on with your evidence. I'll stop you if I want to."

The inspector's eyebrows rose slightly.

"Very well, sir," he said calmly. "Mr. Milne arrived and was taken in to her——"

"I didn't suppose he was left outside. Let's stick to the essentials, inspector, or we shall be all night."

"Mr. Milne," said the inspector expressionlessly, "spoke to her several times but she did not recognise him. We went outside and it was in conversation with Mr. Milne that I first learnt that Mrs. Lucian had been attacked by her husband before."

The coroner's head came up sharply. "Before this affair?"

"Yes, sir."

"She hadn't said so."

"No, sir. Mr. Milne also told me——"

"Never mind that," said the coroner, waving a hand. "We shall have his evidence later. What happened next?"

"We were told that she was quieter and might recognise Mr. Milne. We returned to her and she recognised him and talked to him. She was worried about what would happen to her husband if she died." He hesitated. "I don't think she fully realised the situation, sir."

"How d'you mean?"

"She seemed to think that somebody might be able to—to explain what had happened and excuse it. Mr. Milne promised to look after her husband. She seemed very relieved."

"Look after him?" said the coroner, looking up.

"Yes, sir."

The coroner's small mouth twisted slightly but he made no comment.

"She then addressed me and said that Mr. Milne had warned her that this might happen and that she hadn't taken any notice."

"She said that?" said the coroner sharply.

"Yes, sir. She said that twice. It corresponded with what Mr. Milne had told me."

The coroner made a note. "All right. What else did she say?"

"Nothing else, sir. She then became unconscious and I understand remained unconscious till she died."

"Right. Then that's the end of that part. Now you may as well carry us straight on. Next thing was you got a phone call from Mrs. Milne?"

"Yes, sir. The deceased man had gone to Mr. Milne's house."

"Yes. Well, we'll have what happened there later. Next time you saw him was on the roof?"

"On the ledge, sir."

"Yes. On the ledge. All right. Go on from there."

The room was very cold. An icy draught seemed to blow along the floor. Milne's head was hot, but his feet were numbed with cold. He saw the military-looking Mr. Lucian pull his black coat more closely around him. Pat's hand on his arm was trembling slightly as though she was shivering. He wondered vaguely why she had not worn the ermine coat and then reflected that perhaps one couldn't very well go to an inquest in an ermine coat. But if not, why not?

The inspector said, "Mr. Milne," again, and the coroner repeated "Mr. Milne?" again with that husky question mark.

"He went up? Why'd he go up? Job for the police, wasn't it? Or the firemen?"

The inspector said, "He thought he might be able to persuade him to come down. He was the only person there that Mr. Lucian knew. I didn't feel justified in stopping him."

The coroner gave a little grunt. "Looked pretty funny if he'd got a bullet in him, wouldn't it?"

"I thought the risk was justifiable. Mr. Milne was very keen to go up."

"Dare say he was. But it wasn't a question of what he wanted, was it? Still—he went up. Then what?"

"While Mr. Milne was going up I sent men on to the roof with ropes. Mr. Milne reached the top of the ladder and stood on it for some minutes. He appeared to be talking to the deceased, who hadn't moved. Then the deceased suddenly turned round and appeared to say something. Then I heard a shot and saw him fall forward against the building."

The coroner stared at him for a moment and then gave a curt nod and threw down his pen. "All right. We'll get what Mr. Milne said to him and what he said to Mr. Milne later. All you know is that Mr. Milne went up to make him see reason and he promptly shot himself."

There was a sharp little movement beside Milne, which seemed somehow to run all round the court.

The inspector flushed slightly. "I should like to add, sir," he said stiffly, "that throughout Mr. Milne showed the greatest concern for his patient."

"I'm sure he did," said the coroner off-handedly. "But

I'm not talking about Mr. Milne. I'm talking about what happened. Those are the facts, aren't they? All right then, inspector. Now then——" he waved a hand towards the solicitors. "Any of you gentlemen——?"

Mr. Grandison rose.

"I should like to put just two questions to the witness, sir, if I may?"

"Go ahead Mr.—Mr.——"

Grandison turned to the inspector. "I should like to ask the inspector," he said, speaking almost comically slowly, "what Mrs. Lucian's attitude towards Mr. Milne appeared to be? I mean was it one of trust and confidence?"

"Very much so, sir."

"I see. And then over the last incident. Do you consider that in going up the ladder Mr. Milne took any risk?"

"Yes, sir. I consider he took a grave risk."

"I see. His action, in fact, was that of a brave and conscientious man?"

"Yes, sir. It was."

"If it'll save any time," said the coroner restlessly, "your point's quite taken, Mr.—Mr.——"

"I merely wished it to be clear, sir——"

"Quite. Quite. That's all right. Got it down here. Now—any of you other gentlemen?"

The tall man in dark glasses leapt to his feet with startling suddenness and said very loudly indeed, "You received every proper courtesy and help from the staff of the City and Home Counties Syndicate?"

The inspector looked a trifle startled.

"He means the night watchman," said the coroner sardonically. "He wasn't asleep, was he?"

"Not when I saw him, sir."

"That's all right, then." The coroner waved a hand. "There's no suggestion against your clients, Mr.—Mr.——"

"Parkinson," said the tall man in a sort of hoot, sitting down as though someone had struck him behind the knees.

It was his turn at last, though it had been a long time coming. It seemed as though he could hardly remember a time when he had not been sitting there bullying himself into attention, like a sleepy man trying to keep his eyes open. He was cold and cramped, and it was good to stand up and stretch himself. He glanced round the court and caught sight of Garsten's silver hair, and smiled vaguely and foolishly in Garsten's direction.

The coroner said hoarsely, " Now, Mr. Milne, if I might have your attention——"

He brought his eyes back quickly and found himself looking at the coroner with a mixture of fear and courage and contempt—a mixture that reminded him of school. That was because the thin, stringy neck and the angry grey eyes reminded him of—of—— He was a Scotsman and he taught history. It was a Scots name but he could not remember it.

The coroner said, " You are Mr. Felix Milne ? "

He started to say yes, he was, but his voice cracked and he gave a little cough to clear his throat. The coroner never cleared his throat, though it always sounded as though he would at any moment.

" You're a psycho-analyst or a psychiatrist or some sort of consultant on mental trouble ? "

" Yes. I'm an analyst."

" You're not medically qualified ? "

" No."

" In fact you're a—a—— ? "

" I'm a quack," said Milne stonily.

The coroner looked at him unsmilingly. " Well, you said it. I didn't. I was going to say a lay practitioner. Anyhow people consult you and you treat them ? "

" Yes."

" Right. Well now, I shall have to ask you a few things about yourself. You mustn't mind this, Mr. Milne. After all, you're being put before me as an expert witness on this man's mental state, and I've got to satisfy myself about the value of your opinion. Now, what training have you had for this work you do ? "

" Training ? " said Milne stupidly. He had lost the thread for a moment.

" Yes. Were you trained for this work or d'you just do it by the light or nature of what ? "

"I was at Cambridge," said Milne slowly. "I was an exhibitioner in science. I read medicine. After my third year I went to Vienna instead of going on with the usual medical course. I studied under Loewe."

"Loewe? He's a psycho-analyst?"

"Yes. I worked in his clinic for two years."

"Is he a doctor?"

"Loewe?" Milne smiled slightly. "Oh, yes. He's pretty nearly everything you can be from that point of view."

The coroner stirred slightly irritably. "All right," he said. "You mustn't mind these questions. I've got to ask them." He swept aside the protests that no one had made almost with anger. "Anyhow, this man Lucian came to you?"

"Yes."

"D'you know why he came?"

"His wife suggested it."

"Ah," said the coroner, making a note.

"I think she chose me because I wasn't a doctor. Lucian hated doctors."

"Why did she want him to see anybody? What was the matter with him?"

"She said he'd tried to strangle her."

"I see." The coroner stared at him for a moment with the angry grey eyes. "You didn't hesitate to take him on as a patient, in spite of that?"

"I hesitated a lot."

"Still—you took him on?"

"Yes," said Milne wearily.

"Right. Well, what did you think of him when you saw him?"

"I liked him," said Milne vaguely. He pulled himself up with a jerk and added, "I formed the opinion that he was markedly schizoid."

"You mean he suffered from split mind, as they call it?"

"No, I don't mean that he had schizophrenia. But he had most of the symptoms of a schizoid."

"What symptoms?"

"He was—withdrawn. Apathetic. He showed very little interest in things—and so on."

"And these symptoms might get worse?"

"Yes."

"It didn't occur to you that a man who'd tried to murder his wife and showed symptoms of madness might be dangerous to play about with?"

Milne felt himself flushing slightly. "It occurred to me that he might become dangerous. I wasn't proposing to play about with him."

"Well, treat him then. Psycho-analyse him—whatever it is you do?"

"I thought analysis might help him. I wasn't sure, but I decided to try it for a short while and see."

"Well, you've certainly done that, haven't you?"

Milne stared back into the grey eyes without reply. Beneath the anger in them, there was no mistaking the lustful enjoyment.

"Well, anyhow," said the coroner with a shrug, "let's leave that side of it. It's no use crying over spilt milk. You treated him?"

"Yes. For just over two months. I saw him eighteen times altogether."

"And what did your treatment amount to?"

"The normal preliminary stages of analysis."

"Preliminary stages? You saw him eighteen times and that was just the preliminary stages?"

"Yes."

"The whole treatment goes on for years, doesn't it?"

"It may."

The coroner gave a little snort, hesitated, and then said, "Well, well, never mind. What did these preliminary stages consist of?"

"Mainly in getting him to talk about his war experiences, which I thought were the immediate cause of his trouble. Until he could talk freely about them the analysis proper couldn't begin."

"You were removing his repressions, eh?"

"Not exactly. That would have been a later stage."

"Oh, that's a later stage? Did you do anything else beyond making him talk?"

Milne hesitated for a moment. "Apart from that I just

observed his general behaviour, and noted his dreams and so on."

"Oh, yes, his dreams come into it a lot, don't they? If he dreams of an umbrella that means one thing and if he dreams of a cabbage that means something else?"

"Dream records have a certain value," said Milne tonelessly.

"Well, there may be something in it. I don't know. Anyhow you went on seeing him up till the day before this happened, and when you last saw him you had no reason to suppose that this was going to happen?"

There was a dead silence. The coroner looked up in surprise. He waited a moment and then said, "Well, Mr. Milne? You had no reason to suppose that this was going to happen?"

Milne stared at him in silence for a moment. Then his eyes wandered slowly away towards the back of the court.

"I had no *reason* to think so," he said slowly.

"What d'you mean by that exactly? D'you mean you guessed there was something wrong?"

Milne's eyes came back to the yellow, rather startled face.

"Yes," he said. "Yes. I think I did."

"And you took no steps about it?"

"No. I thought I was probably wrong and I let him go."

The coroner sat back in his chair and stared at him for a moment in amazement. Then he looked slowly round the court.

"Well," he said, addressing nobody in particular, "that's frank at any rate." He turned quickly back. "Mr. Milne—you realise that a man and a woman have lost their lives in this matter?"

"Yes."

"And you've nothing to add to that—you knew that this man had previously made a murderous attack on his wife, you guessed that there was something wrong—some deterioration in his condition—and you took no step—didn't warn her or anything? You just assumed that your guess was wrong?"

"Yes," said Milne wearily. There was no way of explaining that it was much worse than that—that he had stopped because he had a headache and had put it out of his mind, and left the question mark to kill Mollie rather than go on.

He was getting tired now, and there was a dull ache in his shoulder-blades.

The coroner said, " It never occurred to you that he'd go to your house, of course ? "

" No," said Milne. " I don't know why not, but it never entered my head."

" I don't see any particular reason why it should have," said the coroner, with the air of a man who can afford to be just. " And you say you talked for about ten minutes ? "

" Perhaps a bit more than that."

" What did you talk about ? "

" He wasn't very rational. He was confusing his wife and his mother and was rather incoherent."

" He knew he'd killed his wife ? "

Milne hesitated. " That's a little difficult to answer. He knew he'd killed a woman. But as I say, he was identifying his wife and his mother. He was also confusing a Japanese he had killed in the war with his father."

" Anyhow, you had no doubt that he was insane ? "

" No doubt at all."

" Well, it was awkward for you of course with your wife there and an armed madman. What did you do ? "

" I tried to get him to give me the gun. He wouldn't. At first he wouldn't let my wife go, but afterwards he suggested that she should go to bed. As soon as she had gone he said he knew that she would telephone for the police, and pulled the gun out."

" Then he knew that he'd committed a crime ? "

Milne shifted his aching shoulders wearily. " It's difficult to say," he said vaguely.

" Well, he took the gun out. Then what happened ? "

" I told him to give it to me. He said, ' Sure,' and held it out with his left hand. As I went to take it he hit me with his right hand and bolted."

" Then you rang up the police ? "

" Yes."

The coroner sat for a few moments looking at the envelope.

" He said, " This is addressed to Dr. Milne. Did he think you were a doctor ? "

" No," said Milne with a shadow of a smile. " He knew I wasn't. That just means that he was disliking me when he addressed the envelope. ' Doctor ' was an insult with him."

" Why should he send you five pounds ? Just that he was crazy ? "

" I think he had some idea of paying for the treatment."

" He owed it for fees, eh ? "

" He may have thought so."

There was a long silence. The coroner was looking down at his desk and drumming on it softly with his fingers. Milne closed his eyes for a moment and passed a hand across them. When he opened them again the coroner had looked up and was staring at him again.

" All right, Mr. Milne," he croaked at last, " I think that's all I want from you. But before you go, I'd just like to check over one or two things to make sure I've got it straight. If you don't agree or you've got anything to add, you say so. See ? "

He glanced at his notes, and went on very slowly.

" You knew this man had made a murderous attack on his wife before you ever saw him. You saw him and thought he had those schizoid symptoms. You warned his wife that he might attack her again. The day before this happened you saw him and thought there was something wrong. You decided to do nothing about it." He looked up. " That right ? " he said quietly.

There was a long pause. Milne passed a hand across his eyes again.

" Not altogether," he half muttered.

" All right. Then you tell me what's wrong with it. Take your time. I don't want to take advantage of you. It's just my job to get these things straight, y'know."

Milne said suddenly, " These cases aren't like that. You never know. You work on a series of guesses. Sometimes you guess wrong——" he faded away into silence.

The coroner waited a moment. " All right," he said with

an almost imperceptible shrug. " Then just this last question, Mr. Milne." He leant forward. " Are you satisfied that in handling this case you used the reasonable degree of skill and care that it was your duty to use ? Understand me—nobody can demand that a man shall be a genius. But are you satisfied that as far as in you lay you did the best that could be done, and that no particular responsibility for the death of this man and this woman lies at your door ? "

There was a moment's dead silence, and then a slight shuffle as Mr. Grandison rose to his feet.

" With the greatest deference, sir——" he said, throwing his head back so as to bring his half-spectacles to bear.

" Well, Mr.—Mr.——? "

" With the greatest deference, sir, is that quite a fair question to put to Mr. Milne ? "

" He needn't answer it if he doesn't want to," said Lefage shortly.

" Quite. Then——" Grandison looked significantly at Milne.

The coroner shrugged his shoulders.

" All right," he said. " You advise him not to answer. It's up to you, Mr.—Mr.——" He sat back in his chair with the air of a man who washes his hands of a matter. " Then I've finished with Mr. Milne. You want to ask him anything ? "

" If I may, sir ? "

" Go ahead."

Mr. Grandison inflated and deflated his cheeks thoughtfully.

" You had a good deal of regard for Mr. and Mrs. Lucian, Mr. Milne ? Apart from your professional acquaintance you liked them both ? "

" Yes."

" You have shown that you would willingly risk your life to save your patient from coming to harm ? "

" Yes."

" And at all times you acted as you thought for the best?"

He hesitated for a moment and then said " Yes " dully and let it go.

He was back in his seat. He felt not only cold but chilled and dead, and he no longer shivered. Pat's hand was on his arm, and he could feel the fingers gripping tightly. She had used perfume. She seldom did, but to-day he could smell it—the faint, sweet smell that he half-liked and half-hated. He thought that he must do something to comfort her, so he put his hand on hers and patted it and mumbled, " Soon be over now."

Garsten had changed his seat. Milne could see his silver hair next to Grandison. The coroner was still croaking at somebody. McIlwain. That was the man's name at school. McIlwain.

Grandison got up and said, " Before you do so, sir, I wonder if you would be prepared to hear one further witness ? "

" Who's that, Mr.—Mr.—— ? "

" Doctor James Garsten, sir. Doctor Garsten informs me that he has some knowledge of this case and would be glad to assist the court if you wished——"

" Yes, yes. All right. Let him come forward."

He saw with sudden bitter anger that this was quite different. There was the silver hair and the Wimpole Street address. And anyhow Garsten wasn't talking to McIlwain. The coroner nodded and said, " Know your name of course," and one knew that he didn't and thought he ought to and wished he did.

The coroner said, " Well, Dr. Garsten, can you help me in this unfortunate business ? You had some knowledge of the case, eh ? "

Garsten nodded the silver head. " Yes, sir."

" Then just tell me about it, will you ? How you come into it and so on."

" I come into it," said Garsten calmly, " through being a colleague of Mr. Milne."

" A colleague ? "

" Yes. Mr. Milne and I have been closely associated in clinical work for some time, and we are in the habit of consulting one another about our cases."

The coroner said, " Oh—I see." There was a moment's

pause. " And Mr. Milne consulted you about this case ? "

" Yes. We discussed it on a number of occasions."

" Did you actually see the patient ? "

" No," said Garsten regretfully. " That was impossible owing to his strong emotional reaction to doctors. But Mr. Milne kept me informed of the progress of the case and of the methods he was employing."

The coroner shifted uneasily in his chair. " So what you're saying, Dr. Garsten, is that this case was handled to some extent under your supervision ? "

" Oh, no."

" Ah—I thought you meant that."

" No," said Garsten quietly. " I certainly would not presume to supervise the work of Mr. Milne, who is one of the finest clinicians in London. But he did me the honour of consulting me about the case at all its stages."

The coroner's lips were very tight. " And did you approve of the treatment that was given ? " he said curtly.

" I did. I cannot see how it could have been bettered."

" Mr. Milne did what you would have done yourself ? "

" He did what I should have tried to do."

The coroner shrugged his shoulders. " In view of what happened after, I'm a bit surprised to hear you say so, Dr. Garsten."

Garsten bent his head. " Quite," he said gently. " But you'll forgive me for saying, sir, that one's view of these things after a tragedy like this has taken place is very different from the view that the clinician gets when he is dealing with his patient."

" But Mr. Milne said himself that he thought something was wrong the last time he saw the man," said the coroner sulkily.

" He did, sir. And if I may say so, I think the remark may have been misunderstood."

" How ? It's a plain statement."

" Too plain to convey its full meaning perhaps," Garsten hesitated with beautifully calculated deference.

" Well, what you think its meaning was, Dr. Garsten ? "

" Since you ask me, sir, I think Mr. Milne was referring to a type of experience with which every analyst is familiar."

Garsten passed a hand over the silver hair. " A clinician," he said sonorously, " receives impressions of his patients' condition not only from visit to visit but almost from minute to minute. They are not based on anything tangible, and he cannot—*dare* not—act on them. You asked Mr. Milne if he had reason, previously, to think his patient's condition was deteriorating. He replied that he had not. I happen to know that immediately before, he had every reason to think that Mr. Lucian was much better. But you also asked Mr. Milne if, on the occasion of this particular last visit, he had felt that there was anything particular wrong. Mr. Milne, in trying to give his evidence completely objectively, felt obliged to mention this vague feeling that all was not well that day. But the evidence of Mr. Milne himself and of others who saw Mr. Lucian that day makes it clear that there was nothing obvious—nothing on which drastic action could be based. I myself must have had these vague intuitive feelings about patients hundreds of times. But I should no more think of taking immediate action on a vague feeling that something was wrong, than of neglecting precautions because of a vague feeling that everything was all right. One cannot base treatment on anything but the facts."

There was a long pause. The coroner shifted restlessly again. " What you're saying is that it was only a guess and he couldn't have acted on it ? "

" Yes. That, I think, is almost exactly what he said or implied."

" And that to say he should have acted is just being wise after the event ? "

" Yes."

" And it's your opinion as an expert, Dr. Garsten, that all proper skill and care was employed and—and in fact that nobody's to blame. That's it, eh ? "

" Yes, sir."

" Well," said the coroner moodily, " it's a point of view. Any of you gentlemen want to ask Dr. Garsten anything ? "

The handsome young barrister representing Mr. Ogden Lucian rose and said bluntly, " You never saw the patient, Dr. Garsten ? "

" No."

" And yet you're quite sure that the case was perfectly handled ? "

" No case is perfectly handled. But this one, in my view, was handled with skill and integrity."

" Well, you speak as an expert in these matters, Dr. Garsten. But perhaps you'd agree that to the plain man who uses his common sense this might appear to be a clear case of an error of judgment ? "

Garsten leant forward slightly. " To the plain man who uses his common sense," he said silkily, " everything is *always* clear—after the event."

The coroner sat staring moodily before him in silence, making vague jabs at his blotter with a pen. Everything was very still, except for a distant undertone of traffic.

At last Lefage raised his head. " Well," he said huskily, " I've now heard the evidence on this tragic affair and it's my duty to record a finding. Partly easy, partly not. No doubt about the cause of death or the state of mind of the deceased man. But coroner's got another duty. If he finds that anything else was contributory cause—carelessness or negligence on part of anybody else, his duty is to say so."

He paused and looked round the court with the fierce grey eyes.

" Confess I've been very exercised in my mind over this case. Here's a man—young man with a fine record—kills his wife and then himself. He'd attacked her before. He was under mental treatment. We're told that it was realised that he might become dangerous at any time. Here's Mr. Milne who was treating him says he had an idea or a premonition or whatever you like to call it that he was worse. He doesn't do anything about it. Mr. Milne's very frank—very open. There was no need for him to admit that. But he does admit it." He shrugged his shoulders moodily. " Then along comes Dr. Garsten. He's an expert. He says ' I was consulted and I've no criticism to make. Anybody who has is being wise after the event. Mr. Milne may have had an idea but he'd no evidence to go on. He did what I should have done—what anybody would do '."

He paused and shook his head.

"Well—I've thought about it. Pretty anxiously. And I've come to the conclusion that the least said on this part of it the better. Dr. Garsten may be right. Nobody can really say. We still don't know much about the human mind though we talk a lot of jargon about it nowadays. Mr. Milne was frank with me, and later on in the whole business he acted like a brave man and did his best for his patient. I'm going to leave it at that."

There was a very slight stir as he paused.

"But one thing does come out of this very clearly," said the coroner emphatically. "The public ought to know and —and professional men ought to know, that mental disease, or the symptoms of it, is a thing to take very seriously, or there may be tragedy, as there was here. As soon as there's the least suspicion of it—most highly qualified advice at the earliest possible moment. Only safe way. That needs to be more widely realised." He picked up his pen. "Find that Adam Lucian murdered Mollie Sinclair Lucian and then took his own life while the balance of his mind was disturbed," he said in one breath.

XVI

AS THEY were coming out, Patricia said, "We must see Jim. Where is he? We must see him."

Grandison came up and shook hands. He blew his cheeks out and said, "Well, well. Might have been worse. I thought at one time it was going to be a bad business."

Patricia said, "Thank you very much, Mr. Grandison."

"Not at all, Mrs. Milne. There wasn't much I could do." He tilted back his head and looked at Milne through his glasses. They made his eyes look grotesquely big. "Of course, Mr. Milne, your own evidence——" he shook his head. "Frankly, I thought you'd done for yourself. Still —you told me you were going to do it your own way and you did and you got away with it, so there's no more to be said. But really. I thought at one time——" He shook his head again.

Milne said, " So I got away with it ? "

" I should certainly say you did, sir." Milne shrugged his shoulders in silence. " My dear boy, he could have added a rider to his verdict throwing the whole blame on you. Nothing whatever to stop him. No appeal, and no means of objecting. And that's exactly what I thought he was going to do. Until Dr.—whats-his-name—Dr. Garsten —until he got up."

Patricia said, " Yes. We must go and find Jim. You will excuse us, Mr. Grandison ? "

" Of course, Mrs. Milne. And if I may say so, your husband owes a good deal to his colleague. But for him——"

Milne had turned away and was walking slowly out of the court. He saw two or three people look at him curiously. Patricia caught him up and put a hand through his arm. She said again, " We must see Jim."

Milne said, " He'll be gone." He had a foolish hope for a moment that perhaps Garsten would have gone. Garsten was good all right. He might have known, and gone.

Garsten hadn't gone. He was just getting into his car. Patricia said, " Jim ! "

Garsten turned and said, " Oh, hallo ! " and took off the black felt hat and looked at them with a rather tentative smile.

Patricia said, " Hallo——" Her lips were trembling. She stopped and looked at Milne. He knew he must say something to Garsten—that she was waiting for him to say something.

He said coldly, " What the hell did you want to barge in like that for ? "

Garsten grinned broadly. " I'm terribly sorry, Felix," he said guiltily. " But I just couldn't resist it. You know I can never keep my hands off the trades union."

" To hell with the trades union," said Milne wearily. " What did it matter anyway ? You might have landed yourself in a muck. I'm not sure that you haven't as it is."

" Nonsense," said Garsten. " With a bit of luck I shall have got my name in the papers. Probably spelt wrong, but think what the space would cost if I'd had to buy it."

"I shouldn't think it's done either of you any actual *good*," said Patricia quietly. "But——"

"Oh, but you don't understand!" said Garsten. "You don't know about old Lefage. That's the first time in living memory that he's given a verdict without a rider saying that somebody ought to be sent to gaol. He's an awful old boy. That's the trouble about coroners. They can say any damn' thing. And do, some of them."

There was a moment's silence. Then Patricia said, "Well, anyhow—thank you very very much. It's a feeble thing to say, but——"

Garsten looked puzzled for a moment. Then he smiled. "Oh—I see——" he jerked his thumb towards Milne. "Oh I wasn't interested in *his* sweet eyes, bless you. He can bloody well look after himself. It was just that I wanted to have a crack at the old boy's prejudices. He's one of those people who's honest according to his lights, but his lights aren't very well focused. Now I suppose we've all got to get ourselves back to civilisation. Have you got a car here, Felix?"

Milne hesitated and said, "We can get a cab."

"No—why should you? Jump in. I'll run you back. You come in front, Felix. There's a lot of junk back there."

The big Daimler was very smooth and quiet. Garsten drove with gloves, seeming to stroke the wheel with loose, easy hands. Milne watched his hands and hated their competence with a dull, detached hatred.

As they sat and waited for the traffic lights, Garsten said quietly, "You aren't terribly good at that sort of thing, are you?" He said it in his ordinary voice. It was the first time that day that Milne had heard Garsten's ordinary voice. Previously it had been too heavy or too light.

He said, "Why not?"

"You misunderstand the object of inquests," said Garsten rather bitterly. "An inquest isn't the place to start searching for the truth—particularly if you're a professional man. An inquest is a place for arriving at a comfortable verdict that no blame whatever attaches to anybody. The sort of thing you did spoils the game. They don't like it."

Milne said, " What the hell do I care whether they like it or not? Lucian's dead and so's his wife."

" So what? " said Garsten, his eyes on the road. " You didn't kill him."

" No," said Milne bitterly. " I didn't kill him. I handled his case with skill and integrity. Dr. Garsten says so. And then I let him go and he killed her and killed himself. What's that to do with me? My job's to take his money and prove that I'm a hell of a chap."

" Well, you don't seem to have succeeded in taking his money much. The five pounds was interesting. I'm not sure that you were right about that being an insult."

Milne said, " You're all the same. Some of you are good doctors and some of you are bad doctors, but you're all doctors. You know the game. You may pretend you think it's all bunk. But you play it. I don't believe in Wimpole Street addresses and sponge-bag trousers and a professional manner. I don't believe in witch-doctoring. And I don't believe in it any more when it plays on my side than when it plays on the other."

" Nor I," said Garsten gently, snicking into third gear.

" Why couldn't you let him go? " said Milne bitterly. " Do you think it mattered to me what he said or thought or did? Why not let him say that it was my fault? It doesn't alter the facts."

" I tell you," said Garsten, " I wasn't interested in you."

" Oh, for Christ's sake," said Milne disgustedly.

Garsten grinned at the road ahead. " All right, Felix. Maybe that was a bit amateur. Anyhow I enjoyed myself a lot. Sorry if I made it worse for you. I think it was better that way from Pat's point of view."

" Pat? " said Milne bitterly. " She'll never forgive me for not falling on your neck."

Garsten said, " The person Pat will never forgive is me. I can see that one coming all right. You may, but she won't. Greater love hath no man, than that he lay down somebody else's charming wife for his friend."

Patricia said, " Won't you come in for a bit? "

Garsten shook his head. " No, I must cut straight back,

thanks." He jerked his head towards Milne. "He's like a bear with a sore bottom. Give him a bun or a nice cup of tea or something. Cheerio."

In the hall Milne stopped and took off his hat and coat. Patricia stood quite still and silent as he did it. As he went towards the consulting room, she said, "Want me? Or not?"

He looked at her for a moment and then mechanically put his arms round her. She was crying.

He said, "No. Not for a bit. Don't cry. There's nothing to cry about."

She clung to him very tightly and he smelt the perfume again. He said, "Nice Rhino," and stroked her hair vaguely. He wanted to tell her that it would be quite all right soon, that he had come back, and that it was only for the moment that he was like this.

Patricia let go and said, "I'll go and see about some tea. We'll have it by the fire."

Milne said, "All right," and went into the consulting room and shut the door.

He sat down at his desk and looked round the room. It was not a very professional room. It might have been any man's study. But it looked professional enough to curl his lips. He looked at the couch and the big chairs and the card index cabinet and the record files, and they seemed intolerably false and smug and self-satisfied.

He sat back in his chair with closed eyes and tried to sort things out. But there was no longer a straight issue to be considered and weighed and decided and acted upon. Between him and the real question there was a queer film of disappointment and baffled irritation. Until that last quarter of an hour—until Garsten had interfered—it had run so smoothly and inevitably. But for Garsten there would have been the clear, damning verdict. He could have listened to that and then put it out of his head and ignored it, and made up his own mind. But Garsten had come in and muddled the issue with his special pleading; and now nobody knew the truth, and himself least of all. In Scotland they could find murder Not Proven and leave it at that. But there was always at least one person who knew the truth. Here there was nobody.

He started to go over it again in his mind, but it no longer meant anything. He had been over it before, and had always left his own verdict until after the inquest. And now it had been thrown back at him, no further on.

He could get no further on the facts, but he opened his eyes and looked round the room again, at the chair in which Mollie had looked very small, and the couch on which Lucian had looked very big, and at the path that Lucian had gone limping down, and then there was no real doubt about it. He noted carefully the masochistic pleasure and relief of that feeling and got up and went over to his record files and started to pull them out and throw them on the table. They were beautifully kept. He knew and always had known that they were a useless bluff and a swindle—a way of convincing him that emotional guess-work was a careful science. He opened one at random. It was a record of Lady Maresfield's dreams. He laughed quietly to himself and ripped the thick wad of sheets out of the folder, tore them carefully into small pieces, and dropped them into the waste-paper basket. They filled the basket loosely, and he put the sole of his shoe on the pieces and crushed them down to make room for more. Tread softly, because you tread on my dreams. Poor old Lady M. She would cry and threaten suicide, and then she would buy a Pekinese and that would do just as well. Or else she would really commit suicide and then there would be another inquest. But damn it, they might blame you for treating people, but they could hardly blame you for refusing to treat them.

He had forgotten some of the cases, and sometimes he stopped and read a bit, tearing up each page as he came to the end of it. But this made him very slow, and he started to put one or two aside to be read and scrapped at leisure. It worried him to find that he was doing this and he sat back and looked at the full waste-paper basket and at the pile put aside. The top one of the pile was the file on Whiteley, and he decided quietly and coldly that there was absolutely no reason to wish to read Whiteley's file again, and picked it up and started to tear it out of its covers. It was thick and resisted him. He tore it in sudden wild anger.

Patricia came in. She stopped short and said, " Hey—what are you up to ? "

Milne said, " I'm scrapping all this junk." He pulled again at the Whiteley papers, but they still did not come so he took a thinner wad, and ripped them out and tore them up carefully.

Patricia came over and looked and said, " Why are you tearing these up ? "

Milne said, " They clutter up the place, and I shan't want them now. They were never any good really."

Patricia looked at him for a moment and then said shortly, " Don't be a bloody fool. Put them back and come and have tea."

" I don't want any tea," he said childishly. " I want to finish this."

She did not say anything. That surprised him. He thought perhaps she had not understood so he said, " I'm through, and I've got to get rid of the whole thing."

" You mean," she said slowly and politely, " that you're giving up practice ? "

" Yes. I am."

He stiffened himself for it—the protests—the tears. But they didn't come. She raised her eyebrows and said, " Well, well." Milne felt his throat contracting till it ached.

He looked away and said with difficulty, " What else could I do ? "

Patricia said gently, " You could start by showing three-ha'pence worth of guts, honey."

He was wildly relieved and angry. He almost shouted, " What the hell d'you mean ? I tell you I'm through with the whole bloody business."

" Because somebody criticised you ? "

" Criticised me ? They didn't criticise me. They agreed to say no more about it. Dr. Garsten of Wimpole Street assured them that I'd done my best and they decided to give me the benefit of the doubt. That ignorant old fool. He didn't think I meant any harm. I told him I knew, that time when Lucian went down the path and I let him go. I told him. But they hushed it up. Garsten squared it. D'you think I'm going to spend the rest of my life being patronised and excused by people like that ? "

Patricia was looking at him thoughtfully. " It's just as well you're not a surgeon," she said, " if this had to happen every time an operation went wrong."

Milne said, " It's a pity we didn't think of that at the inquest. It's just the sort of argument they'd like." She smiled quietly and that was too much. He said incoherently, " You bitch ! " and his eyes filled with tears, and he turned away.

She came over to him then and put her arms round him, but she didn't say darling, darling. She said, " Come on, now," in a queer voice that he didn't know. But he knew the feel of her arms and that was good.

He said, " No can, Pat."

" Sure can," she said calmly. " Got me."

" No, I haven't," he said, breaking away. " That's the trouble. I haven't got a bloody thing." He stood there staring at her. " It's all part of the same thing. It's all paying out, this job. And if there's nothing coming in, you can't go on. I've got nothing to give away."

She hesitated for a moment. The doorbell rang in the silence. She said slowly, " Don't I give you—anything ? "

He said, " Give ? You give me everything, but I don't give back. That's why I'm going to stop. It isn't fair. It all goes out to these people, and then I'm sucked dry and there's nothing left for you. Where's the sense of it ? It sucks you dry, and then at the end of it you don't know whether you've done more harm than good. That's why I'm through. Because then I can come back to you, and have something to give you and be really yours. As long as I'm doing this bloody stuff I shall never be any use to you."

The doorbell rang again. Patricia said, " Damn that bell. I must go. I don't think there's anybody in."

She went out. He turned and stood looking out of the window. He felt very tired, but it was coming straight at last. The bit about Lucian and tearing up the papers had had a cracked note. But this last was true enough.

Patricia came back and said, " Look, darling—you've got a patient. I'd forgotten."

He said, " No. No more."

Patricia hesitated. " Shall I tell him to make it to-morrow ? "

He said, " No. No more."

" You can't just drop them, darling."

" No," he said, getting up. " I can't. But I can tell them. And I will. Send him in."

" What are you going to tell him ? "

" I'm going to tell him that I'm going out of practice. That this job needs God, and I'm not God. I'm going to tell him to go and suck somebody else's blood because I need mine. I'm going to recommend him to Dr. Garsten of Wimpole Street who's a real doctor who doesn't make mistakes——"

Patricia gave a queer, sudden grin. " Well," she said gently, " you know your own technique best, but I think he'll be a bit surprised if you say all that. It's little Charlie Oakes."

Milne said, " Charlie Oakes ? " He stood silent for a moment and then suddenly started to laugh. " Forgive me if I appear to laugh, but this is funny. That's the size of it all right. That's me. I have a certain talent for dealing with people's mental difficulties. Sometimes I have headaches, and then I let them go away and shoot their wives and commit suicide. But at other times I treat them with skill and integrity and cure them of wetting their beds. Or nearly cure them. That's what I do."

" Well ? " she said quietly. " What's wrong with that ? "

Milne said, " Wrong with it ? There's nothing wrong with it. It's magnificent. And if it weren't, there's nothing to be done about it. Where is he ? "

" In the lounge."

Milne went towards the door. On his way he paused and said, " You know I'd left you ? That if it hadn't been for this business—— ? "

She said, " Yes. I know that."

He caught her and kissed her hard and bitterly and then almost pushing her away went into the lounge. Charlie Oakes was standing with his cap in his hand. His hair had been plastered down with water.

Milne said, " Hallo, Charlie. I'd forgotten about you. Come on in."

As they went into the consulting room Charlie said defensively, " You said come here to-day. Not the Clinic."

" Yes, that's quite right," said Milne, shutting the door. " So I did. Come and sit down. How's life ? "

THE END